A
WELL-DESERVED
MURDER

Katherine John

Published by Accent Press 2008

Copyright © 2008 Katherine John

ISBN 9781906125141

The right of Katherine John to be identified
as the author of this work has been
asserted by her in accordance with the Copyright,
Designs and Patents Act 1988

Printed and bound in the UK

Cover design by Red Dot Design

For Diane and Neil Langford, absolutely the best neighbours in the world. Unfortunately not mine, but my father's. However, if I didn't know about the other kind, this book may never have been written.

Never pick a fight with a man who buys
ink by the gallon.

Mark Twain

CHAPTER ONE

Kacy Howells cut the last of the lower branches from the willow tree, switched off her power saw and surveyed her handiwork. The tree looked neat and tidy. It would blend in with the other trees she had cut, shaped and fixed bird-boxes to. Finally she had the well-ordered view she wanted from her kitchen window. Except for ... she looked at the ragged silver birch. The farmer, Bob Guttridge, had warned her twice not to cut any more trees on his land, but once it was done, what could he do? The trees might be on his land, but he had made no effort to manage the woodland that backed on to her garden. And she was the one who had to look at it from her kitchen window ...

She switched on her power saw again and in seconds the tree was on the ground. Birch trunks were so slim – and satisfying – to slice into. She picked up one end and dragged it to the wire fence that separated the farm's woodland from her garden and tipped the trunk over. Climbing after it, she picked up the end of the trunk and hauled it towards the five-foot deck she'd had built that overlooked the garden next door.

Her neighbours had sat out there every summer and spring evening until she'd built the deck, deliberately placing it in a position to overlook as much of their garden as possible. Her husband George hadn't been too keen at first. Joy and Alan

Piper had moved into their house the same time as George's parents over thirty-five years before. They'd been his neighbours since he was six years old. But she knew how to handle George. Knew all his little secrets, and made certain he knew his position inside their marriage.

The house may have been his before their marriage but since then she'd had two children that were registered in his name. If she divorced him citing his preference for young – very young – boys she was confident of obtaining the house and a restraining order that would keep George away from it – and her and the children.

She walked up the steps onto the deck, cleaned the electric saw with a rag, opened the door of the summer-house and laid the saw in the chest she used to store her electrical and cordless tools. She locked the chest, slipped the key onto the rack above it and opened one of the two "secret" cupboards she'd had built into the walls – the one she used to store her hand tools. George only knew of this one. She suppressed a smile at the thought of what she stored in the other.

She lifted out an axe, walked down the steps and proceeded to chop the birch into logs. If she rolled them under the decking with the other debris from the trees she'd cut down, the farmer would be hard put to prove that she was the one "managing" his woodland. Irritating man. He'd neglected the woodland for years and yet had the gall to complain that she was trespassing whenever he saw her on it.

She left the axe embedded in the chopping block, disposed of the logs and looked at her watch. Time had run away with her. Another five or ten minutes and *he*'d be with her.

She climbed back onto the deck, entered the summer-house and opened the second "secret cupboard". How could she have allowed herself to get carried away? She tested the rubber and leather straps fastened to the wall. Flicked through the items on the shelf above. Rubber rings … spray cans of nipple dust … handcuffs – whips – she'd hurt him last time and he'd complained – but he couldn't possibly object to her soft plaited lamb's leather whip. A jar of liquid chocolate, two wooden massage rollers … large as well as small …

She heard the wooden step creak under the weight of his foot. She peeled off her sweatshirt, slacks and underclothes, hung them on a peg inside the door and, stark naked, turned around. She looked through the open door. There was no one in sight. She braced herself. The last time he'd hidden behind the door, he had jumped on her and played his favourite game – masterful owner takes unwilling slave. She stepped out through the door and looked left and right. Still nothing. Had she imagined the creak?

Suddenly his shadow blocked out the sun. She opened her lips in readiness to receive his invasive, wet kiss. A hand gripped the back of her neck, squeezing painfully, forcing her to her knees before an excruciating pain in her head darkened the scene.

Dazed, disorientated, she struggled to collect her thoughts but hurting and blind she could sense nothing beyond the warm, wet and sticky fouling of her hair and an irritating trickling down her neck. She lifted her right hand …

The second blow severed her hand at the wrist before cleaving into her skull. She was aware of acute pain in her teeth and the crunching of bone in her skull. Her agony was excruciating, all-encompassing. She could feel nothing beyond it; see nothing through the thick blanket of suffocating grey.

The last sounds she heard were her attacker's laboured breath and the thud of her body as she slumped onto the deck – the last sensations, the sun-warmed solidity of the wooden planking beneath her – the last perfumes, the sharp astringent smell of wood, tinged with an iron stink that permeated her mouth.

She didn't have time to connect the metallic taste with her blood.

CHAPTER TWO

'Noddy gave you sound advice, Alan. You should take it.' Peter Collins sat back so the waitress could set the roast beef sandwiches he and his cousin, Alan Piper, had ordered on their table.

'Sound advice that will send my neighbours even further round the bend,' Alan predicted gloomily. 'Given what they've already done, can you imagine what they'd get up to if they saw a CCTV camera set up between our houses?'

'Stop stealing your property.' Peter reached for the mustard, opened his sandwich and spread on a liberal helping.

'I haven't thanked you for your help. I'm not sure the community police would have taken my complaint seriously without the statement you sent them.'

'Revered journalist like you, course they would have,' Peter teased. 'I told them I was in shock. You don't expect a woman – and I use the word loosely – to stalk her neighbours by snaking around the border of her garden using her elbows and knees like a commando so she can eavesdrop on a private conversation.' Peter cut his sandwich in two. 'I can still see the look on her face when she looked up and saw us staring down at her. I expected her to at least say "sorry" before running into the house. But she didn't say a word, not a single bloody word.'

'That's not the first time it's happened. One of

my …' Alan hesitated.

'Sources?' Peter questioned.

'Don't ask.'

'I wouldn't dare. Although I'd give a great deal to know who tipped you off about the White Baron. Not that anyone on the force is complaining. We've been after the bastard for years. The amount of crack cocaine and heroin on the streets has halved since he was sent down. Of course there's always the other half.'

Alan didn't take the hint. Peter had been a police officer too long to miss the obvious. The villain most likely to shop another was one in direct competition. But the first rule he had learned as a journalist was the identity and anonymity of sources was sacrosanct. Reveal them and it wouldn't only be the information that would dry up. The blood flowing in your veins might too.

He changed the subject. 'It's foul living next door to stalking kleptomaniacs. I've caught myself counting the plants in my front garden. If one disappears I'm never sure whether it died or I should go and bang on their front door.'

'How many paving bricks did they take?'

'Two square metres.'

'Two square metres at 19p a brick …'

'Knock it off, Peter. It's not funny,' Alan protested. 'One day it could be you.'

'Could be.' Peter demolished half of his sandwich in two bites. 'Two minutes after I moved in with the love of my life she started making noises

6

about trading in her flat for a house. It doesn't help that Trevor Joseph has one, complete with wife, baby, cat and full wedded bliss.' He referred to Inspector Trevor Joseph, his colleague and closest friend.

'Take my advice, keep out of suburbia. Buy a place on its own in the middle of nowhere.'

'That would be a prime burglary risk,' Peter the law officer recited automatically.

'I don't know how much more I can take,' Alan muttered, obsessed with his problem neighbours.

'So far, you've been the good boy. You've done everything by the book, kept a diary, listed their ridiculous complaints about you and everything they've stolen from you. The community constable was right, bless him. Put up a CCTV linked to a video recorder and film their movements every time they come near your property. They'll soon back down.'

'I wish to God I'd never bought half his garden off him. When he knocked on my door and said he couldn't afford the mortgage any more I should have let him move into a semi on the estate.'

'You should have,' Peter agreed cheerfully.

'I felt sorry for the kid. His mother had just died, he had to buy his brother out of his share of the house … how was I to know he'd marry the bitch from hell a couple of years down the line?'

'"No good deed goes unpunished",' Peter quoted Clare Boothe Luce. 'Serves you right for being bloody charitable.'

'Not that charitable. The land gave Joy and me a view of the woods. She used to love sitting out there in the evening.'

Alan's wife Joy had died of cancer a year ago and Peter felt helpless every time Alan mentioned her. He wondered if Alan and Joy had been close because they hadn't had kids. That was something else "the love of his life" was talking about. He knew his reluctance to start a family was down to pure selfishness. Things were so mind-bogglingly perfect between them, he didn't want to risk what they had by bringing another being into their lives. Especially one that would demand round the clock attention.

Alan managed a small smile, 'I haven't been that good. And, I suspect that if I do take the Community Police Officer's advice and put up a monitor, they'd only chuck a brick at it.'

'Then we'd charge them with criminal damage.'

'And they'd end up in a magistrates' court where they'd get a ticket to a "Support The Misunderstood Criminals group", a stern "don't do it again" and remain free to return to their house where they'd tear down more of my fences and steal even more of my property.'

'There are no guarantees in this life, especially when you're dealing with lunatics,' Peter qualified. 'What do you mean you haven't been "that good"?'

'You want to know what they left in front of my garage this morning.'

'You haven't answered my question,' Peter said

warily. Alan had an odd sense of humour which wasn't always understood by his friends, let alone his enemies.

'Journalists move in mysterious ways.'

'And rarely truthful ones.' Peter sipped his orange juice.

'They left an axe – a bloody axe.'

Peter frowned. 'An axe with blood on it?'

'Not bloody in that sense,' Alan replied irritably. 'One was lying in front of my car this morning. I had to move it.'

'And you saw them put it there?'

'No.'

'Then how do you know they left it?'

'Who else would have done it?'

'Axes cost money. You should have run over it.'

'And risk damaging my tyres?' Alan shook his head.

'Your obsession with these nutcases is unhealthy. Ignore the stupid bastards!'

'Obsession!' Alan's voice rose two octaves. 'They build a deck overlooking my garden then complain to the police that I'm watching them when they spend all their time on a five-foot platform in view of the patio I've used for over twenty years. They build a monstrous shed on the platform and paint it bright blue and yellow …'

'Everyone's entitled to express themselves,' Peter interrupted.

'In fairground colours?'

'Perhaps they love cartoons.'

'If Mickey Mouse was sick he wouldn't throw up anything that vivid.' Alan was on a rant and nothing was going to stop him. 'They stole my paving bricks and used them to raise their pots in their front garden so I could see exactly what they were doing. They tore down my fence, dug up and stole my plants. They took delivery of the flowers Joy's friends sent her when she was in hospital and kept them for days until they were dead. And to top it all they dug up my gatepost and stole my gate and post, and I was the one who had to fork out for a new fence to make my garden secure. And you lot advise me to pay out even more money to put up a camera linked to a recorder.'

'Not "you lot". Community police officers aren't real officers.' Peter pulled the lettuce leaves from the other half of his sandwich and discarded them.

'They aren't?'

'They haven't had their polite gene removed.'

'Very funny.' Alan eyed Peter. 'It's not a laughing matter.'

'I'm sorry.' Peter wiped his fingers on his paper napkin. 'The idea of your neighbours tiptoeing around in their pyjamas in the dead of night, digging up your gatepost and stealing your gate is hilarious. It's not even as if it's your usual sized gate. It must weigh a ton. The locals said they couldn't believe it when they went around to retrieve it. Or his explanation that he was "keeping it safe for you". It took two of them to find it, even when he told them where it was. They didn't expect to find it buried under half a ton of tarpaulins.'

'So you did check up on the locals' progress?'

'The community policing service needed monitoring. I volunteered for the job.' Peter's tone was so casual, Alan knew his cousin had made it his business to follow their progress. 'They acquitted themselves well. I wouldn't be as restrained as they were in dealing with kleptomaniac lunatics.'

'You need bigger and heavier community officers.' Alan sipped his pint. 'The one who retrieved my gate was terrified they were going to have him for breakfast.'

'He was the one who told you to get CCTV?' Peter checked.

'I told him I subscribed to Robert Frost's philosophy.'

'Frost, do I know him?'

'The writer, you ignoramus. He said, and I quote, "*Good fences make good neighbours*".'

'You have one now.'

'Only after I paid a builder more than a month's wine bill to erect one.'

'Moan, moan, moan. And don't plead poverty to me. You journalists coin it with syndication rights. I've seen your work in six or seven nationals in the last couple of months. That White Baron piece alone must have made you enough to buy a summer palace.'

'Not after tax. I have overheads.'

'Fine wine, dining, cigars …' Peter held up the cigar Alan had given him so the landlord could see it from behind the bar. 'Not that we're allowed to smoke them in this pub.'

'It's no good complaining to me about the law, Sergeant Collins,' the landlord chipped in.

'Suppose not,' Peter conceded.

'But if you have one spare I could enjoy it upstairs when I shut up shop,' he hinted.

'I couldn't afford this one. It was a present.' Peter raised his glass of orange juice in the direction of the landlord.

'This is the first time I've seen you drink anything soft at lunchtime – or any time come to that. Missus curbing your lifestyle?' Alan enquired maliciously.

'Meeting this afternoon. New female broom upstairs doesn't like officers smelling of alcohol.'

'That must cramp your and Trevor's style.'

Peter deliberately moved the conversation on from the personal. 'You put up your CCTV yet?'

'No.' Alan sank half his pint of beer.

'You've no intention of taking good advice?'

'As I said, I haven't entirely been a good boy. I had a better idea.'

'What?'

Alan tapped his nose. 'I'm waiting on results. Soon as I get my patio back, you and your lady love – Rose?'

'Daisy,' Peter growled.

'Must come round for a barbecue.'

'What have you done?'

Alan glanced at his watch. 'Tell you next time.'

'And which innocent character is the emperor of the gutter press assassinating this afternoon?'

'Haven't made my mind up – yet.' Alan hesitated. 'Off the record …'

'Isn't everything always off the record with you?'

'What do you know about that missing girl?'

Peter narrowed his eyes suspiciously. 'What missing girl?'

'The beauty queen who disappeared after winning the competition. "Miss Eco-friendly" or "Miss Alternative Lifestyle" …'

'If you mean, "Miss Green Earth" I know jack shit,' Peter answered. 'Why? Do you know more?'

'Just asking.'

'I know you. You never "just ask" about anything. You've had a tip-off?'

'Not in so many words.'

'No?' Peter queried sceptically. 'Because if you have, and kept it to yourself, you could be charged with withholding evidence.'

'It wasn't worth mentioning.'

'Then why mention it? Stay silent and it could be construed as perverting the course of justice,' Peter warned.

'I don't know anything.'

'A pound to a penny if you stretch out your tongue it will be black.'

'Grow up. We're not six years old any more.'

'You're behaving as if you're a fully paid-up member of Enid Blyton's Secret Seven.'

13

'All right.' Alan moved his chair closer to Peter's. 'I had a call this morning from someone who said they know where she is and why she's in hiding. They want to meet so I can print her side of the story.'

Peter pulled out his notebook. 'What story?'

'If I knew the answer to that, I wouldn't need to meet them.'

'When and where?'

'You expect me to tell you that so you and your colleagues can tramp in with your size fourteen boots? No way. Besides, it might be nothing.'

'And, it might be something.'

'If it comes to anything, you'll be the first to know,' Alan assured him.

'Man or woman?'

'What?'

'Who phoned you, man or woman?' Peter pressed him.

'Don't know. They used one of those electronic voice changer things.'

'Phone number?'

'They rang the office switchboard and asked to be put through to me. And don't suggest I look at the records. That phone rings off the hook. We get up to 500 calls an hour.'

'In other words you didn't try to trace it.'

'No.'

'Record it?'

'You think I have time to record every crank call that comes in?' Alan left his chair. 'Like I said, if anything comes of it, I'll let you know.'

'It's not every day a beauty queen goes missing or you read unsubstantiated articles about them being sold into white slavery on the North African coast.'

Alan held up his hands in mock defence. 'Not one of mine.'

'This week,' Peter sniped.

Alan checked his watch again. 'I have to file a piece before I meet my snitch, or not as the case maybe.'

'Piece on what?' Peter asked.

'Police incompetence,' Alan joked.

'Spell my name right.'

'Don't I always?'

'Unfortunately.' Peter picked up his coat and followed Alan out the door.

Alan filed his report, on the abandonment of a rape trial, by three forty-five. He left the office, bought a box of chocolates and drove out of town via home so he could pick up a sleeping bag in case his contact wanted to move on and it would turn into an all-nighter. He dropped the chocolates into a neighbour's house as a combination "thank you and sorry for being insensitive" gift.

Back in his car he headed for a B-road that wound through the hills. The motorway would have been faster but he'd heeded the caller's warning not to use it. He had to concede it was easier to spot a second car or a tail if you were watching a country road. Twice he heard helicopters overhead and wondered if whoever had phoned him could afford to rent one.

Deciding he was paranoid, he turned off the road and on to a lane that led to a well-known beauty spot. After nine miles of winding track he pulled into a picnic area. He drove slowly around the perimeter to check it was as deserted as it appeared to be. Eventually he parked beneath a tree at the furthest point from the entrance because it gave a clear view of both the area and the approach road. He turned off his ignition, gazed blindly at the rain-sodden scene and mulled over the telephone call that had brought him here. After a few minutes he opened his briefcase and pulled out one of the notepads that was never far from his side.

'You want a scoop?'
'Every journalist wants a scoop.'
'I know where the beauty queen is.'
'Where?'
'Not in a rich Arab's harem.'
'I never thought she was. So, where is she?'
'You think I'll tell you on the phone.'
'How do I know you're not a crank caller?'
'Because she has a birthmark on the top of her right thigh.'
'You can see it on every photograph of her taken during the swimsuit finals.'
'Can you see the one that runs into her pubic hair?'

16

There was no way of checking the information, as the caller undoubtedly knew. It was every journalist's dilemma. A story he was ninety-nine per cent certain was crap, but the one per cent dangled like the promise of a lottery win – with about the same odds.

'You want a scoop you have to pay for it.'

'You get nothing until I know your information is genuine.'

'Meet me at the picnic spot on the north side of Connor's lake. You know it?'

'Why not somewhere closer?'

'Because that is close – for me. Take the scenic route not the motorway.'

'You want me to drive on B-roads?'

'I need to know no one is following you. I'll be there between seven and nine tonight. Don't look for me; I'll find you and if I see the police or anyone else besides you there, you won't see me.'

Alan closed his notepad and reached into the back of the car for the sleeping bag. He unzipped it, threw it over himself, snuggled down in his seat and waited … and waited … and waited …

Alan woke with a start. It was pitch black and hailstones were thundering on the roof of his car. Shivering, he peered into the darkness. He could make out nothing beyond the white blur hitting the windscreen. He switched on the ignition and his headlights. The car park yawned back at him, shadowy, empty and iced with white frost. He turned on the fan and heater and looked at his clock – nine thirty. The peculiar robotic voice echoed in his head.

'I'll be there some time between seven and nine tonight. Don't look for me; I'll find you and if I see the police or anyone else besides you there, you won't see me.'

'Bloody lunatic!' He wasn't sure if he was cursing himself or the hoax caller. He allowed the car a few minutes to warm up before driving slowly around the picnic area again. Reluctantly he pulled away the sleeping bag and tossed it onto the back seat, fastened his seat-belt and drove away.

The hail and rain had stopped and a full moon was shining, pale and waxy when Alan drove down his cul-de-sac at eleven o'clock. When he and Joy had moved in some thirty-five years before, they'd taken the trouble to get to know the neighbours, but most of the friends they'd made had long since moved on, and he'd lacked the will to make the acquaintance of the families who had replaced them.

Without realising it, he had become more and more isolated within his own street. Driving from house to work and back, spending what little free time he had with colleagues, work contacts, police and "sources". Since Joy had died, the house had become no more than a place to eat, sleep, and get drunk in after a day's work. And, given his immediate neighbours – an increasing source of irritation.

The light was switched on outside the garish shed his neighbours had erected on their monstrous oversized deck. It had been deliberately placed to shine directly into his living-room, necessitating yet more expenditure on thicker blinds and curtains. He parked his car in front of his drive. Since he'd erected a five-foot fence between them, he rarely bothered to open the wooden gates and put his car in the garage.

He stepped out, locked his car and went inside, heading straight for the kitchen and the fridge-freezer. Taking a can of lager from the fridge, he opened it, poured it into a glass and walked up to the woodland patio he and Joy had sat out on almost every spring, summer and autumn night – until their neighbours had built their edifice overlooking it.

He tried to ignore his neighbours' deck as he walked down to the fence that backed on to the woods but it proved impossible. The halogen lamp glared, blinding him. He recalled all the summer evenings he and Joy had sat out here, sharing a bottle of wine and watching the wildlife in the woods. No foxes or badgers would go near that light. It was as though the idiots next door were hell-bent on despoiling and tainting everything around them. Petty, ugly people leading petty ugly lives.

He looked at the illuminated decking in front of the shed his neighbours grandly referred to as a "summer-house". There was a pool of red on the planking. It stood proud, in glaring contrast to the blue and yellow painted wood. Something was lying on it, something pale … white … tendrils of dark hair spattered with black and red globules … an axe …

The images knitted together forming a picture. He reached for his mobile and dialled 999.

CHAPTER THREE

'He is adorable. I can't wait to have one of my very own.' Daisy Sherringham tenderly stroked the cheek of Trevor and Lyn Joseph's two-month-old son with the back of her finger as he lay in her arms.

'That can be arranged. But it will take time and effort,' Peter Collins said dryly.

'He's not so adorable at four in the morning,' Trevor complained. 'We haven't had a night's sleep since he arrived.'

'Who wants sleep?' Lyn leaned over Daisy's shoulder and gazed at her son. 'You're gorgeous aren't you, Wumpelstilskin? You're goochy goochy gorgeous …'

'Do you think women ever gooed like that over us?' Peter asked Trevor as they watched Lyn join Daisy in blatant baby adoration.

'Trevor, perhaps, but not you,' Daisy answered. The telephone rang. 'Goodnight, Trevor. Don't wake me up when you come stumbling in at four in the morning, Peter.'

'Who says it's work?' Peter topped up his glass from the bottle at his elbow.

'Who else would it be at this hour?' Daisy answered. 'But look on the bright side; at least we managed an entire dinner party this time. Don't worry, Peter, I can travel home in a taxi by myself. I'm a big girl now.'

Trevor picked up the receiver. 'Trevor Joseph.'

He frowned as he listened. 'I've had a couple of drinks. Send a car and driver. I'll be with you as soon as it gets here.'

'Trouble?' Peter looked at him.

'Could be. Want to come?'

'Don't I always?'

'Might be interesting.'

'Why?' Peter shrugged on his coat.

'A body has been found in the street where your friend the journalist lives.'

'He's my cousin, not friend. I had lunch with him today and all he did was complain about his neighbours. Perhaps they stole one thing too many from him and he finally snapped.'

'I hope you're joking.'

'You didn't hear him go on – and on – and on – about them.'

'Let's look at the evidence before we start on the theories, shall we?' Trevor kissed Lyn and dropped a kiss onto his baby's head. 'See you in the morning, sweethearts.'

'Marty won't thank you for calling him that when he's older.' Peter kissed the cheek Daisy offered. 'I'll be back as soon as I can.'

'Why don't you stay here tonight, Daisy?' Lyn suggested.

'Thank you, but I need my car.' She deposited the baby carefully in Lyn's arms. 'I'm operating before nine in the morning. Skin grafts on a burn victim. Poor mite's only four years old.'

'Oh no! What Happened? No, don't tell me, I

can't bear the thought of a child being hurt. Motherhood does that to you. It makes all children's pain, even ones you don't know, somehow personal.'

'I can imagine. And, after work, four of us are leaving for a medical conference. In New York. So if you need any American shopping …'

'Conference,' Peter sneered. 'You're off for a jolly and a shopping trip.'

'Anything to get away from you and your moods, darling,' Daisy mocked him.

Trevor flicked the blinds. 'Driver's here. We'll drop you off on the way, Daisy.'

'Thank you. It's kind of you to think of me. Peter never does.'

'I heard that.' Peter returned from the hall with his jacket.

'You were meant to.' Daisy picked up her wrap and handbag. 'Thank you for a lovely dinner. Our turn next.'

'It'll have to wait until the case is closed,' Lyn warned.

The forensic team had already arrived and were erecting tenting, screens and spotlights in the garden of a house at the end of the cul-de-sac. Trevor wondered why they'd bothered with spotlights. The halogen lights that illuminated the decking area were brilliant and could be seen from the road, although the decking itself was partially screened by the back of the house.

He climbed into the paper overalls and overshoes a young constable, Sarah Merchant, handed him.

'You're here bright and early,' he commented.

'Chris and I were on duty, sir, we took the call.'

'Trevor, nice to see you back in home territory. I feel safer walking the streets knowing you're around.' Patrick O'Kelly, the on-call pathologist was sitting in the boot of his hatchback, pulling on his boots.

Trevor zipped up his overall and joined Patrick. 'Your sense of humour never changes.'

'Thank you.'

'It wasn't a compliment,' Trevor said. 'Had a chance to have a look yet?'

'Only the digital photographs the first officer on the scene took. Axe in head. Looks simple, but as you know …'

'The ones that look simple never are.' Peter glanced towards his cousin's garden. On the patio, overlooked by the neighbours' monstrous five-foot-high deck and even more monstrous shed, he could make out the shadowy figures of Alan and a uniformed officer.

Patrick followed his line of sight. 'That's the neighbour who spotted the body and called the emergency services.' He left the back of the hatchback, slammed the door and shouted to his assistant, Jenny.

Trevor watched Patrick and Jenny skirt around the house and approach the deck. They were careful to walk on the plastic sheets the forensic team had used to cover the drive and garden. Sarah appeared at his side, notebook and pencil in hand.

'I telephoned the station and told them to set up an incident room, sir.'

'Thank you, we'll need as many officers as can be spared at first light to carry out a fingertip search of the garden,' he said, as they followed Patrick to the raised deck.

'Yes, sir,' she scribbled as she walked.

'Arrange interviews with all the neighbours. I know it's late but try and get them done in the next twenty-four hours while their minds are fresh. I'd like you to correlate the evidence as it comes in.'

'Yes, sir. Thank you for your confidence.'

'Thank you for being efficient.' Trevor looked back down the street. 'There are how many houses here? – Twenty?'

'Twenty-two, sir.'

'I want every house visited, even the ones at the far end. Find out who is the …'

'Busybody of the street, sir?'

'You learn fast. Did the victim live with anyone?'

'Husband and children, sir.'

'They at home?'

'No sign of him or the children, sir.'

'Was the house open?'

'The back door wasn't locked. No sign of a break-in, but if there was an intruder he could have walked in as we did. The house could be cleaner. It's cluttered with the usual paraphernalia you'd expect from a family. Overflowing toy baskets. Bins of dirty washing in the kitchen. DVDs scattered around the machine. Clothes heaped on chairs in the bedrooms.'

'Send forensics in to check out the house when they've finished with the shed, deck and garden.'

'Will do, sir.'

Trevor glanced at his watch. 'You said DC Brookes was here?' Christopher Brookes, a young constable, had recently been seconded to serious crimes along with Sarah.

'Yes, sir.'

'Everyone hates knocking on doors, especially at this time of night, but both of you go up and down the street now. Leave the ones that aren't showing a light until morning, but visit every house that is. Ask if they saw or heard anything.'

'Sir.' Sarah left him.

Trevor walked up the garden towards the deck. Both deck and shed were massive, totally out of keeping with the scale of the garden. Sarah had mentioned children but it was far too large for a playhouse, more like a workshop or potting-shed for a keen gardener, but when he looked around all he saw was a scrubby lawn, balding in patches and borders of straggly perennials vying for space with weeds. Close up the shed was painted like an ice cream kiosk. Garish, lit up like an amusement arcade it wouldn't have looked out of place in Disneyland or Blackpool.

'No accounting for taste.' Patrick was kneeling

on the decking in front of the shed, examining the naked corpse of a woman through an oversized magnifying glass.

Trevor remained on the ground four and a half feet below him. 'You talking about the victim or the garden?'

'This make-shift theatre.'

Trevor stood back. Patrick was right. The decking was high enough to be a stage; open the front of the shed and you'd have a theatre.

'Fifty to sixty years old, dyed brown hair, brown eyes, five feet four inches, birthmark on left breast and right leg, stretch marks on torso.' Patrick didn't look up from the magnifying glass.

'Cause of death?'

'Blow or blows to the head from the axe embedded in her skull. From the blood pattern and spray, she was alive at the initial impact. She also lifted her right hand, possibly in an attempt to protect her head. It's severed at the wrist. But although there would have been considerable bleeding it didn't contribute to her death.'

'She was hit more than once?'

Patrick moved the magnifying glass up to her skull. He peered at the hair- and gore-clotted wounds. 'There are three distinct and separate cuts, but the axe could have hit the same spots more than once. It looks likely given the width of the cuts and bone fragmentation at the edges of two of the wounds. Given the severity, she would have lost consciousness within seconds. Death from shock

27

and bleeding would have been within minutes. But the attacker kept chopping. One of the cuts is *post mortem*.'

'Frenzied attack?'

'I'd say whoever did this wasn't feeling very friendly towards the victim at the time of the assault.'

'Thank you, Patrick.' Trevor was cold, tired, and in no mood for any more of the pathologist's humour. 'Any sign of sexual assault?'

'Not obviously so.' Patrick sat back on his heels. 'As you see, she's naked but her clothes are hanging on hooks in the shed. Either she undressed herself or we have a neat and tidy killer. Both are possibilities. DNA and forensics might come up with something to help you decide which.'

'Is there a hot tub?'

'No, and no pool.'

'No indications why she was naked?'

'Perhaps she was a nudist or liked to give the neighbours a thrill. There has to be a reason why this shed was built on such a high platform.'

'Like what?'

'You're the detective.' Patrick looked down at the corpse. 'No body piercing, not even earrings and no tattoos. Strange thing is I'd expect more blood after axe blows to the head. Any injury to the skull bleeds profusely. Also there are footprints and smudges on the deck around the injuries.'

'Indicative of what?' Trevor asked.

'How would I know? It's possible someone

mopped up after she was killed but don't take that as a given, I'm not into guessing.'

'Why would anyone do that?'

'I have absolutely no idea.'

'Would the killer have been bloodstained?'

'Could be if he wasn't wearing protective clothing.' Patrick rose cautiously to his feet and looked around. 'Jenny, check we've photographed every inch of this site, will you?' He jumped down off the platform, landing beside Trevor. 'I've done all I can here. I'll do the PM first thing in the morning.'

'Time of death?'

'You know I hate that question.'

'And you know I have to ask. Any idea?' Trevor pleaded.

'It was a warm afternoon but the air temperature's not far off freezing now and we had hailstones an hour or so ago. Rigor's set in and the body's wet. So I'll venture that she's been dead at least three to four hours. But it could have been earlier.'

'Can't you be more specific?'

'No.'

Trevor knew better than to push Patrick. 'Anything on who we should be looking for?'

'Someone strong enough to wield an axe and crack her skull. Beyond that, at this stage I can't help you.'

Trevor looked up and saw Peter talking to a uniformed constable and Alan Piper in the garden next door. 'Thanks, Patrick, see you in the morning.'

'I'll keep the coffee and chocolate biscuits on ice.' Patrick knew Trevor found his habit of storing his milk, coffee and snacks in mortuary drawers distasteful.

Trevor walked around to the drive next door. Peter met him at the gate.

'Saw you coming.'

'I heard Alan found the body.'

'He saw it from his patio.' Peter led the way around the house into the back garden.

'You do realise you won't be allowed to work on this case?' Trevor checked with Peter.

'Personal involvement and all that. Yes. But regulations can't stop me from calling in on my cousin for a friendly family chat.'

Trevor looked at his watch but it was too dark to see the face.

'We're insomniacs,' Peter said cheerfully. 'Aren't we, Alan?'

'Hello, Trevor. Good to see you, wish it was under different circumstances.'

'A quiet drink in a pub would be better.' Trevor nodded to the officer who'd stepped back when he'd arrived. 'They could do with some help to square off the garden next door in preparation for a search, Constable.'

'Yes, sir.' The constable walked away.

'What time did you notice the body, Alan?' Trevor steered the conversation firmly on a professional track.

'I came home about eleven o'clock, went into the house, poured myself a beer and came straight up here. I suppose it would have been around ten past eleven.'

'Back from where?'

'A fool's errand.'

'You told me,' Peter reminded. 'You may as well tell him.'

'And if I don't?'

'I will,' Peter warned.

'I got a call this afternoon from someone who said he knew where the missing beauty queen was.'

'The one the tabloid press would have us believe has been sold into white slavery?' Trevor asked.

'That's the one. Whoever it was wanted me to meet them at Connor's Lake.'

'That's over forty miles away.'

'Fifty-five door to door,' Alan corrected. 'They said they'd be in the picnic area between seven and nine. I waited, no one showed.'

'You saw no one.'

'It was bucketing down hailstones. I suppose someone could have come and gone …' He heard Peter snort. 'All right I went to sleep.'

'For how long?' Trevor persisted.

'An hour, maybe more.'

'And before you drove up to Connor's Lake?'

'I was in court all morning following a rape case that was thrown out for lack of evidence. Then I had lunch with Peter in the Black Boar before returning to the office. And I stayed there until I drove to the lake.'

'So you left town … when?'

'About half past four.'

'Did anyone see you after that?'

'If they looked inside my car and recognised me driving, yes.'

Trevor pulled out his notebook. 'I'll need your registration. We'll track it on the motorway. You did take the motorway?'

'No.'

'You went over the mountains?' Trevor said incredulously.

'Whoever phoned, told me they wouldn't show if I used any other route or tipped off the police. I knew if they were watching it would be easier for them to make sure I was alone if I drove on a B-road.'

'So, you drove the long way round, no one showed, you came back here, fetched a beer from your fridge, then what?'

'Walked up here.'

'You often walk up here when it's cold and dark?'

'It's the only bloody time I can come up here. See that?' Alan pointed at the enormous deck that held next door's shed. Before the bad taste morons next door built that, Joy and I used to sit here every evening. They deliberately erected that to overlook our entire garden and since then, neither I – nor Joy during the last few months of her life – had a moment's privacy. Every time I walk outside my back door one or other of the bastards is there, peering over the fence.' He fell silent for a moment. When he spoke again, he was calmer.

'Sorry, it infuriates me to consider how they impacted on our life and upset Joy. She used to love it here. She couldn't even sit here when she was dying. They were constantly back and forth with their sneaking and listening in on every bloody word we said.'

'Did you complain?'

'Oh yes. Ask him.' Alan pointed to Peter. 'You're not supposed to speak ill of the dead but he saw "her next door" crawling along the ground listening in on our conversation.'

'I can vouch for that,' Peter agreed.

'They even fixed the light on that stupid garden shed so it shines directly into our living room.'

'No need to tell Trevor your temper's still running high,' Peter murmured.

'Did you try talking to your neighbours when they were building this …' Trevor looked back at the deck and shed and words failed him. He was trying desperately to remain impartial but he had to agree, he would hate something as large, ostentatious and privacy-destroying, in the garden next door to his house.

'I tried to reason with them but gave up when they started stealing things.'

'What kind of things?'

'At first it was small things. They tore down a

fence at the back of my garage and took all the plants. When I challenged them they said the plants had died, although they all looked perfectly healthy to me a short time before. Then, I had a load of paving bricks delivered, and a couple of square metres disappeared. Some reappeared under pots in their garden. The final straw came when they stole one of my gates and a gate post.'

'Did you contact the police?'

'The joking police,' Peter muttered.

'I'll pretend I didn't hear that, Sergeant Collins,' Trevor reprimanded him. Peter didn't voice an objection. Trevor insisted on observing the formalities when working on a case.

'The Community Police came round, they retrieved the gate and gatepost, warned me my neighbours were aggressive and I could expect more trouble from them. They advised me to put up CCTV.'

'The Community Police were helpful?'

'Very. Peter suggested I contact them. He and I were enjoying a quiet drink in the garden last summer, when Peter spotted Kacy slithering along the ground like a snake, but we've already told you about that.'

'It was a personal highly sensitive chat.' Peter kept a straight face.

Trevor allowed the comment to go unchallenged. He could imagine the kind of personal sensitive conversations Peter and Alan shared.

'You said her name was Kacy?'

34

'Kacy Howells.'

'Did either of you say anything when you saw her?' Trevor eyed Peter, trying to decipher his expression in the darkness.

'We both challenged her, she ran off into the house without a word.'

'Which is why I advised Alan to contact the … community police,' Peter explained. 'Alan's face is well known locally. His photograph appears above his columns in the local and national papers. He does the occasional TV appearance. I was concerned he'd picked up a stalker.'

Sarah Merchant strode up the path towards them.

Trevor effected the introductions. 'DC Sarah Merchant, Alan Piper.'

Sarah smiled at Alan. 'I recognise you from your photograph in the paper, sir.'

'See what I mean,' Peter said.

Sarah turned back to Trevor. 'I spoke to a Mrs Walsh, who lives in the house that faces down the length of the cul-de-sac on the other side of the Howells, sir. She said she saw George Howells drive off with the children early this morning. The Howells talk to very few people in the street but the children are left to roam at all hours. The youngest, who's about four, told Mr Walsh that they were going to spend a few days with their grandmother because their daddy had to go away to work.'

'What does he do?'

'Civil servant.'

'My kind of people,' Peter said disparagingly.

'Mrs Walsh saw us arrive and asked me what was going on. I told her we were investigating an incident. She asked if anyone was hurt and added, "If anything has happened to Kacy Howells don't expect anyone in this street to be sorry. She's crossed everyone at some time or another and it would be good to see the kids get some proper mothering for a change. They might find one with a foster family that wouldn't put them out on the street with the milk bottles and take them in at night with the cat".'

'So our victim wasn't popular with Mrs Walsh as well as you, Alan.'

'Some people "would be enormously improved by death",' Peter quoted.

CHAPTER FOUR

Trevor had only managed two hours sleep before he walked into the station at eight o'clock. He went to his office and checked his e-mail and voicemail before walking down the corridor to the incident room Sarah had organised. She was working on one of a bank of computers.

'Have you been home?' Trevor asked.

'I'm not tired, sir.'

'It's Trevor in the office and that wasn't what I asked.'

'Chris and I decided to record what information we had before returning to the street to interview any residents who are home during the day. Chris is in the canteen.'

'You eaten?'

'Yes.'

'Less than him evidently.'

She turned her swivel chair to face him. 'I'm not keen on fry-ups, sir.'

'Then you'll never make a real police officer.'

'I've downloaded the photographs the pathologist e-mailed us and printed them off with the ones that were taken at the crime scene last night.'

'Thank you.' Trevor took the file she offered him. 'Any stay-at-home mothers in the street?'

'No, sir and just one part-timer.'

'Kacy Howells,' Trevor guessed.

'She worked in the same office as her husband for twenty hours a week.'

'After you've finished the interviews, you and Chris go home and get some sleep. That's an order.'

'But …'

'Be back at eight thirty this evening for a case conference. The PM results should be in and we might have some information from forensics.'

'We'll be here.'

Trevor's immediate superior Dan Evans entered the room with Peter. Peter was heavily built and six feet two inches but Dan dwarfed him. The Welshman was massive and looked intimidating, yet he was the gentlest man Trevor knew.

'Good morning, I see you've heard the news.' Trevor opened the file Sarah had given him and spread the photographs on a table.

'Peter wants to work on the case. Do you have any objections?'

'Not if upstairs know he's related to a witness and are happy about it.'

'I'll talk to them this morning. First photographs?' Dan looked over Trevor's shoulder.

'Patrick e-mailed some of these. He's doing the PM this morning. The others were taken at the scene last night.'

Trevor moved a couple onto a glass screen. Sarah had already pinned up a scale sketch of the house, garden, deck and shed.

'Relatives been informed?' Dan checked.

'In the early hours. The husband was on one of

those management consultancy team-building courses the civil service are so fond of and private business gave up on years ago. In the Lake District. We found a contact number next to the phone in the Howells' house, which was just as well as the organisers had confiscated the participants' mobiles. I left it to the locals to tell him about his wife's murder. Two of our constables are bringing him down today.'

'Has he an alibi for last night?' Peter asked.

'Cast-iron,' Trevor revealed. 'He and twenty colleagues spent the night camping next to one of the lakes.'

'Rather them than me in this weather,' Peter said.

'Rather them than me in any weather,' Dan added in his slow Welsh lilt. 'I'm not built for camping.'

'His children are with their maternal grandmother. She's been told that her daughter has been murdered. A family liaison officer is with them.'

'How old are the children?' Dan asked.

'Four and six. The father wants to break the news to them.'

'Poor souls. So, what have you got?' Dan asked.

'Hopefully, later this morning some useful information from Patrick and forensics. I have appointments with both.'

'Any suspects?' Dan checked.

'It's early days but we already know that her two immediate neighbours disliked her. She wasn't a popular woman – apparently,' Peter added the last word when Dan gave him a hard look.

'First case conference?' Dan checked.

'Eight thirty this evening.'

'I'll be here.'

'Thought you were working on the drug war murders. I heard the tally was up to seven dead.' Peter moved a chair in front of the screen.

'Four corpses, three missing, they could be in hiding but I doubt it. The case won't stop me from keeping an eye on other investigations in the department.'

Trevor glanced through the rest of the photographs of the murder scene. 'There's nothing in these that I didn't see last night.' He picked up the photographs Patrick had taken in the mortuary. 'These, I'll go over with Patrick when I see him this morning.'

'If you need help, phone.' Dan went to the door. 'Good luck with your case.'

Dan nodded. 'We'll get the villains responsible.'

Trevor and Peter didn't doubt he would. Dan had one of the best clean-up rates in the station.

'If you're helping – help,' Trevor admonished Peter after Dan left.

'I'm studying the sketches of the murder scene.'

'Through closed eyes?'

'I was resting them for a moment.'

'Rest over; drive me to the morgue.'

'Now that's an invitation from a superior no officer can resist.' Peter patted his pockets for his car keys.

Trevor had worked with Patrick O'Kelly on several cases and valued his expertise. He was one of the best and most highly respected pathologists in the country. But Trevor had never entirely become accustomed to Patrick's idiosyncrasies. He found him and his attractive blonde assistant, Jenny, sitting side by side on a dissection slab, drinking latte from specimen beakers and munching chocolate biscuits.

'Coffee?' Patrick asked Trevor and Peter when they walked in.

'No thanks,' Trevor refused.

'Go on, live dangerously. I'll get Jenny to rinse out a couple of beakers that haven't even been used to hold specimens.'

'I've just had breakfast,' Trevor refused firmly. 'What you got for us?'

'Not much more than I had last night. Want to see her again?'

'Not unless you think it will help.'

'Injury pattern might.' Patrick jumped down from the slab, walked across the mortuary and opened a door that led into a small, cold room dominated by a bank of drawers. He checked the tags before pulling one out and folding back the sheet that covered the body. He pointed to one particular cut on the head. 'The blow that killed her. As you see it practically cut the brain in two.'

'Delivered with force?'

'I'd say so, yes. Now look at these other blows.'

'Not as deep, slighter …'

'This one is glancing.' Patrick took a pair of gloves from a pack on top of the drawers, slipped them on and parted the corpse's hair.

'Which means our attacker wasn't physically fit?' Peter guessed.

'Possibly not as in weight-training gym fit, no,' Patrick replied cautiously.

'So, it could be a woman?' Trevor suggested.

'Or someone trying to fool us that the killer was an older, weaker person or a younger one …'

'Is there anyone we can rule out?' Peter enquired testily.

'I'm not a clairvoyant, Sergeant.'

'Pity.'

'If I were, you and the inspector would be out of a job. To recap on what I told you last night, Trevor, death was as I described, one axe blow killed her, the others were unnecessary extras.'

'First blow?'

'From the pattern I'd say third.'

'Because she struggled?'

'The only evidence we have that she fought back is the severed hand. Bruising on back of neck occurred before she died. From the pattern of the blows and the angle of the wounds, I'd say she was kneeling when she was killed. DNA samples, her own and those found on her and on the deck and the shed are with the lab. No semen or obvious sign of sexual assault. The murder was brutal and lacked finesse.'

'Any identifying marks on the axe?' Trevor asked.

'None I saw.' Patrick answered. 'You're thinking the murderer brought it with him?'

'It's worth finding out.'

'If it didn't belong to the Howells it would be a give-away,' Peter said. 'On the other hand, a man carrying an axe up a cul-de-sac would risk being noticed.'

'If it did belong to the Howells and it was lying on the deck, it could be that someone lost their temper and lashed out,' Trevor mused. 'Where's the axe now?'

'Forensics.' Patrick picked up the sheet.

'Our next stop.' Trevor took a last look at Kacy Howells' head before Patrick covered it.

'Lot of help aren't you?' Peter grumbled good-naturedly at Patrick.

'Try to be. If you stumble across any more bodies, put them in your car and drop them outside my jurisdiction, there's good fellows.'

'There are five distinct sets of fingerprints on the axe.' Alison, the middle-aged senior technician in the laboratory replied to Trevor's question. 'Also smudges that suggest it was handled by someone wearing gloves. Patrick sent us through the victim's DNA and prints. We're waiting on her husband's, children's, other members of her family and visitors to the house.'

'Might be an idea to fingerprint the neighbours,'

Peter suggested.

Trevor nodded. 'Tell Sarah to organise it. What else have you found?'

'A false panel that concealed a cupboard in the shed. These were behind it.' Alison led them to a table in the centre of the room. She pulled away a sheet of thick plastic.

Peter covered his eyes. 'I'm too young to see this lot.'

'I knew you'd want results fast, Trevor, so they've all been checked for DNA and prints. They're safe to handle.'

'The last time I saw this many sex aids was in a display case at Anne Summers.' Trevor picked up a set of handcuffs.

'Two sets of those were fastened to the panel at ankle level. There were also leather belts attached to the wall at neck and waist height and two above head height, probably wrist straps. The whips were hung on a bracket besides the fastenings.'

Trevor replaced the handcuffs on the table. 'Looks like Kacy Howells had at least one sexual partner who was into sado-masochism.'

'I didn't know vibrators came in so many shapes, sizes and colours. A bunny for God's sake!' Peter held up a purple plastic rabbit. 'Where do you put its ears?'

'Ten of these were new, clean, and still packed in the proverbial brown envelopes,' Alison told them.

'Which leads us to surmise what exactly?' Peter asked.

'Did you work on that massage parlour murder, Alison?' Trevor checked.

'Yes. And congratulations on getting your man.'

'Your department deserves the congratulations. You found the DNA and effectively handed us the villain on a plate. But, if I remember correctly, there were fewer toys there and they had a dozen girls working out of those premises.'

'So, why would one suburban housewife want this lot?' Peter picked up one of a set of identical spray cans and read the label. 'One can of nipple dust I would find peculiar, fourteen seems downright weird.'

'You finished with the shed?' Trevor asked Alison.

'Yes, we stripped out what we wanted so it's safe for you to go in there without contaminating the scene. We lifted the decking and brought in the planking, together with the furniture and cushions. We're running tests on them.'

'And the house and garden?'

'The team is still working there.'

'You'll …'

'E-mail or fax results through as soon as we get them. Constable Merchant gave us our orders on the telephone first thing this morning.'

Trevor's phone rang. He stepped away from the bizarre display to take the call. When he finished, he turned to Peter.

'We need to get back to the incident room. Thank you, Alison. You're doing a great job. If there's anything to be found I'm one hundred per cent convinced you'll find it.'

'Do I get a bunch of flowers when you solve the case?'

'And a box of chocolates,' Trevor called back.

Sarah Merchant had tracked down a dozen copies of the amateur porn magazine and distributed them to the senior officers working on the case; she'd also handed out computer print-outs of a website that was carrying the advertisement that had attracted her attention.

Peter opened his copy of the magazine at the marked page and saw a photograph of Kacy Howells' head transposed on to a computerised, pornographic image of a naked female body, under the heading,

Want fun? Send me a present and your phone number and if the gift is large enough, I'm yours. Cheese on toast can be arranged.

Below it was a telephone number.

Trevor looked up from his own copy. '"Cheese on toast?" Am I missing something here?'

'You've never been offered any when you've taken Lyn down the pub?' Peter asked.

'No.'

'I'm surprised. Lyn's very tasty. "Cheese on toast" is a euphemism for wife-swapping.'

'How the hell do you know that?' Trevor asked Peter.

'Because I lived in hope when I was married.

46

Not that anyone ever offered. Or that I was surprised. One look at my ex's face was enough to put anyone off.'

'You checked the phone number?' Trevor asked Sarah before Peter could elaborate. Peter and his first wife had been divorced for seven years but the memory had remained bitter – on Peter's side.

'Supplied by the magazine, sir. It's an answering service provided by them.'

Trevor didn't prompt her to call him by his Christian name again. Old habits died hard and he realised it was going to take time. 'Did Kacy Howells place the ad?'

'We have people looking into it, sir. I spoke to the editor of the magazine. He was asked to forward all messages to Kacy Howells' landline and mobile number at weekly intervals. The numbers he'd been given are the Howells'. But their landline number is in the directory and the mobile number is on the answer phone so anyone could have picked it up by calling the Howells when they were out. The magazine has a safety policy. They insist ads are paid for by a credit card in the name of the person being advertised.'

'Was it?'

'Yes, sir. The application for the card was made a month ago and the credit card company has a record of it being used twice. Once, two weeks ago to pay for this ad, which was placed online, and to pay for sex toys and aids, again bought online. It was a sizeable order of sex aids. Over two hundred pounds' worth. The balance on the credit card was paid off over the counter of a local bank in cash yesterday. I asked the cashiers if they can recall who paid it. So far I haven't had any luck but I have requested the bank's CCTV tapes.'

'So, Mr and Mrs Howells could be swingers?' Peter looked from Sarah to Trevor.

'It's possible, sir.'

'There's something else?' Trevor sensed.

'You saw the sex toys forensics found in the shed, sir. We found more in unopened packages in the house. We also found chocolates and enough flowers to stock a florist.'

'When did this ad go in?'

'Magazine came out three days ago, sir.'

'Which would explain all the newly stamped plain brown envelopes. Popular lady or a set-up?' Trevor turned his chair around and threw the question at Chris and Peter as well as Sarah.

'Could be either,' Peter observed: 'But the only ones who could have sent her presents are people who knew where she lived. There's no address with the ad, and although the magazine agreed to forward messages, I doubt they'd send on gifts. Am I right?' he asked Sarah.

'You are, sir. I checked with the editor as soon as I heard about the sex toys.'

'How did you find this?' Trevor held up the magazine.

'I asked an officer to visit the office where the Howells worked and carry out a routine search of

George and Kacy Howells' desks. She went there first thing this morning and found the magazine in a bin bag. The cleaner couldn't remember which bin it had been in. She empties them all into one sack. The officer found over two dozen copies of the magazine in the building.'

'Don't tell me, they'd been sent anonymously?' Trevor didn't know why he'd phrased it as a question.

'According to the magazine editor they'd been ordered and paid for along with delivery when the ad was placed. And on the same credit card,' Sarah confirmed.

'It has to be a set-up,' Trevor said, 'no outwardly respectable civil servant would advertise his wife and his services for wife-swapping in a porn magazine and send copies to the office. They'd risk losing their jobs, and that's without the ridicule and snide remarks they'd be subjected to.'

'The entire staff of the office could be at it, in which case it would pay to advertise.' Peter pulled a chair out from a table and sat on it.

'Has the husband arrived here?' Trevor asked.

'He was taken to his mother-in-law's house, sir,' Sarah informed him. 'He wanted to see his children.'

'Bring him in this afternoon. I'll question him here. If he objects, tell him we're doing it to save his blushes. In the meantime we carry on interviewing the neighbours. Starting with your cousin, Peter.' He went to the door and turned back. 'I thought I'd ordered you and Chris to go home and get some sleep, Sarah?'

'You did. We decided to work through.'

Realising there was no point in trying to force them to go home, Trevor said, 'Don't forget to put in your overtime sheets.'

'We won't, sir.'

'I'll telephone Alan,' Peter volunteered.

'Ask him to come in at lunchtime. That will give us an hour to go over the information Sarah and Chris have come up with.'

'Oh joy,' Peter said tonelessly.

'This would be a good one to start with, sir.' Sarah pushed a computer print-out across the table towards Trevor and handed out copies to Peter and Chris.

Trevor read the name on the top. 'Mrs Walsh?'

'I talked to her again this morning. She was very helpful.'

'She even gave us a diary, not that it proved easy to prise it away from her. I had to promise to copy it and get it back to her ASAP as well as give her a new notebook.' Chris handed Trevor a small red book. 'It's a breakdown of every tradesman who comes into the cul-de-sac, the time they usually arrive, the time they actually arrive, which doors they knock on and how long they spend in every house.'

Trevor flicked through the pages. 'This is the original?'

'Yes, but I've already copied it,' Sarah told him.

Trevor noted that the pages were dated. He turned to the day before. 'I see the paperboy went to about half the houses in the street and NO MILKMAN is written large on every page.'

'Mrs Walsh was upset when he retired. He used to deliver fresh vegetables and dairy products as well as milk.'

'When did he retire?'

'Five years ago.'

Trevor couldn't recall the last time he'd seen a milk-float on the street. Did everyone order their milk along with their groceries on the internet these days and have it delivered as Lyn did?

'The window-cleaner went to seven houses and stayed an hour and half at the Howells' house?'

'Their windows must have been very dirty,' Peter observed.

'The window-cleaner's not the only one who made long visits to the Howells' house, sir. If you look back, there's mention of visits that range from half an hour to two hours in length from the fishmonger, postman and various delivery van drivers.'

'How reliable is your Mrs Walsh?' Trevor asked Sarah.

'I'd say a hundred per cent, sir. She didn't stop writing the diary when we were with her. She keeps a stop watch on the table next to her. And it wasn't just the routine of the Howells she timed. She watches all her neighbours and clocks them all in and out, including Alan Piper the journalist who lives the other side of the Howells. Apparently he lost his wife fairly recently, and since her death he has taken to visiting a divorcee who lives in the street several times a week.'

Trevor looked at Peter. 'That is one you can question Alan about, Peter.'

CHAPTER FIVE

Peter walked down the corridor to Trevor's office, knocked once and entered. 'I left a message on Alan's mobile but he won't be able to pick it up for at least four hours. He's with the Queen.'

Trevor turned from his computer where he was reading the interviews Sarah had already inputted with the Howells' neighbours. 'What Queen?'

'As far as I know we have only one. She lives in Buckingham Palace, and Windsor Castle and Balmoral ...'

'I need all my energy for the case. Spare me the list of royal residences, extravagances we have to pay for and republican arguments.' After reading an article on how many boiled eggs Prince Charles wasted at his country house every shooting season, Peter had spent hours on a calculator in an effort to prove it was equal to his yearly tax bill.

'*Your* Queen is opening a hospital that's been up and running for six months. Alan's covering it for the national and local papers. In honour of the occasion our Health Trust has cancelled all outpatient appointments and non-urgent operations, which no doubt delighted everyone on the waiting lists. But we can't have Her Majesty rubbing shoulders with inferior mortals, especially sick ones, now can we?'

'Did you call in just to tell me that Alan can't be contacted?'

'No. George Howells is here. He volunteered his own and kids' DNA when we told him we needed it for elimination purposes. We've also taken Kacy Howells' parents' and brother's.'

'What about George Howells' parents?'

'Both dead and his brother hasn't been to the house since he married.'

'Problems?'

Peter shrugged. 'George said Kacy didn't get on with him and his wife.'

'How is George Howells?' Trevor asked.

'Shell-shocked. Family liaison has remained with his mother-in-law and children. Sarah is looking after him.'

'That girl's going to wear herself out.'

'You know the youngsters in this department. Keener than rats downwind of a sewer. All they can think about is promotion. When I left her she was feeding George Howells sympathy, tea and biscuits in interview room 3.'

Trevor reluctantly left his desk. He always felt incompetent and inadequate whenever he had to interview the relative of a murder victim. He hadn't needed a counsellor to tell him it was down to a misplaced sense of guilt. There was no way that he, or any other police officer, could prevent a random murder. Dan Evans and hard-learned experience had taught him to view crime scenes and corpses dispassionately. Calm analytical thinking was essential to accumulate evidence that would stand up in court, achieve conviction of the guilty and justice for the victim. Relatives brought a personal aspect to a case. A sharp, unwelcome reminder of his own and his family's mortality. And, since the birth of his son, thoughts of death had become even more unpalatable.

Peter joined Trevor at the viewing window outside the interview room. A slightly built, nondescript, fair-haired man with watery blue eyes was sitting, hunched over the table in the centre of the room, a cup of tea and a plate of chocolate biscuits at his elbow. Sarah was sitting at his side, a sympathetic expression on her face, her hand resting on the table close to his.

'Doesn't look the type to have a wife who puts it about, does he?' Peter commented.

'We can't be sure she did.'

'Come on, all those sex aids? Don't tell me she bought them to titillate him.'

'You can't judge a book by its cover.'

'You do all the time,' Peter contradicted him. 'And he's not the "cheese on toast" type. They're flash Harrys with bouffant hair or toupees, fake tan, designer sunglasses …'

'And you know this, how?' Trevor continued to watch George Howells.

'Experience,' Peter continued unabashed. 'But from what I saw of his other half, she didn't look the type either. Not a painted fingernail, scrap of make-up or hint of French knickers in sight.'

'It's good to have an expert on wife-swapping on my team.'

'He doesn't look straight.'

'You referring to his sexual or criminal tendencies?'

'He's gay,' Peter pronounced emphatically.

'Even if it was possible to tell whether someone is gay or not simply from looking at them, the crime that put Oscar Wilde behind bars was struck off the statute book years ago.'

'And thank the Law Lords for it. But his penchant for the same sex must have strained a marriage where the wife had as many vibrators as his had. On second thoughts, perhaps that's why she bought them.'

'That's if they were bought by her. Do you have a copy of the magazine? I left mine in my office.'

Peter produced it from his pocket. Trevor took it from him. 'Do me a favour, go through the witness statements Chris and Sarah have taken so far and see if anything strikes you?'

'You don't have to keep doing that.'

'What?'

'Saying "Do me a favour" every time you want something. You've been promoted. There's no need to pretend I'm anything but your underling.' Peter grinned. 'Just don't forget I'm the one living with the doctor and you're the one married to a nurse so our family incomes are even.'

Trevor smiled. 'So you're only living with Daisy for her wage packet?'

'Absolutely. Have you any idea what that woman earns? Well, can't stand chatting here all day, the boss has given me a job to do.'

Trevor watched Peter walk away before opening the door of the interview room. Sarah and George Howells both rose to their feet.

'Mr George Howells, sir,' Sarah effected the introduction. 'Mr Howells, Detective Inspector Trevor Joseph, the senior officer in charge of the investigation.'

Trevor held out his hand. George shook it. His palm was damp, his wrist limp, his grip feeble.

'Inspector.'

'My condolences on the tragic loss of your wife, Mr Howells.'

George blew his nose in a tissue that he tucked up the sleeve of his camel-coloured V-necked sweater. His hands fluttered back down to the table. 'Thank you.' His voice was high-pitched.

'Please, sit down.' Trevor took the chair opposite George and Sarah.

'I'll get more tea. Would you like a cup, sir?' Sarah collected the cups.

'Would you like more tea, Mr Howells? Trevor asked.

'No, thank you. All I seem to have done since the police arrived at our camp site early this morning is drink tea.'

'I am sorry to have to question you at a time like this, Mr Howells, but speed is of the essence in a murder investigation.' Trevor produced a notepad and pencil, but he also switched on the recorder. After giving details of the date, time and investigation he launched into formal questioning.

'When did you last see your wife, Mr Howells?'

'Yesterday morning. We breakfasted together with the children as we always do. Then I packed the car with the children's and my own bags and drove the children to my mother-in-law's before going on to the office where a coach was waiting to take the staff who'd been selected for the course to the Lake District.'

'What time did you leave the house?'

'Around seven thirty. Half an hour earlier than school time. The bus was time-tabled to leave the office car park at eight. Not that it did. There are always late-comers. Some of my colleagues are very poor time-keepers.' He was talking quickly and, Trevor sensed automatically repeating previous comments he'd made without thought to relevance.

'Do your children spend much time with your mother-in-law?'

'Not usually, but I had to attend this course. It was an honour to have been chosen. Most of the others were a full grade above me. Kacy … we're both on flexi-time at the office – we take turns to take the children on the school run. Of course, Kacy does … did … most of the journeys because she works … worked fewer hours than me. But it's not as easy for her because she doesn't drive. Never has. Never wanted to. Lacks the confidence needed to be a driver.' His voice trembled every time he corrected the tense from the present to past. 'Because it was half-term Kacy decided to put in more hours while I was away, which would give her more time with the children afterwards.'

'Wouldn't it have made more sense for your wife to have worked less hours when the children were off school?' Trevor suggested.

'She was thinking of us as a family. If we both finished work early we could spend our evenings together.'

Trevor thought back to what Mrs Walsh had told Sarah.

If anything has happened to Kacy Howells don't expect anyone in this street to be sorry. She's crossed everyone at some time or another and it would be good to see the kids get some proper mothering for a change. They might find one with a foster family that wouldn't put them out on the street with the milk bottles and take them in at night with the cat.

The most difficult aspect of an investigation, where too much information was flying around at the outset, was knowing who to believe.

'How long was the course you were on?'

'Four days.'

'Were you expecting your wife to go into work yesterday?'

'No.' George picked up his empty cup and stared into it. 'She said she wanted a day to clean the house from top to bottom so it would ready for us when we came back. I'd arranged to pick up the children when I returned on Thursday evening.' He pulled the damp tissue from his sleeve again and Trevor gave him a few minutes to compose himself.

'How would you describe your life with your wife and family, Mr Howells?'

'Normal. Kacy worked part-time; we have a nice house with no mortgage. I inherited half of it from my mother and bought my brother out of the other half. We have the children …'

'Have you been married long?' Trevor broke in.

'Seven years.'

'And your wife was –' Trevor referred to the notes Sarah had made and given him. 'Fifty years old. Nine years older than you?'

'Yes.'

'Where did you meet?'

'At work.'

'You married when she was forty-three and you were thirty-four?'

'Yes.'

'Did you live together before your marriage?'

'For a few weeks. We'd only been seeing one another for a couple of months.'

'Couple? Two, three?'

'Three, I suppose,' George answered.

'That's not long to go out with someone before marrying them.'

'Kacy wasn't getting any younger. She wanted children.'

Trevor considered Peter's opinion. If he had met George Howells in a pub, he, like Peter would have assumed he was gay. Something of absolutely no interest unless the person concerned was involved in a crime, where his or her sexuality might have a bearing. And given the number of sex aids in the Howells' shed, Kacy and George's sexuality was a factor to be considered in this investigation. He only wished he knew exactly where it fitted into the scenario.

He made a mental note to check the date of the Howells' marriage against the birth of their eldest child. Could Kacy have been having an affair with someone she didn't want to – or couldn't marry? And, as a result, on finding herself pregnant, targeted George as an economic option because he had a mortgage-free house?

'Did you or your wife have any other long-term partners before your marriage?' Trevor questioned.

'What's that got to do with Kacy's murder?' George flushed crimson.

'So far, Mr Howells, we have a motiveless crime. Your wife was axed to death on a platform in your garden. She was naked …'

'Naked? I don't understand.' George appeared bewildered.

'Neither do we, Mr Howells. The pathologist who carried out the post-mortem found no evidence of sexual assault, which is why I asked about your wife's previous partners. At this moment we are not discounting anything. Including an angry, possibly jealous, rage from a lover – or previous partner.'

'I see.' George stared down at the floor.

Trevor thought it odd that George didn't protest that seven years was a long time to nurse jealousy.

'Did you have a previous partner, Mr Howells?'

'No – no – not really.' His face went from crimson to vermilion. 'I mean I went out with other girls and all that … but nothing serious.'

Trevor was tempted to ask him to elaborate on the "all that" but he persevered with his line of questioning.

'And your wife?'

'She lived with someone.'

'For how long?'

'Eighteen years.'

'His name?'

'John Evans.'

'You know him?'

'He works in the same department as us. In the civil service,' George added superfluously.

'Was the break between John Evans and your wife amicable?'

'Not really. Kacy moved out of the house they'd lived in together. He gave her some money to cover her share. Not everything she was entitled to, but he'd made sure the house was in his name. She went to a solicitor but he said it was a difficult situation because John Evans had bought the house before they had cohabited. John even produced a rent book and tried to say that Kacy had never been more than a tenant in his house which was a blatant lie. People can be mean when it comes to making financial redress.'

Trevor thought he could detect Kacy Howells' voice in the complaint.

'A few weeks after Kacy moved out of John Evans's house he married another girl from the department.'

'He and Kacy remained friends?'

'Hardly,' George squeaked in indignation. 'Kacy hasn't spoken to him or the girl he married since. And neither have I.'

'That must make things difficult in the office.'

George stiffened his back. 'Kacy and I keep our heads down and do our work. Our superiors find our efforts more than satisfactory.'

Glad George Howells wasn't on his team, Trevor held his pen, poised over his notepad. 'Do you have John Evans's address?'

'You can contact him at the office. I have no idea where he is living.'

'I thought you said his wife moved in with him.'

'That was seven years ago. I told you, I don't talk to him.'

'What about your social life, Mr Howells?'

George Howells could have been reciting from his CV. 'I enjoy sport and cycling. I attend football and rugby matches in winter and cricket in the summer. I sit on various committees at work.'

'Who do you socialise with?'

'Friends.'

'From the office or neighbours?'

'Sometimes both,' George replied evasively.

'And your wife?'

'Since she had the children she has been very busy between working part-time and taking the children back and forth to school. I am not able to help as much as I'd like to and she spends a lot of time in the garden ...' He buried his face in his tissue.

Trevor recalled his first sight of the garden the night before and the photographs that had been taken of it in daylight. It wasn't the garden of a keen gardener. Rather one that had been laid out thirty or more years ago, neglected and allowed to go to seed. Its only concession to current outdoor fashion, the decking platform and oversized shed.

'So while you attend football, rugby and cricket matches, your wife works in the house and garden.'

'It's her choice.' George hesitated then added. 'I take the children to matches sometimes.'

'That wasn't intended as a criticism, Mr Howells. I am trying to form an impression of your wife's daily routine. What about friends?'

'She saw her parents and brother occasionally. As we both work there isn't much time for socialising outside of her family.'

'Her family. What about yours, Mr Howells?'

'I only have one brother and a couple of cousins. I don't see much of them.'

'They live away?'

'No, but it's difficult to keep in touch when you have a young family.'

'Does your wife have any special friends, male or female?'

'Not really. No.'

Trevor unrolled the magazine he was holding

and flicked through until he came to the full-page spread of Kacy Howells' head tacked on to an obscene cartoon body. He turned it around so it faced George. 'What can you tell me about this, Mr Howells?'

The blood drained from George's face. He stared, mesmerized at the page. 'This is – it's obscene.' He closed the magazine and thrust it back at Trevor.

'Have you seen it before?'

'In the office. Someone sent copies there and left one open on my desk.'

'Did you ask your wife about it?'

'No, I assumed it was a sick joke.'

'And, believing that, you still didn't ask your wife about it?' Trevor questioned incredulously.

'I decided it was best to ignore it.'

'Have you any idea who might have done such a thing?'

'No.'

'An article like this in a pornographic magazine would be covered by the libel laws. You didn't want to see whoever placed it punished?'

George fidgeted nervously. 'I told you, I thought it best to ignore it.'

'Has anything like this been printed about your wife before, Mr Howells?'

'No!' George shouted.

'The magazine was printed three days ago. Did your wife have an argument with anyone during the last few weeks that might cause someone to want to annoy her or get back at her by doing this?'

'No. Kacy never argued with anyone.'

Trevor allowed the lie to pass.

'It's just a magazine,' George whimpered. 'I thought they'd soon be binned and forgotten.'

'Is it a magazine that is delivered regularly to your office?'

'If it is, I've never seen it before.'

'Excuse me, sir,' Sarah interrupted. 'I don't know if Mr Howells is aware that an online version of that page has been put on a public-access website.'

'No, I didn't,' George acknowledged. 'But I don't surf the internet. I think it's a waste of time.'

'You don't have a computer in the house?'

'Two. Kacy uses hers for delivering learning programmes to the children. And I have one I use to keep our financial records and business and personal correspondence.'

'And neither can be connected to the internet?' Trevor asked.

'We have internet access. But only Kacy uses it – for shopping.'

'The officers who searched your house found a number of floral bouquets and boxes of chocolates that had been sent through the mail to your wife.'

'What do you mean a "number"?' George was instantly on the defensive.

'You didn't know about them?'

'I left the house yesterday before the postman arrived. If there are "a number" of things Kacy would have taken them in.' George's defensive attitude was hardening into aggression.

'I'm sorry I have to ask these questions, Mr Howells,' Trevor apologised. 'But we need information if we are to apprehend whoever is responsible for murdering your wife. Did you and Mrs Howells participate in wife-swapping?'

'How dare you!'

'I am investigating the murder of your wife, Mr Howells,' Trevor reminded him forcefully.

'Kacy and I are – were – a normal couple, Inspector. I don't know where you get your filthy ideas from.'

Trevor reached for the magazine and again opened it at the full-page spread of Kacy Howells. Kacy's face smiled up at them from the obscene, cartoon body beneath the headline

"Want fun? Send me a present and your phone number and if the gift is large enough, I'm yours. Cheese on toast can be arranged."

Trevor slid it in front of George again.

George's face crumpled and he stifled a sob.

'Could your wife have placed this advertisement without your knowledge?'

'I don't know.'

'Was your wife secretive?'

'We spent time apart, she in the house, me in work, but that's normal in a marriage once you have children.'

'Do you know what the expression "Cheese on Toast" means?'

'No.'

'It's a euphemism for wife-swapping. Did you and your wife have an open marriage, Mr Howells?'

'I don't know what you mean.'

'Did you and your wife have sex with other partners, Mr Howells?' Trevor asked bluntly.

'No, most certainly not.'

'Then we can assume that if she was responsible for placing this advertisement, the "cheese on toast" referred to her and another man?'

'How dare you! How dare you …'

'I think this is a good time to take a break.' Trevor announced that he was stopping the tape and switched off the recorder. 'Constable Merchant, would you please get Mr Howells a cup of tea?'

CHAPTER SIX

Trevor found Peter waiting for him outside the door.

'Do you think George Howells really didn't know about his wife's collection of salacious toys?' Peter asked.

'Your guess is as good as mine.'

'My money's on his ignorance. I doubt he'd know what to do with them.'

'Did you look through the witness statements?'

'The ones Sarah has inputted on the computer – yes.' Peter opened the door that led into the corridor. 'There's nothing in them.'

'Speed-reading again?'

'You think I missed something?' Peter challenged.

'I came to the same conclusion. I hate the onset of an investigation,' he added feelingly.

'When we can't make a move because we're waiting on results,' Peter agreed.

'It's the not knowing which way to proceed that gets to me.'

'You only like the exciting bit when you can stand in the middle of a room of suspects and say "One of you is a murderer"?'

'Been watching too many Agatha Christie stage plays lately?' Trevor mocked him.

'You going to ask George about his wife's credit card next?'

'Do we have their bank statements and personal

papers?' Trevor checked.

'The search is ongoing at the house. George Howells signed a waiver stating that we can take whatever we need. But that was before your little set-to.'

'It was questioning, not a set-to.' Trevor led the way into his office to find Sarah Merchant making room on his desk for a tray of tea and biscuits.

'You, Sarah, are an angel of mercy and all I do is give you extra work. Set up an interview schedule with Kacy Howells' parents and brother will you please? And any other visitors to the house.'

'When do you want to see them, sir?'

'Tomorrow morning, I'll call in on Kacy Howells' parents on my way here. It would be convenient if the brother could be there as well as her mother and father.'

'I'll try and arrange it, sir.' Sarah left the office and closed the door.

'You'll have to sit in on the interview with Alan unless you want it off the record,' Peter warned.

'It's going on the record and I will sit in.' Trevor lifted his feet on the desk. 'But now I am taking a break to make a personal call, and I want you out of my office.'

'Does that mean I can make a personal call too?' Peter looked at his watch. 'Daisy should be at the airport by now.'

'You can telephone the world provided you pay for the calls.'

'Give Lyn and Marty my love.'

'Close the door on your way out.' Before Trevor could dial out, the telephone rang. He picked it up. 'Trevor Joseph.'

'It's your favourite pathologist.'

'Patrick. You have more information – time of death –'

'Can't you bloody police officers think of anything other than the time of death?' Patrick complained.

'It would help …'

'I don't have anything on the time of death, end of discussion.'

'Then, why ring?'

'Jenny is thorough, bless her. Does all kinds of unnecessary tests in the name of furthering her experience and knowledge.'

'On Kacy Howells?'

'No, Jack the Ripper,' Patrick retorted, 'who the hell did you think I was talking about? She froze a section of her brain, sliced it and examined it. The results were surprising for a fifty-year-old woman.'

'Do I have to come over there and beat it out of you?'

'There were regions of brain atrophy, increased water content in the white-matter areas and high ADC values in the hippocampus, temporal lobe grey-matter and the corpus callosum …'

'English, Patrick,' Trevor pleaded.

'We can't be one hundred per cent certain but Jenny's findings indicate Kacy Howells was in the early stages of Alzheimer's or dementia.'

Trevor struggled to recall everything he knew about Alzheimer's. 'Short term memory loss …'

'Obsessive compulsive disorder, aggression …'

'Thanks, Patrick, that would explain a few things about her anti-social behaviour.'

'If we find anything else, I'll let you know.'

Trevor replaced the receiver, looked at his coffee, decided he didn't want it and made his way back to the interview room.

George Howells was red-faced and damp-eyed, but as a result of Sarah's efforts, he was noticeably calmer.

Trevor sat down pressed the record button, logged the time and continued the interview with an innocuous question. 'Tell me about the committees you sit on?'

'They are civil service committees. Social clubs, cricket teams …'

'You go out several evenings a week?'

'Five evenings, but only for an hour or two.'

'Your wife knew what time you would leave the house and when you would return?'

'Yes. But this magazine is disgusting rubbish …' George thumped it with his fist leaving a damp patch. 'We have – had – a happy private life.'

'You really have no idea how this advertisement came to be placed?' The pain on George Howells' face was so acute; Trevor hated having to pursue the matter.

'No.'

'Payment was made by a credit card in your

wife's name.'

'Kacy was a good wife – a good mother, she hated what she called the sleazy side of life. She wouldn't watch …'

'What, Mr Howells?' Trevor persisted when George fell silent.

'Dirty films on television.'

'And what did she consider dirty?'

'Anything to do with naked bodies, sex – you know the sort of thing.' George tried to peel apart the layers of his damp tissue.

Sarah took a pack of tissues from her pocket and handed George a clean one.

Trevor turned to Sarah. 'Would you get the photographs forensic sent over. The ones of the items we found in the chest, cupboard and behind the panel in the shed, please, Constable.'

Sarah left the room.

George continued to dab at his eyes, nose and mouth.

'Can you think of any reason why someone would want to kill your wife, Mr Howells?'

'No.'

Trevor sensed that George was close to breaking down. 'Please, think again. You have no enemies? No one you or Kacy annoyed in any way?'

'No one that I can think of.'

Trevor found it odd that George Howells didn't mention their ongoing dispute with Alan Piper given that Alan had contacted the community police. 'Your wife was killed by an axe blow to her head.

Do you own an axe?'

'Kacy has a lot of gardening tools.'

'She uses an axe for gardening?'

'She likes to chop wood. We have a wood-burning stove. We don't light it very often because of the smoke. She has an electric saw as well. She uses it to trim the trees outside our garden.'

'Your trees, Mr Howells?'

'You're entitled to cut trees that overhang your garden provided you keep the branches and hand them back to the owner,' he recited as if he were repeating a phrase he'd learned by heart.

'And the owner of the land that backs on to your garden is happy with that arrangement?'

'No one seems to own the land at the back of our garden. Kacy ...' George bit his lip, and Trevor recalled Alan mentioning that Kacy Howells had torn down a boundary fence between their gardens and tried to claim a section of his land.

'If you work land for seven years you can lay claim to it,' George said lamely. 'The land doesn't seem to be registered.'

'It doesn't necessarily follow that land isn't owned by someone just because it isn't registered, Mr Howells. But we were discussing axes. Do you own one?'

'I've seen Kacy using one. She keeps her tools locked in a chest in the summer-house, away from the children.'

'Summer-house?' Trevor questioned quizzically.

'On the patio in the garden.'

'The wooden shed on the deck?'

'Kacy called it the summer-house.'

'Would you be able to identify the axe if I showed it to you?'

George shook his head. 'I don't use Kacy's tools and one axe would look very like another to me.'

'You didn't help your wife with the gardening?'

'I cut the grass with the lawnmower when it needs doing. I leave everything else to her.'

'So you never go into the shed or open the chest or the cupboard we found behind the panelling?'

'No, but I know that she keeps her tools in the chest and the cupboard behind the panelling.'

'She didn't keep tools in the second cupboard.'

'There's a second cupboard?' George looked at Trevor; his eyes bloodshot as well as watery.

'We found one.'

'As I said, I had no reason to go into the summer-house. The lawnmower is kept in the garage.'

Sarah returned, closed the door behind her and gave Trevor a file. He opened it, removed a sheaf of photographs and handed them to George.

'You're looking at a photograph of items we found in the second concealed cupboard in your shed.'

'I keep telling you we don't have a shed.' George's voice grew shrill in anger.

'Summer-house – whatever you call it.' Trevor had no intention of getting side-tracked into a discussion on the shed or patio which had been a point of contention between the Howells and Alan Piper.

George was nonplussed. 'I don't understand.'

'Neither do we, Mr Howells,' Trevor agreed. 'I doubt a sex shop has this many sex aids in stock at any one time. Was your wife offering sexual services to men for money?'

'You're being disgusting …'

'You're very fond of that word, Mr Howells. I take it that if your wife was offering sexual services you were unaware of it.'

'She was doing no such thing. And you are *disgusting*.'

Trevor moved on to a less provocative question. 'Did your wife have a credit card?'

George refused to be mollified. 'Yes.' He spat out the word.

'Do you have independent cards or joint cards on the same account?'

'Both. Kacy has one of her own, as I do. We also have a joint card.'

'Any reason why you have independent as well as joint cards?'

'We use the joint card for household expenses. The independent cards for personal expenditure.'

'Expenditure you don't want one another to know about?' Trevor suggested.

George was instantly on the defensive again. 'I don't like your inference, Inspector.'

'Most couples on a fixed income have a joint card to simplify their expenses.'

'Married couples are entitled to a personal life.'

'But in my experience rarely personal finances, unless they are both high earners.'

'That's certainly not the case with me and Kacy.'

'The two credit cards we found in your wife's purse in her handbag have been checked against the card that was used to pay for the advertisement in the magazine. Neither was used, so your wife either had a third card, or someone held a fraudulent one in her name.'

'You searched my wife's handbag?'

'You signed a waiver, Mr Howells,' Trevor reminded him. 'Did your wife have any other credit cards that you were aware of?'

'No, just the two credit cards and a banker's card.'

'Can you think of anything else? Any snippet of information? A name of a friend or relative your wife might have confided in who could give us information that might help us to further this enquiry?'

'I told you we lead … led … lead,' the dam finally burst and George sobbed uncontrollably.

'Would you like me to call a doctor, sir?' Sarah Merchant asked.

George waved her away.

Sarah and Trevor waited for him to compose himself.

'I want to return to my children,' George said as soon as he'd recovered enough to speak.

'Constable Merchant will arrange a car. I

apologise again for having to question you so soon after your wife's death, Mr Howells. But whoever killed her is violent and dangerous. We need to apprehend the person or persons responsible, quickly before they attack someone else.'

George looked up but he had difficulty meeting Trevor's eye.

'I will need to question you again after we have received the results of the forensic tests that are being carried out in your house and garden,' Trevor warned him.

George mumbled unintelligibly.

'One thing I can assure you; is that we will do everything in our power to apprehend those responsible for murdering your wife. I would also like to warn you that withholding information during a murder investigation is a serious charge but one I wouldn't hesitate to bring, if it was warranted.'

George allowed Sarah to escort him out of the room.

Trevor returned to his office. He sat behind his desk. As he hit the button on his computer to disperse the screen-saver there was a knock at his door. Trevor shouted, 'Come in,' and Chris Brooke entered with a tray.

'Lunch, sir.'

'I didn't order any.'

'When the rest of us ordered sandwiches from the canteen, Peter – Sergeant Collins – added an order for you because he said you'd most likely forget.'

'He did, did he?' Trevor took the top sandwich and opened it. 'Ham and salad, thank you. Any more information come in?'

'Not yet, sir. But we've sent the family's fingerprints to forensics.'

'I've gone through the statements Sarah inputted. Have the teams who are interviewing the neighbours discovered anything new?'

'Not much, sir. No one has reported seeing or hearing anything above the usual noises.'

Trevor took a bite from his sandwich. 'What are the usual noises?'

'A farmer who owns the land behind the Howells, and lives on the hillside above it, said he heard Mrs Howells using her electric saw around midday. He looked down and saw her felling trees on his land. He said he intended to have a word with her about it.'

'A grateful word for managing his woodland?'

'More like an angry "stay your side of the fence" word according to the officer who interviewed him. Apparently Kacy Howells was always walking on his land and couldn't leave it alone. He is convinced that she was under the misapprehension that if he did nothing with the land, she could cultivate and eventually claim it. From what the interviewing officer told me when he came in, Kacy Howells appeared to be obsessed with her neighbours' lives and frequently stole their property.'

'As Alan told us.' Peter joined them; sandwich in one hand, coffee in the other.

'You raised Alan yet?' Trevor asked.

'He's on his way. Apparently the Queen didn't invite him to lunch, just the opening so he missed out on the five course, taxpayer-funded, champagne-fuelled binge.'

'Ask Sarah to make sure an interview room is empty, would you please?' Trevor ordered Chris.

'Yes, sir.' Knowing he'd been dismissed, Chris left.

Peter dropped his coffee and sandwich on Trevor's desk, sat in the visitor's chair and propped his feet on Trevor's waste-bin.

'You listened in to the second half of the questioning.' Trevor said to Peter. It wasn't a question.

'Yes.'

'Any thoughts?'

'A few. Starting with their marriage. For all George's insistence, there's no way it was normal. Forget the murder for a moment. Why did he marry her? Short of loneliness I can't come up with a single reason why a bloke like him who was enjoying the bachelor life would saddle himself with an unstable mouse of a woman.'

'Patrick came up with some information that might shed light on the unstable.' Trevor told Peter about the call he'd received from the pathologist.

'No – I still refuse to feel sorry for her. Even the community police officer who retrieved Alan's gate

80

and post and suggested Alan put up CCTV warned him to watch his property and take care of himself because she was aggressive.'

'If she was incubating Alzheimer's …'

'If!'

'Possibly George Howells wanted children.' Trevor finished his sandwich and reached for his coffee.

'In which case George should have picked a woman the right side of forty. They were lucky but a lot of women her age have trouble conceiving. And if it was just kids he wanted, he could have adopted, fostered or bought himself a nice little subservient Thai bride.'

'Perhaps he'd heard that marriages to brides bought on the internet last only until the brides get UK citizenship along with half the groom's assets in the divorce courts.'

'Sir,' Chris Brookes knocked again. 'Forensic results have come in that we thought you'd want to see right away.'

Trevor took the print-out from Chris. 'Thanks, if anything else of interest arrives you'll bring it in?'

'Of course, sir.'

Trevor opened the file and read the first page.

'Talk?' Peter demanded impatiently.

'These are initial results from fingerprinting. Remember I said there were four sets of prints on the axe?'

'Yes.'

'One set belonged to Kacy Howells.'

81

'Which is to be expected if the axe was hers.'

'Two remain unidentified.' Trevor looked up at Peter. 'The other set belongs to your cousin.'

CHAPTER SEVEN

Alan Piper had been in the police station many times in his capacity as a journalist. He went to the front desk, gave his name and was surprised to find himself hustled into an interview room.

Trevor and Peter were waiting for him.

'Nice meeting with the Queen?' Peter asked.

'Very funny. You've done enough duty around royals to know what their events are like. A lot of standing round waiting and watching the interminable handshakes before listening to the endless speeches.'

'Tea?' Peter broke in.

'You know me.' Alan answered.

'I do and we have no wine, vodka or beer.'

'In that case a coffee would be good.'

Peter opened the door and shouted down an order to the incident room.

'Made any progress?' Alan took a notebook and pen from his top pocket.

'Some,' Trevor answered guardedly, looking to Peter.

'You can put that away,' Peter said to his cousin. 'I'm about to switch on the recorder.'

'Bit formal, aren't we?' Alan asked.

'You're a material witness to a murder. And you found the body. That makes it formal.' Peter stated the date time and case number. 'Mr Piper, tell us exactly when you saw the body of Kacy Howells?'

Alan delivered the same story he had the night before. It didn't deviate in any respect. Experience had taught Trevor that could be down to one of two reasons. Either Alan Piper was telling the truth because he had no reason to lie – or he did have reason to lie – and had carefully concocted and rehearsed the story until he was word perfect.

'You mentioned the file the community police opened regarding your dispute with the Howells. Is there anything you can add to the information you gave the officer who retrieved your property from their garden?' Peter continued.

'Such as?' Alan looked surprised.

'Something you forgot to mention at the time,' Peter suggested.

'I kept a full diary of events. Their thieving of my property, times, dates, stalking activities of Kacy Howells …'

'That we can get,' Peter commented.

'What more do you want?' Alan looked from Peter to Trevor, who was sitting slightly away from the table, his arms folded across his chest.

'What can you tell us about the Howells' marriage?'

'They were the ones spying on me and making my life hell, remember,' Alan said flatly.

'Were you surprised when George Howells married?'

'Very.'

'Why?'

'Like everyone else in the street who had

watched him grow up we assumed he was gay.'

'Did you ever see him with another man?'

'Many times, and before Kacy started spending weekends with him, never with a woman.'

'What did you think of Kacy Howells when you met her?'

'That she was a shy, quiet, mousy woman.' Alan made a face. 'Just shows how easily I can be taken in. I soon discovered that she was an evil, thieving, grasping, envious …'

'Bitch?' Peter finished for him.

'This interview is being recorded,' Trevor reminded.

'Have you ever visited the Howells' garden?'

'Not since George Howells' mother died nine years ago. I used to cut her lawns and help her out with the heavy gardening jobs after her husband died.'

'Why didn't George Howells take over?'

'Because he was useless at any kind of practical work.'

'Did you use Mrs Howells' tools, or yours, to do these jobs?'

Alan frowned. 'Sometimes mine, sometimes hers. I can't remember. For God's sake, it was over nine years ago. What is this, Peter? Come on, do you know something I don't?'

Peter glanced at Trevor who pretended he hadn't noticed. 'Your fingerprints were on the axe that killed Kacy Howells.'

Alan stared at Peter for what seemed like several

minutes, although it could only have been seconds.

'Have you any idea how they could have got there?' Peter pressed.

'No … no, wait a minute. You remember that pub lunch we had yesterday? I told you then that the Howells had put an axe in front of my car that morning. I had to move it before I could drive off. You said, "Why didn't you run over it?" …'

'And you answered "because I didn't want to damage my tyres". Or words to that effect.'

Trevor pulled his chair forward. 'Is that right?'

'It is,' Peter and Alan confirmed in unison.

'So what did you do with the axe?' Trevor looked intently at Alan.

'I moved it.'

'To where?'

Alan thought for a moment. 'I left it on their side of our communal drive. They leave all kinds of rubbish in front of my car. Usually I pick it up and leave it on their wall. But I remember thinking that I didn't want the axe to fall and hurt a child and the Howells' kids are always roaming the street.'

'What kind of rubbish?' Peter asked.

'Anything they don't want. Garden rubbish, cuttings, grass, dead leaves. If their bin bags overflow and burst they leave their tins and bottles lying in our communal drive.'

'How did you pick up the axe?' Trevor asked.

'How … like you pick up an axe,' Alan answered.

'By the handle or the blade.'

86

'Not the blade, that's for sure, it looked sharp.'

'Think, Alan. How did you handle the axe? It could be important,' Peter stressed.

'I can't remember,' Alan snapped impatiently. 'I saw the axe, it annoyed me, I picked it up and set it aside. I thought out of harm's way.'

'We need an axe.' Trevor switched off the recorder. 'Go and see if there's one in the station.'

'Under your desk?' Peter lifted his eyebrows.

'Try lost property,' Trevor replied.

Peter returned less than five minutes later with an axe. 'This is smaller than the one that killed Kacy Howells but I thought it might do to illustrate a point.'

Trevor looked at it in amusement. 'Where did you find it?'

'I'd rather not say.'

Trevor continued to stare at him.

'The canteen cook had it in the boot of his car.'

'Why?'

'Perhaps he uses it to chop up road kill. I've often wondered about the quality of the meat he serves.'

Trevor set the axe on the table in front of Alan and switched the tape back on.

Alan looked at it for a moment, then picked it up by the handle, and the top of the blade.

'Alan Piper has picked up axe,' Trevor said for the benefit of the recording. 'That is how you picked it up from the road?'

'Possibly. I didn't realise at the time that it was

87

going to have any significance.' Alan set the axe down again.'

Trevor nodded to Peter. 'Proceed with the interview, Sergeant Collins.'

'Do you know your neighbour, Mrs Walsh, Mr Piper?'

'Every bugger in the street knows Mary Walsh.'

Peter knew the answer to his question but mindful of the tape recorder he still asked it. 'Why?'

'Because she monitors the comings and goings of everyone in the street.'

'Including yours with the divorcee who lives opposite her?'

'Judy Mason.'

'Is that her name?'

'It is. She was a friend of Joy's. She visited us every day when Joy was dying. She helped out with practical things like washing, cleaning and cooking. Now we share an occasional meal. Sometimes I provide the steaks, sometimes she does. I always provide the wine. She's the only woman I can talk to about Joy. But my relationship with Judy Mason is based on friendship and nothing whatsoever to do with Mary Walsh or the Howells,' Alan said firmly.

'Does Judy Mason know about the problems you had with the Howells?'

'She's one of the few neighbours who do. I tried carrying Joy out on to the woodland patio a couple of times when she was dying. Judy helped me. Kacy Howells always made it her business to sit on her platform and stare at us. It made Joy uncomfortable

88

so I erected a screen near our back door. We didn't have the same view but at least we could sit out there in peace.'

'What about the rest of your neighbours. Did they have any problem with the Howells?'

'I don't know. Judy was the only one I discussed it with, and then only after she saw Kacy Howells virtually stalking Joy and me.'

'So you don't know if any of your other neighbours had problems with the Howells?'

'I hardly see them. Since Joy died I spend most of my time at work or in the pub.'

'Or with Judy Mason,' Trevor reminded him.

'Once or twice a week,' Alan agreed without rancour. 'What happens now you've found my prints on the axe?'

'We check out your story. Look at the other forensic results. Try to build a case.'

'And me?' Alan looked from Peter to Trevor.

'We warn you that you may be called in for further questioning at any time.' Peter formally closed the interview and stopped the recording.

'And ask you not to leave town,' Trevor added when the tape stopped.

Peter glanced at his watch as Trevor finished the early evening team briefing. 'Half past nine. It's been a long day, children.'

'Let's hope forensic come up with something tomorrow that we can use.' Trevor watched Chris and Sarah pick up their jackets from the backs of their chairs. 'There's no need for you two to come in before nine. I won't be in until after I've seen the victim's parents. You did schedule that interview for half past nine, Sarah?'

'I did, sir. At their home. And the brother will be there.'

'Thank you.'

As the room emptied, Peter sat back in his chair and propped his feet on the edge of a table. 'Something must have cropped up for Dan to give the briefing a miss after he said he'd be here.'

'It could be the breakthrough he's been waiting for.' Trevor opened his briefcase and pushed a couple of files into it.

'In the middle of a drugs war?' Peter asked sceptically. 'Dealers are too petrified to talk, in case they're the next to end up at the bottom of the bay wearing concrete boots.'

'Let's hope it's not more murders.'

'Drink?' Peter asked hopefully.

'I have a wife, baby and home to go to. Don't tell me you've quarrelled with Daisy again.' Peter's relationship with the woman he insisted was "the love of his life" was at best tempestuous.

'She went to New York, remember. Could this be old age eating your brain cells? She told you last night. I mentioned it at lunchtime …'

'Sorry, I've a lot on my mind.' Trevor smiled at the forlorn expression on Peter's face. 'I remember her saying something about a medical conference. But it could be an excuse. If I lived with you I'd need to take a break now and again.'

'Very funny.'

'And, because you've been forced to return to the bachelor life, you want me to suffer too.' Trevor snapped his briefcase shut.

'The single life was good – wasn't it – while it lasted?'

Trevor laughed. 'You make it sound as though you're heading for the morgue.'

'I've all the shackles of a married man and none of the benefits.'

'You talking about your unmarried state or Daisy being away?'

'Daisy being away. And don't you dare mock.'

'Who's mocking? Hate being home alone.'

'How do you know?' Peter demanded suspiciously.

'Because I feel the same way whenever Lyn stays overnight at her parents, not that she does very often. Since we moved in together I hate walking into an empty house, even though I lived alone for years.'

'I thought it was just me. The thought of going back to the flat and opening the door on absolute silence makes me ...'

'Want to stay in the pub all night.' Dan joined them, shook off his jacket, ran his hand over his balding head and pulled up a chair.

'So that's where you spend your evenings,' Peter gibed.

'Not me. But I know you and your habits.'

'I'm a new man since I moved in with Daisy.'

'We've seen the difference, although I'm still trying to work out how you hypnotized her.'

'With my charm.'

'We've never seen any sign of it,' Trevor commented.

'Sorry I'm late,' Dan apologised to Trevor.

'You look as though you could do with a week's sleep. Tough day?'

'I wasted it exploring false leads. And, every single one ended in a solid brick wall.' Dan lowered his massive bulk onto a chair. 'All we've established is general evidence that won't hold up in court on its own. We know, but can't prove, that the White Baron is employing hit men from his cosy prison cell. We also know but can't prove that the Red Dragon is doing the same, which makes it bloody hard to investigate the murders. The professional hitmen know what they're doing and thanks to TV documentaries and crime shows they also know how we collect forensic evidence. We have a fair idea who the hitmen are. But there the information ends. I've tried everything – putting on the squeeze – bribery – rewards – threats – immunity and I haven't come up with a single piece of hard evidence that I can use. The White Baron remains tucked up in his cell, and word has him getting conjugal visits and privileges way above what's permissible by the prison system but again, we can't prove a thing. The Red Dragon is elusive as ever, not that we've a clue as to his identity. The streets are awash with drugs, even more so than when the White Baron was trading and every villain we pull in for questioning pleads the fifth amendment even after we tell them the fifth amendment doesn't apply in Britain only American TV crime shows.'

'Interesting case.' Peter lifted his feet down from the table. 'Glad it's not mine.'

'Two more corpses were found floating in the river an hour ago. Both shot in the back of the head.'

'Professional executions,' Trevor murmured.

'That makes six dead and three still missing. The drug war's out of control. After the White Baron was convicted I thought things would calm down but it's worse because his lieutenants and the Red Dragon are fighting to take over his empire, which as far as anyone can make out the White Baron is still ruling from his cell.'

'Anyone contact you claiming knowledge of the identity of the Red Dragon?' Trevor knew that Dan had put out word of a substantial reward to the first "nark" to shop the Dragon.

'Not a one,' Dan answered shortly. 'For all the evidence and information we have on the bastard he could be a ghost.'

'Or The Shadow.' Peter grabbed his jacket and rummaged in his pockets for his car keys.

'Come again?' Dan asked.

'Didn't you read comics when you were a kid? The Shadow creeps about doing strange and peculiar things, sometimes heroic, sometimes nasty depending on the version you read. And all anyone sees of him is his shadow on the wall in certain light.'

'I see,' Dan said wearily.

'No doubt you only read improving literature like *War and Peace* when you were a kid.'

'Forensic manuals and pathologists' reports. I was a sick-minded child.' Dan looked at Trevor. 'You made any progress?'

'We're waiting on forensics.'

'No suspects?'

'Everyone at this stage.'

'I heard Alan Piper's prints were on the murder weapon.'

'So you are keeping a close eye.' Peter finally found his keys.

'Alan told Peter that he found an axe lying on the road in front of his parked car. Given the situation between him and the Howells he suspected them of leaving it there. He moved it so he could drive off.' Trevor picked up his briefcase.

'I take it this was before the body was found?' Dan asked.

'The lunchtime before,' Peter answered. 'And much as he disliked the woman, Alan didn't kill Kacy Howells. I know him. He's capable of writing evil things about those who cross him but quite incapable of murder.'

'You'd stake your life on that?' Dan eyed him quizzically.

94

'I'd stake my career on it,' Peter retorted.

Trevor headed for the door. 'Let's see what tomorrow brings. Thanks for calling in Dan.'

'I may have hit a dead-end on my own case and be seriously doubting my ability to help anyone else, but I'm always at the end of a phone.'

'Want to sit in on the family interviews tomorrow?' Trevor asked Peter

'Whatever the boss wants.'

'Pick me up at my place at nine.'

'Why do I have to do the driving?' Peter grumbled.

'Because I'm looking forward to enjoying breakfast with my wife and son,' Trevor called back as he left.

'Go on, rub in your domestic bliss to us lonely bachelors,' Peter shouted after him.

Dan left his chair as Trevor headed for the door. 'Let's go for a drink, Peter. You never know, we may even meet a snitch who'll have some information he can't wait to pass on.'

'The only thing I'm likely to pick up in a pub is a dose of something nasty, but when your boss's boss invites you to have a drink with him, you have to humour him.'

Dan and Peter went to Dan's favourite haunt, Platform 10, which was housed in a disused railway station. It was the last pub in town that had an outside toilet – which said more about the quality of the beer served than the facilities. The bar was crammed tight to the doorway. There was barely room to breathe and no free tables or seats in the place.

'I'll get in the first beers,' Dan offered.

'I'll get us a table.' Peter looked around for a familiar face. Finding three he pushed his way through to the table they were sharing and stood, arms folded across his chest, staring at them. With two minutes the three young men had finished their drinks and walked out of the door.

'The pay may not be great but we do have a few perks in our line of work.' Peter sat down and took the pint Dan handed him.

'Breaking and entering?' Dan asked.

'You can tell by looking at them, can't you? Two also had handling stolen goods and one grievous bodily harm.' Peter glanced around the room. 'Disturbing number of straight people here.'

'That's why I like the place, that and it's round the corner from my flat. I call in most nights.' Dan sipped his pint.

'I've managed a fair amount of free time since I moved in with Daisy. But I don't spend much of it in the pub.'

'Because you prefer staying in with her?'

'She's prettier than most villains.'

'The joys of married life.' There was a wistful tone in Dan's voice.

'You never talk about your Missus,' Peter hinted. Like everyone else in the station he knew Dan was a widower but his wife had died before he'd been posted to their station.

'Not much to say and, what there is, is personal,' Dan closed the conversation. 'Steady.' Dan grabbed the arm of a plump, middle-aged man who either fell or was pushed against their table.

'I'm not drunk.' The man straightened up.

'Never said you were,' Dan said easily.

The man glanced at Peter before moving to the door that led to the outdoor facilities.

Peter glanced across the table at Dan. 'Good pint here,' he said loudly.

'Landlord knows how to keep his beer,' Dan agreed.

Two men walked into the bar through the door that led to the toilets. Peter hadn't been monitoring the comings and goings but he decided to take a risk. He finished his pint. 'When you have to go, you have to go. I'll pick us up refills on my way back.'

The man who had bumped into Peter and Dan's table was waiting for Peter just inside the door of the Gents.

'You took your bloody time,' he whispered.

Peter eyed the two empty cubicles and deserted washroom. A high-pitched giggle grated from the other side of the wooden partition that divided the Gents from the Ladies. He walked into both cubicles, flushed the lavatories, returned and turned on both taps in the wash-basin. Just as he'd hoped the water gushed noisily from the antique plumbing.

He dropped his voice to a barely audible murmur. 'Got something, Snaggy?'

'The Red Dragon executions.'

'Not my case but I can pass on a message.'

'It's worth a grand.'

'Cash on results you know that.'

'I need money – fast.'

'And who've you fucked off?'

'None of your business.' A door banged and Snaggy bent over the sink and pretended to wash his hands. 'Lofty's flashing money. Word is, the Dragon's paid him for a job well done.'

'What job?' Peter recalled Dan telling him about the corpses found floating in the river.

'Last night.'

A man walked in. Snaggy walked out. Peter washed his hands and waited until he was alone again. Snaggy didn't return, but he appeared at his elbow when he was buying beer at the bar.

'Money here, same time tomorrow,' he murmured in Peter's ear. 'I'll try to find out more.'

Peter knew better than to turn round. He handed the barmaid a ten-pound note, smiled at her, and said, 'And two packets of crisps, love. Salt and vinegar if you have them.'

'So, Snaggy's one of yours too,' Dan said when Peter set a fresh pint of beer in front of him.

'One of everyone's in the station. He says he's desperate for money and in my experience that's when he's least reliable.' Peter fought the crowd for enough space to pull his chair out from under the table.

'Anything of interest?'

'To you maybe.' Peter bent his head close to Dan's. 'Word is Lofty's flashing money around for a job well done and the Red Dragon's the poorer for it.'

Dan shook his head. 'You're right, Snaggy's way off beam. We heard the Nape brothers wasted the two we found today and that was before we fished them out of the river.

'That's Snaggy for you.' Peter handed Dan one of the packets of crisps. 'Starters on me. Fancy a curry for the main course?'

CHAPTER EIGHT

'Coffee, orange juice and croissant?' Lyn offered when she opened the back door to Peter the next morning.

'He hasn't time, love.' Trevor kissed her on his way out of the kitchen.

'I was just about to say yes,' Peter grumbled.

'I buy fresh every day. Come tomorrow,' Lyn offered. 'One of the joys of having a little mite who gets you up before six every morning is an early morning stroll to the baker's. Sometimes I arrive before he puts out his first bake of the day.'

'I'll be here half an hour early tomorrow,' Peter promised.

'Who says you'll be picking me up tomorrow morning?' Trevor grabbed his keys.

'What kind of key-ring is that for a police inspector?' Peter pulled at the two-inch silver teddy bear on the ring.

'It was a present from my mother to Trevor when Marty was born,' Lyn explained.

'You two can stop grinning like Cheshire cats. The last thing I want to do is offend my mother-in-law by ignoring her gifts.'

'Some gifts cry out to be ignored,' Peter advised.

Trevor kissed Lyn again. 'Take care of yourselves.'

'We will. I may even have time to sneak in another cup of coffee before Marty wakes.'

'Don't work too hard and don't pick Marty up every time he whimpers.'

'You want me to let him scream and get a hernia?' Lyn followed Trevor and Peter outside and stood on the patio waving as Peter drove off.

'Ah, domestic bliss. What it is to see your boss with a soppy expression on his face first thing in the morning,' Peter slowed at the junction at the end of the street.

'Lonely night made you jealous?'

'You bet.' Peter turned the corner. 'So, what we looking for in Kacy Howells' family?'

'Whatever we can find, let's just hope …'

'We recognise it when we see it,' Peter recited.

Kacy Howells' parents lived in a run-down terrace on the outskirts of town. Trevor left the car and checked the house number while Peter parked the car. The place was dilapidated and decaying and, given his background as a farmer's son, Trevor guessed that the terrace either had been, or still was, tied agricultural workers' housing. The wooden window frames and door weren't just in need of a lick of paint. They were crumbling with rot. The roof was bowed; the net curtains at the windows, yellowed with age or dust and the long, thin front garden littered with rusting pieces of machinery and sun-bleached plastic toys.

'Home sweet home,' Peter recited.

'Just remember …'

'They're in mourning,' Peter interrupted. 'I will.

But you know me and this kind of unnecessary filth and mess.'

Trevor did. He also recalled his surprise the first time Peter had invited him back to his bachelor flat after they had begun working together. He had expected Peter to live like him, in a chaotic state of overflowing laundry baskets, discarded beer cans and take-away cartons. But Peter's place was as clean as a monastery kitchen and as tidy and impersonal as a monk's cell. In sharp contrast to his working space in the station which was invariably littered with sandwich, crisp and chocolate wrappers and soft-drink cans.

Side-stepping past what looked like the remains of a car engine and a couple of lawnmowers, Trevor made his way to the front door. There was no bell and no knocker so he hit the wood with his knuckles.

George Howells opened the door a minute later. His pale blue eyes were still watery, ringed by red and underscored by black shadows. His fair hair tousled, his face starkly pale.

'Inspector, have you any news?'

'None as yet, Mr Howells. I'm here to interview your wife's parents and brother.'

George stepped outside. 'I haven't told them about that magazine or the photographs of the things you said your people found in the summer-house …'

'The sex aids the investigative team did find in what you refer to as your summer-house,' Trevor corrected. He spoke softly, but he didn't leave any doubt as to who was in control of the questioning.

'My mother-in-law is frail and elderly …'

'We are conducting an investigation into your wife's murder, Mr Howells. And that means questioning everyone connected to your wife, including her relatives.'

'I'm certain they can't help you …'

'I'll be the judge of that.' Trevor looked him in the eye. 'May we come in?'

George showed them into a tiny, cheerless front parlour furnished with pieces that would have been considered old-fashioned forty years before. 'I'll get my in-laws.'

A sludge-coloured vinyl two-seat sofa faced a pink-tiled fireplace that held a gas fire. Two matching vinyl chairs were placed either side of the hearth, two upright chairs stood in front of the window. Trevor took one of the upright chairs, Peter the other. Trevor lifted his briefcase onto his lap, opened it and removed a file, before closing the case and placing it at his feet.

Kacy's parents and brother entered. George made the introductions. Trevor heard children's voices, shrill with temper in the other room.

'My sister-in-law is looking after my children as well as her own. My son and daughter are very upset,' George told Trevor.

'They know what's happened?'

'We told them that their mother has gone to heaven to be with the angels.' Kacy's mother stifled a sob in her handkerchief.

'Please accept our condolences, Mrs Jenkins, Mr Jenkins.'

Kacy's mother was thin and hunched, what was left of her hair was grey, her skin yellow and creased. She looked nearer eighty than seventy. Her husband appeared years younger but he had the leathery skin and square physique of an outdoor worker that was difficult to pin a precise age to. Their son was short and square like his father. His hair was greasy, his hands dirty, scarred with half-healed cuts, scrapes and ingrained dirt. His fingernails were cracked, broken and blackened at the edges. Trevor guessed that he was either a mechanic, or judging from the abandoned scrap in the front garden, an amateur.

Trevor placed his notebook on top of the file on his lap. 'I apologise if any of my questions upset you but the more information we have the greater the possibility of apprehending your daughter's murderer. For elimination purposes, Mr Jenkins, Mrs Jenkins, where were you the afternoon and evening of the day before yesterday?'

Mrs Jenkins answered. 'Mark drove me, Jen and all the children to the beach at midday. We had a barbecue there and came back late, about nine o'clock.'

'Did you see anyone while you were there?'

'Our neighbours,' Mark broke in. 'As it was half-term four families from the street went. Kacy and George's kids can be a bit of a handful for Mum.'

Mark looked pointedly at George. 'So when they are here, Jen and I try to help out as much as we can.'

'You didn't invite your sister?' Trevor asked.

'She wouldn't have wanted to come, besides with three adults and four children there wouldn't have been room for her in my people carrier.'

'Mark bought the people carrier so he can take Dad and me on outings. Dad never learned to drive. Mark's good at organising surprises for the children,' Mrs Jenkins brushed the tears from her eyes with the back of her hand.

'When we came back, Jen helped Mum put the children to bed, while I ordered a take-away ...'

'You went out for it?' Trevor interrupted.

'They do a delivery service. We ate it while watching a film.'

'What time did you go home?'

'Home is next door and we went about eleven o'clock.'

Trevor turned to Kacy's father. 'You didn't go with them, Mr Jenkins?'

'No, I attended a meeting of the chapel elders that afternoon.'

'What time?'

'They're held from two to four o'clock.'

'And afterwards?'

'After the meeting finished, a few of us stayed on to paint the chapel, it needed it.' Kacy's father ran his finger around the inside of his shirt collar. He was red-faced and perspiring.

Trevor wondered why he was so nervous. 'When

did you finish painting the chapel?'

'Not much before eleven o'clock. I went home with another of the elders, Matthew Clarke. His wife died a few months ago. He invited me in for tea. Knowing he was lonely I accepted.'

'And you came home when?' Trevor held his pen poised over his notebook.

'Around midnight. My wife was asleep.'

'When did you last see your daughter?'

'A month last Sunday,' Kacy's brother, Mark, replied. 'It was my son's ninth birthday. My wife organised a family tea.'

'Did you meet often as a family?'

'More often than some, not as often as others,' Kacy's father answered. 'Kacy and George work, they're busy.'

'When were you last in Kacy and George's house?'

Kacy's mother looked doubtfully at her husband.

'Last Christmas.' Mark glared at George. 'We were allowed to drop presents off at their front door.'

'You didn't go in?'

'Not in winter, we would have dirtied the place with our filthy boots and common ways. Summer's different. If Kacy has any jobs that need doing she calls on me and Dad. We can build her fences after she's quarrelled with her neighbours. And erect her decking and sheds as long as we stay outside. Our Kacy married up in the world, Inspector Joseph. She didn't like us going round there and reminding her,

George and their neighbours of where she'd come from.'

'That's unfair,' George protested. 'Kacy loved having you around …'

'So much so, she never asked us. And when I drove Mum, Dad, Jen and the kids over once unexpectedly you wouldn't let us in.'

'We were going out …'

The last thing Trevor wanted to precipitate was a full-scale family argument. 'So you didn't see one another very often?'

'Christmas, birthdays and whenever George and Kacy wanted to dump their kids on Mum or Jen and me.'

Trevor scribbled a note. 'Could you give me the names and addresses of any of Kacy's friends?'

'She didn't have any,' Mark snapped.

'Mark, please,' his mother admonished. 'Kacy was highly strung. You two never got on.'

'Face it, Mum, she was a nasty snobbish bitch. She never kept a friend for more than a month or two when she was in school. When she joined the civil service she lived with that bloke for years but only because he put up with her bullying. When he finally broke away from her and found a woman he wanted to marry Kacy refused to move out until she paid her off, even though she hadn't put a penny into his house …'

'How dare you!' George's face glowed bright red. 'To say such things about your sister when she's not even buried …'

107

'You think it would be better to wait until she's under the ground?' Mark challenged him. 'Dear God, she picked you all right. A wet wimp, who did everything she ordered you to because it made you look respectable and hid the fact that you were gay. Not that's there's anything wrong with being gay. My best mate is. But coming out wouldn't suit you, would it, you bloody hypocrite, because your minister wouldn't like it? And you'd miss being a big man in your chapel ...'

George left his chair. 'Kacy was right to want to keep you at bay, Mark. You're poisonous. You envied us.'

'Envied!' Mark sneered. 'How long did it take her to drive a wedge between you and your brother and the rest of your family? One week after the wedding? Two? I heard the way she talked about your brother. How he refused to give her the share of the antiques he took from your parents' house after your mother died. She even wanted your mother's jewellery when the poor women had died before you two got together. She was a greedy grasping ...'

'How dare you ...'

'I dare because you're a stupid bastard who can't see what's under his nose. Kacy was a tart who'd sleep with anyone who fancied her, not that there were many ...'

Peter jumped up and caught George's fist before it connected with Mark's face. 'This isn't helping anyone, Mr Jenkins, Mr Howells.'

Trevor saw Peter steeling himself to take a blow but Mark stepped back. Peter waited a few seconds then released George's hand.

'You're right, copper. This isn't helping anyone. As I said, I live next door, house on the right as you walk up the garden. If you want me, come round. I work in the garage in the back. You going to be much longer?' Mark went to the door.

'Hopefully not,' Trevor answered, 'why?'

'I don't want my missus looking after his,' Mark pointed at George, 'brats longer than she has to.' Mark left the room. They heard him talking to the children in the next room.

'Mark and Kacy never got on,' Mrs Jenkins wiped tears from her eyes. 'But then that's normal in families where there's an older sister and younger brother. Kacy felt she had to look after Mark and he didn't like her telling him what to do.' She looked up at Trevor. 'She was a wonderful wife and mother.'

'Wonderful,' her husband echoed unconvincingly.

Trevor glanced at George who was sitting in the chair studying his fingernails. He didn't even nod agreement to his in-laws' praise.

'This is filth.' Mrs Jenkins flung the magazine Trevor had given her on the floor. It fell open at the page featuring Kacy. She turned aside and burst into tears. 'Our Kacy would never do anything like that,' she choked out between sobs. 'We brought her up to be a decent girl.' She stared at George. 'You …'

'I've already told them that Kacy wouldn't have had anything to do with a disgusting magazine like that, Mary.'

Mr Jenkins bent down, retrieved the magazine and stared at the page. It could only have been for a few seconds but even that was too long for his wife.

'How dare you look at such obscenity, and with your daughter's face plastered on it. How dare you! Isn't it bad enough that she's been murdered in cold blood without someone murdering her reputation as well? This is worse than having an axe in her head. It strikes at the very core of her being – the way people will remember her …'

'God protects the innocent,' Mr Jenkins chanted the phrase automatically and Trevor sensed that he hadn't considered the meaning of what he'd said in relation to his daughter's murder.

'God didn't protect Kacy from whoever murdered her.' Even angry and bitter, Mrs Jenkins's voice was soft. Trevor marked her as a mild-mannered woman who had been taught subservience at an early age and never thought to question it.

'There's more to heaven and earth than we know. This life is short, the after-life is for all eternity …'

'Please,' Mrs Jenkins begged, 'No bible quotes. Not today. Our daughter is dead. Do you know what that means, Dad? Kacy is dead. We'll never see her again. Never ever …'Mrs Jenkins gulped in air before succumbing to hysteria. Her husband slipped his arms around her shoulders.

'Of course we'll see her again, Mum. And when we do she will be cleansed of sin and cloaked in glory.'

George Howells rose to his feet. 'Inspector, Sergeant. Please leave.'

Trevor retrieved the magazine and returned the photographs of the sex aids to his folder. He hadn't had time to show them to Kacy's parents.

'I told you not to give that magazine to Kacy's parents,' George reproached them as he escorted Trevor and Peter to the front door.

'Would you like us to stop investigating your wife's murder, Mr Howells?' Peter challenged.

George flushed. 'No.'

'Then, help us to do our job. Investigating a murder means investigating the victim's life.' Trevor stood back while George opened the front door.

'That magazine has nothing to do with Kacy's life,' George insisted.

'That advertisement has everything to do with Kacy's life.' Trevor followed Peter out into what passed for a garden. 'Someone placed that advert, Mr Howells. Someone with access to a computer, Kacy's photograph, and a current credit card in her name. Whoever it was – and we haven't discounted the possibility that it was your wife – they had enough acumen to make it look as though the advert was e-mailed from abroad. If that someone wasn't Kacy Howells we need to find out who they are and

111

why they targeted her. If our methods distress you, please try to remember our priority is the apprehension of a murderer before he strikes again.'

'If you need me or my parents-in-law, we will be here for the next week or two, Inspector.' George closed the front door on them.

'Even allowing for his wife's murder, that bloke's got an attitude problem. And that was a waste of a morning, Joseph,' Peter complained.

'Not entirely,' Trevor countered. 'We now know that Kacy Howells didn't like her family visiting her in her leafy suburban paradise, probably because, as her brother believed, she was a snob who was ashamed of her origins. We also know her parents made excuses for her attitude towards them. And, my instinct tells me that we need to thoroughly check out her father's alibi.'

'Not much of a family man if he prefers chapel elders' meetings and painting the chapel hall to an outing with his grandchildren.'

'You noticed he didn't comment on Kacy's photograph in the magazine?' Trevor questioned.

'I did.'

'He couldn't take his eyes off it but he didn't look shocked.'

'Almost as if he had seen it before,' Peter agreed. 'I've never trusted people who call themselves "Mum" and "Dad" once they have kids. Or tell me that the next time they're going to see their murdered loved ones they will be "cleansed of sin and covered in glory".'

'It was cloaked in glory and you're suspicious of all religion.'

'Too damned right, I am. And religious nuts of any denomination.'

'Try and set religion and republicanism aside for the duration of this case,' Trevor pleaded.

'And look at what we've got? Family ties? Kacy's "Mum" and "Dad" made excuses for her and wooden George's snobbery towards them. And Mark Jenkins hated her with something more than your usual brotherly animosity.' Peter glanced across the wasteland of scrap metal to next-door's garden which was even more rubbish-strewn than the one they were standing in. A car was propped up on jacks and Mark Jenkins was fighting to remove the wheel-nuts.

CHAPTER NINE

Trevor walked down the path and out through where there might have once been a gate, given the evidence of rusting posts. There weren't even remnants of posts separating the jungle of weeds and rusting islands of metal that was Mark Jenkins's garden from the pavement.

Mark didn't look up when Trevor approached but he inclined his head towards his parents' house. 'I suppose *he's* staying on there.'

'If you're referring to your brother-in-law, George Howells, he did say we could contact him there for the next week or two,' Trevor answered.

'He's got a home all bought and paid for with his mum and dad's graft, not his, and from the way Kacy and him used to talk about it, you'd think it was a bloody mansion, so why doesn't he go there?'

'Because we are still working there. Our forensic teams,' Trevor explained in answer to Mark's quizzical look.

'He's always boasting about how much money he's got. Why doesn't he go to a hotel?'

'Perhaps he thinks the children will be better off with your mother for a while.'

'Kacy's kids are better off around Mum. Kacy never wanted either of them. God knows why she didn't abort them; she didn't have a single maternal bone in her body. As for George, he'll do anything to live life on the cheap. Christ knows how much he earns but I'm betting he won't give Mum a pound coin to help her feed him and those kids while they stay with her.'

Trevor opened the file he was carrying and removed the magazine. 'I'd like you to look at this Mr Jenkins. I showed it to George and your parents. It upset them, but given that the magazine was published in paper and internet form three days before your sister was killed, it's one of the leads we are following.'

George turned his head and looked at it but made no attempt to take it from Trevor. 'Big sister finally showed her true colours.'

'True colours?' Peter repeated.

'She always played the Sunday School girl around Mum and Dad. Even went to Dad's Bible-thumping chapel with them twice every Sunday until she left home. But I knew what she was really like. Couldn't escape it. I used to get teased about her mercilessly. Knickerless Kacy they used to call her when she was in the sixth form. In the civil service it was No knickers Kacy. Into all sorts by all accounts, but I only know what people told me in the pub. It wasn't the sort of thing she would discuss with me or my Missus.'

'Do you understand the reference to "Cheese on Toast"?' Trevor asked.

'Course. But I never heard that Kacy and George were into wife-swapping. I wouldn't put it past her, but George?' Mark turned back to his wheel nuts. 'Face it; I can't imagine any woman being thrilled with the thought of swapping her old man for him.'

'You don't like him?'

'I don't like his stinginess with money, his sponging off my parents, the way he and Kacy used to dump the kids on Mum whenever it suited them, but most of all I hate the way he echoed everything Kacy said. First time I met him I thought he was gay and wet. I couldn't make out what he thought about anything, then I realised that before he hooked up with Kacy he was a blank slate. He didn't have a personality. After they married he adopted hers. Kacy always was into exhibitionism, but I couldn't tell you if George followed her down the kinky sex route.'

'What kind of kinky sex?' After a stint on the vice squad Peter knew people's ideas on what was "kinky sex" varied enormously.

'When she was in the comprehensive she often used to take on half a dozen blokes in the bandstand in the park of an evening. One of my mates, Jason White, went out with her for a while. He told me she found it a real turn on when people were watching. She'd wind him up and unzip him in all sorts of places. Trains, supermarkets, football matches, cinemas, clubs, you name it, she'd want to do it there. The more public the place, the better she liked it. He said he found it exciting at first but then he got tired of people staring and being questioned by the police. He found himself a nice quiet girl and settled down. But that's what we all want in the end, isn't it?'

'A nice quiet girl,' Peter suggested.

'I think all blokes are the same when it comes down to it. They visit strip joints and parlours in a crowd with their mates, pay for a lap dance and make a lot of noise pretending they're enjoying it, but sex as a spectator sport palls after a while. It's best done in private.'

'Do you think Kacy settled for that after she married George?' Trevor probed.

'She didn't when was living with her last bloke…'

'John Evans?' Trevor broke in.

'That's him. He got on well with Mum and Dad. And Jen and me liked him a lot. Last time I bumped into John, he told me he had been trying to kick Kacy out for years. He finally resorted to paying her thousands to get her out of his house, although she never gave him a penny towards the mortgage and every month he had to fight to get her to pay anything towards the bills. He told me it was worth every penny to be rid of her because he couldn't stand her antics any more.'

'What exactly were her "antics"?' Trevor checked.

'Having sex with other blokes in their garden in full view of him and their neighbours. It was her speciality at barbecues. A couple of vodkas and she was any- and everybody's.'

'She built a high deck in the garden of her present house,' Peter commented.

'Exactly.' Mark finally managed to loosen the

last nut on the wheel. He removed it and lifted the wheel from the car.

'You think Kacy was being unfaithful to George?' Trevor asked.

'I don't think, Inspector. I know.'

'Do you know the names of any of her current lovers?'

'Her window-cleaner is fond of bragging in the pub, as for the others; check the electoral roll for her street and yellow pages. If she carried on as she did when she was living with John Evans, it will be every male she'd been introduced to between the ages of sixteen and sixty.'

'And Jason White?' Trevor had filed away the name of Kacy's early lover.

'Went to Canada two years ago. Him and his missus are loving every minute of it. The e-mails and pictures they send us are making me and Jen think hard about moving there ourselves.'

'So, after a long morning interviewing, we have a mother who was almost afraid of Kacy Howells, a brother who hated her …'

'Because she slept around indiscriminately and was a snob, neither of which is sufficient grounds for murder,' Trevor reminded Peter.

'A father whose alibi needs checking.'

'You volunteering?'

'No. Ask a female to do it. You know me and male chapel elders. And before you say a word, they will all be male. Chapel elders haven't heard of the

Sex Discrimination Act. Send in Sarah and they'll treat her like a two-year-old. But they'll tell a two-year-old girl, things they wouldn't tell a man.'

'You can interview Kacy's lovers. Make a list of them and get their alibis checked out.'

'That should keep me busy for the next ten years,' Peter quipped.

'I hope not. The sooner this case is closed, the sooner I can take Lyn and Marty down to Cornwall for a break.'

'Optimist. The sooner this case is closed the sooner we can move on to the next one,' Peter corrected him.

'Some forensic results are in, sir,' Sarah greeted Trevor when he and Peter walked into the interview room. 'DNA as well as fingerprints. I put a copy on your desk.'

Trevor sat down and took the coffee Peter had poured him. 'Tell me?'

'The axe handle has Kacy Howells', Alan Piper's, her father's and eldest son's fingerprints and traces of the DNA of all four.'

'So much for the tools being locked away and the children not allowed to touch them,' Peter observed.

'There are also smudges overlaying all of the prints and the smears of Kacy Howells' blood.'

Trevor gingerly picked up his polystyrene coffee cup. His fingertips had always been over sensitive to heat. 'Gloves?'

'The lab thinks latex.'

'So whoever killed her could have picked up the axe wearing gloves. Wouldn't he have left any traces of DNA?'

'According to the lab technicians, if the murderer had gone in the way we do, which is the way it's depicted on every TV crime drama and documentary – suited, booted and gloved, hair covered, not necessarily.'

'Our Mrs Walsh-cum-street clarion didn't pick up on any suited, booted, hatted and gloved murderers walking up the street, or arriving in cars,' Peter observed.

'Given her thoroughness, she would have noticed,' Sarah flicked through the papers in front of her. 'A discarded tissue was found on the decking; it had Alan Piper's DNA and blood on it.'

Trevor looked at Peter. He had fallen suddenly and uncharacteristically silent.

'DNA and blood,' Trevor repeated. 'Is there any margin for error?'

'None, sir,' Sarah assured him. 'Chewing gum was found on the decking, also with Alan Piper's DNA. And Kacy Howells' and Alan Piper's fingerprints were found on paving bricks under the pots on the decking and on two of the pots.'

'Any other fingerprints found on the deck or the chest that contained the tools and the cupboard that held the sex aids?' Trevor asked.

'Apart from the family …'

'When you say family, do you mean just Kacy,

George and the children or her parents and brother as well,' Peter checked.

Sarah scanned the file. Kacy's, her husband's, her children's and father's prints were all over the deck and inside the house. Only two sets of her mother's prints were found on the chairs on the deck. And they were months old. No sets of her brother's, his wife's or his children's prints.'

'What about her father's prints, were they old?' Trevor finished her coffee and tossed the cup into the bin.

'They were fresh.'

Trevor eyed Peter.

'I'll update Chris on the father's alibi.' Peter left his chair and joined Chris at his desk in the far corner of the room.

'What about the sex aids?' Trevor asked Sarah.

'They had all been washed, but traces of Mrs Howells' DNA remained and, so far, twelve sets of unidentified DNA.'

'George Howells' DNA?'

'Not on any of them, sir.'

'Call Alan Piper and ask him to come in right away. You are free to interview him?'

'Me, sir?' Sarah echoed.

'I'll be the one asking the questions.'

'Yes, sir.'

'Until he comes in you can help Peter compile a list of visitors to the house. Arrange to have all their DNA samples taken and get the lab to check them against the DNA on the sex aids. I'll be in my office if anyone needs me.'

Trevor blanched at the mountain of witness statements Sarah had printed and left on his desk. Too large for his in-tray, it was daunting, but somewhere amongst all the minutiae of daily life in the cul-de-sac Kacy Howells had lived and died in, a vital clue could be hidden. He sat behind his desk, opened his computer and started a time-line.

The farmer behind Kacy's house had said that he had seen her working on his trees on his land at midday. He called up Patrick O'Kelly's post-mortem report. Patrick hadn't deviated from the initial assessment he had made at the scene around eleven forty-five, when he said that Kacy Howells had been dead for at least three to four hours, and probably earlier.

Trevor returned to the time-line page. All he knew was that Kacy Howells had been alive – and presumably clothed, because the farmer hadn't commented – otherwise at midday and dead at eight forty-five at the latest. He was left with a window of nearly nine hours. A window that needed narrowing.

The telephone rang, he picked it up.

'Mr Piper's arrived, sir.'

'Thank you, Sarah.'

'Interview room 2 is free, sir.'

'Show him in, I'm on my way.'

Peter was hovering outside the door that led to the interview rooms.

'Sarah's sitting in on this one,' Trevor anticipated and pre-empted Peter's request.

'Do you mind if I observe?'

'Because Alan's your cousin and friend?'

'Because I might pick up on something that you and Sarah miss.'

'Don't enter the room unless I invite you in,' Trevor warned. He pushed open the door. Sarah had brought two copies of the forensic report on the findings on the deck in Kacy Howells' garden, along with a pot of coffee and three mugs.

'Hello again,' Alan greeted Trevor. 'Do you interview everyone who finds a murder victim twice, or did I draw the lucky straw?'

'We need to clarify a few points.' Trevor sat down, hit the record button and went through the preliminaries before opening the report. Sarah had thoughtfully highlighted all the findings relevant to Alan Piper.

'Your fingerprints have been found on paving bricks used to raise pots on Mrs Howells' deck. Could you explain how they got there please, Mr Piper?'

'As I said yesterday, Kacy Howells has been stealing property from my garden for some considerable time. Including approximately two square metres of paving bricks.'

'You say approximately. How did you arrive at two metres?'

'Because I was two square metres short when I laid a path in my garden. I knew I'd ordered sufficient for the job. I looked around and that's when I saw that she'd used my bricks to lift her pots.'

'You explained how your fingerprints came to be on the axe yesterday. You also said that you hadn't been in the Howells' garden for several years.'

'That's right, not since old Mrs Howells died.'

Trevor lifted his head and looked directly into Alan Piper's eyes. 'A tissue and a piece of chewing gum, both impregnated with your DNA were found on the decking where Kacy Howells was murdered. Can you provide an explanation as to how they came to be there, Mr Piper?'

The silence in the room was palpable. The atmosphere tense and escalating. Trevor continued to look Alan directly in the eye.

'I can't explain it,' Alan said finally.

'Do you chew gum?' Trevor glanced at the report to make sure he had the facts right. The gum had contained nicotine.'

'Nicotine gum,' Alan confirmed. 'I was a heavy smoker for more than twenty years. When my wife was diagnosed with cancer I gave it up. Now, I only smoke the occasional cigar. In between I chew nicotine gum.'

'And you've been doing this for how long?'

'About eighteen months.'

'And the Howells built their deck, when?' Trevor continued to monitor Alan's reactions.

'Three – four years ago.'

'Do you ever throw your rubbish into the Howells' garden?'

'Never,' Alan was emphatic. 'The last thing I wanted was the situation between us to escalate. My wife and I suffered enough from the Howells' anti-social behaviour. If we'd given them an excuse I've no doubt they would have behaved even worse than they did, although it's difficult to see what more they could have done to us.'

'There was blood on the tissue – your blood,' Trevor added so there'd be no mistake. 'Can you explain how it got there?'

'I get the occasional nose bleed, graze and cut finger like everyone else.'

'Any recently?'

'Not that I can recall. But I don't make a note of every little cut, scrape and minor injury with a view to being interrogated about them by police officers.'

Trevor sat back in his chair. Alan's fingerprints on the axe that was used to kill Kacy Howells coupled with his DNA being found on the gum and tissue on the deck and his lack of a corroborated alibi was damning, but not damning enough to hold up on its own in court before a judge and jury. 'Tell me more about your quarrel with the Howells?'

'I gave the community police the diary I kept of the Howells' thieving, stalking and anti-social behaviour.'

Sarah scribbled a note. 'I'll ask the community police for a copy, sir.'

'If they've lost it, I can give you one,' Alan volunteered. 'I have the file on my computer. I still update it occasionally.'

'How soon can you get it to us?' Trevor asked.

'I'll run one off when I return to the office this afternoon.'

Trevor scanned the report again. He looked at one highlighted section and read it twice before pointing it out to Sarah, she nodded. Trevor stopped the tape. 'If you'll excuse us, Mr Piper, we need to confer with our colleagues.'

'There's no need to be quite so formal when the tape is switched off,' Alan complained. 'I maybe a suspect but I'm also human.'

'I'd prefer to keep everything on a formal footing at this stage of the enquiries. I would also like to search your house. But it will take time to get a warrant.'

Alan pulled a bunch of keys from his pocket. He singled one out, removed it from the ring and handed it to Trevor. 'Be my guest.'

Trevor pocketed it. 'Would you like another coffee?'

'I have nothing better to do. Although I could go and get that diary if you want it?'

'Not at the moment. Thank you,' Trevor refused.

As Trevor expected Peter was outside. Trevor led the way into the incident room. After ordering a constable to take Alan coffee, he closed the door.

'Why didn't anyone pick up on the sighting of Alan Piper outside his house at four thirty on the day of the murder until now?' he asked Sarah in particular and the room in general.

Sarah answered, 'Because Mrs Walsh only gave

126

us the notes she made on the afternoon of the murder this morning.'

'You said you'd taken her diary after interviewing her on the morning after the murder,' Trevor reminded her.

'She updates it every day. We took her diary the morning after the murder but she hadn't updated it with the afternoon's notes from the day before. This morning, I noticed that the entries stopped at midday on the day of the murder, I rang Mrs Walsh and asked her if she had taken any more notes. She said she had, we visited her and she showed us her rough book ...'

'What rough book?' Peter broke in.

'A cheap exercise book she makes her notes in. She rewrites them in her diary later, sometimes at midday which she did the day of the murder, sometimes in the evening "if there's nothing on television" and sometimes in the early hours if she can't sleep.'

'She trying to rival Samuel Pepys?' Trevor asked.

'Samuel Pepys?' Peter repeated.

'Stop trying to wind me up,' Trevor snapped. 'And Mrs Walsh definitely saw Alan Piper return to his house at 4.14 p.m. on the day of the murder?'

'It's in her rough notes and the notebook we gave her to replace her diary after we took it.'

'Why does she update them?' Trevor questioned.

'Because she uses shorthand to make notes. I asked her for a couple of sample pages.' Sarah retrieved a file from her in-tray and handed it to Trevor.

Trevor studied it. 'This is shorthand?'

'Her own, sir. She did explain it. The inverted V is Mr Piper, the A the paperboy, the square Mr Howells, the circle Mrs Howells.'

'You do understand that some poor soul is going to have to go through all these rough notes, decode them and match them to Mrs Walsh's final transcript.'

'Yes, sir.' There was resignation in Sarah's voice.

'Get a couple of constables to take over the inputting of evidence into the computers while you concentrate on the decoding. But first, give this key to the forensic team.' He handed it to Sarah. 'Ask them to search Alan Piper's house and garden.'

'You can't be serious,' Peter protested.

'Alan handed me the key when I told him I was going to apply for a warrant. If you think he should have objected, feel free to talk to him.'

Peter shook his head.

'And if the forensic team ask me what they're looking for, sir?' Sarah questioned.

'Tell them they'll know it when they see it. I'm going to interview Mrs Walsh. You did say she was house-bound?'

'Yes, sir.'

'Ring ahead to let her know we're coming.'

'We?' Peter left his chair.

'Chris will come with me.'

Peter was clearly disappointed but he didn't argue. 'And Alan?'

'Give him another coffee. I'll be back as soon as I can.'

CHAPTER TEN

Chris drove slowly up the cul-de-sac. The midday sun was strong, the temperature high, the street deserted. Trevor opened the car window on the passenger side. There were no sounds coming from the gardens behind the houses. Only the distant roar of a helicopter engine and the whine of a lawnmower.'

'Spring's arrived and Mrs Walsh's son is cutting the lawn,' Chris remarked as he pulled up outside the house at the end of the cul-de-sac.

Trevor left the car, turned his back to Mrs Walsh's house and looked down the street.

'I wonder if she chose this house because she wanted to watch her neighbours.' Chris locked the car.

'Either that or it became her hobby after she became house-bound.' Trevor turned and nodded to Mick Walsh who'd recognised Chris and switched off the lawnmower.

Mick spoke slowly with the hesitant articulation of the brain-damaged. 'Hello, Constable Brooke.'

'Hello, Mr Walsh. It's a fine day for gardening.'

'It is.'

'But strenuous work, in this heat.'

'Since the accident my doctor has been telling me that I have to do all I can to keep fit. She says that moderate exercise helps strengthen my muscles.'

'And is it?' Trevor asked. Mrs Walsh's son may have had the slow speech and gait of the mentally incapacitated, but he had the physique of a body-builder.

'I think so.' Mick Walsh flexed his biceps proudly. 'We had a telephone call to say that you wanted to speak to my mother again.'

'That's right. Is she inside?' Chris asked.

'She hasn't slept much since they found Mrs Howells. I think it's too much excitement for her weak heart.'

'I'm Inspector Trevor Joseph, Mr Walsh,' Trevor introduced himself. 'I won't keep your mother long; we just need to clarify a few points that she put in her notes.'

'So Mum's diary is useful then?'

'Every witness statement is useful to us, Mr Walsh. If only to eliminate people from our enquiries.'

'Mum always said that it would be useful one day, if only to tell people how we managed to carry on after the accident.' Mick Walsh opened the door and shouted, 'Mum! The police are here,' but Trevor had already seen Mrs Walsh sitting in her recliner at the window of her living room. He didn't doubt that she had already noted down his and Chris's arrival complete with time and car number.

'You know where to find Mum?' Mick asked Chris.

'I do.'

'Would you like tea and biscuits? I always make

my mum a cup of tea around this time.'

'That would be nice, thank you,' Trevor answered for both of them.

Trevor noticed that Mrs Walsh's reclining chair had been placed to give her the optimum vista of the road and a panoramic view of her neighbours' houses and front gardens. He also spotted a pair of miniature binoculars on a side-table next to her chair.

'Mrs Walsh, thank you for your assistance with our enquiries into the murder of Mrs Howells. I'm Inspector Trevor Joseph.'

'Pleased to meet you, Inspector.' She turned her head slowly as if it pained her to move her neck. When she focused her bespectacled dark eyes on Trevor, he was glad he had opted to buy a house in a terrace fronting the sea. One of his balconies overlooked the public beach, but it was easier to spot someone standing on the sand for any length of time, than a peeping Tom or Tomasina concealed behind vertical blinds that had been carefully adjusted to conceal them from the view of anyone looking in from the street. 'You are the officer in charge of the search for Mrs Howells' murderer.'

'I am.'

Mrs Walsh's blue-tinted lenses made it difficult for Trevor to read the expression in her eyes. But his knowledge of her voyeuristic habits made him uneasy.

'That nice young lady who came to see me …'

'Constable Merchant.'

'That's the one; she came with this young man.' Mrs Walsh pointed to Chris. 'They seem very dedicated to their job.'

'As I hope everyone on my team is,' Trevor answered.

'Sit down, Inspector, Constable. Mick,' she called through the open door. 'You're bringing the best Belgium chocolate biscuits for the officers, I hope.'

'I am, Mum.' Mick wheeled in an old-fashioned pink and white trolley, set out with a silver tea-service, porcelain cups and saucers and a silver salver that held a meticulously arranged selection of luxury biscuits.

'Milk, sugar, Inspector?' Mick asked.

'Neither, thank you.' Trevor didn't like tea and rarely drank it, but he was fascinated by the way Mick Walsh, all clumsy six feet four inches and twenty stone of him was obeying his mother's commands like a trained parlour maid. Peter, who didn't give a damn for political correctness, would have called him "a biro short of a refill," yet he snapped to attention whenever Mrs Walsh spoke and did what she asked him, to the best of his lumbering ability.

'Don't fill the inspector's cup too full, Mick; it will slop in the saucer. Now hand him a plate and offer him the biscuits.'

Trevor took the tea but shook his head at the biscuits.

'Are you sure, Inspector? They are very good.

Harrods' best. We have a hamper sent down every month. Constable, you take your tea with milk and two sugars, am I right?'

'You have an excellent memory, Mrs Walsh.'

'At the risk of sounding conceited, I do,' she agreed.

'Your memory and your diaries are the reason we're here, Mrs Walsh.' Trevor set his cup down on the silver coaster Mick Walsh had placed on the highly polished mahogany side-table next to him. The room was beautifully decorated in a traditional way with Persian rugs, wood-block floor and antique furniture. The paintings on the wall appeared to be originals, not prints and he wondered what the absent Mr Walsh had done to house his family in this luxury.

'Take your tea into the kitchen, Mick,' Mrs Walsh ordered her son as he moved towards a chair. 'I don't want you dirtying the upholstery in here with your gardening clothes.'

'Yes, Mum.' Mick walked meekly out of the door.

'When the officers leave, you can clear away the tea tray. The weather's too warm to leave milk out of the fridge and chocolate biscuits on an open salver.'

'I can take the tea things out, Mrs Walsh,' Chris offered.

'No need, Constable, no need at all. Now, Inspector,' she turned to Trevor as if she were the one conducting the interview. 'How can I help you?'

'I saw the entries you made for the day of the murder, Mrs Walsh. Constable Merchant explained to me that you update your diary from the rough notes you make?'

'That is correct, Inspector. If I left them in the rough form no one would be able to read them.'

'You intend them to be read?' Trevor wondered if the woman had delusions about publishing her notes.

'Some day, perhaps. I'm not a celebrity or politician, but my diary provides a record of our here and now. How difficult it is to come to terms with an accident that was caused by a truck driver who hadn't slept for twenty-four hours and wasn't even insured. In addition to struggling to overcome our physical injuries which have severely impacted on the quality of our lives by causing my son and I permanent and severe disabilities I had to fight for minimum compensation. If it hadn't been for my husband's insurance policy – he was killed in the accident –'

'I'm sorry,' Trevor sympathised.

'Mick and I would have been in dire straits. But, it happened a long time ago, Inspector. To get back to my diary, anyone who reads it will discover what it is like to live as a disabled person in a cul-de-sac in suburban Britain in the twenty-first century. Sadly we, as a town and a country, no longer have anything remotely resembling community spirit but since I lost the use of my legs, it helps pass the time.

Occasionally when it's quiet in summer and my neighbours are away on holiday, I even while away an hour or two reading my past entries.'

Trevor looked down the deserted street and wondered if there had been more excitement in the street in previous years.

'It was busier and livelier when most of the houses had young children living in them, Inspector. But all the children have grown up and moved away, except my son, Mick, poor boy. And, believe it or not, in the past my diaries have helped solve many small mysteries.'

'How interesting.'

'Small crimes by your standards. But ten years ago I saw a boy break the windscreen of number 8's new Audi. And eight years ago I was able to identify the boy who picked the sunflowers from the front garden of number 12. I telephoned my neighbours and gave them the names of those responsible.'

'No doubt they were grateful.'

'The parents of the boys concerned were sufficiently embarrassed to pay compensation to the victims of their sons' hooliganism.'

'There would be less crime if there were more people like you living in our suburbs, Mrs Walsh.' Trevor took a pen and notebook from his top pocket. 'But to return to the day of the murder. In your diary, you state that Mr Piper returned to the street at four thirty.'

'Four fourteen, I believe.'

136

Trevor checked the file Sarah had given him and discovered the time was, indeed, four fourteen.

'Mr Piper parked his car outside his house and went across the road to Judy Mason's house. He let himself in with a key. I believe she gave him one after Joy Piper's funeral. While Joy was still alive he used to ring Judy Mason's doorbell. He hasn't since. I remember being surprised when he went into Judy's house that afternoon because it was her day for the hairdresser. She has a facial and a manicure at the same time.'

'How long was he inside the house?' Trevor had the feeling that Mrs Walsh would give him the names of the products the hairdresser used and Judy Mason's final bill if he asked her.

'Five minutes. He shut Mrs Mason's front door, tested it to make sure it was locked and crossed the road to his own house. This is all in my diary notes.' Mrs Walsh added.

Trevor continued to look at Sarah's highlighted extracts. 'Can you recall what he did after he returned to his own house?'

'Obviously I couldn't see what he did when he was inside his house, but he left it at twenty minutes past five, locked the door and drove away. Oh – and he was carrying something.'

'Could you see what it was?'

'No, but it was wrapped in a bundle of cloth. He'd tucked it under his arm.'

'And while Mr Piper was in the street did you see Mrs Howells?'

'No. She spends very little time in her front garden as you can see from the state of it; there are as many weeds there as flowers and the grass always needs cutting. Mrs Howells spends all her time out the back messing with the trees behind her garden which don't belong to her.'

'You see her?'

'Occasionally when Mick takes me out to use the exercise pool and Jacuzzi in the back garden. The doctor recommended I get one to try and use the muscles in my paralyzed legs. Not that it does much good. But although I spend most of my time here or in my bedroom, I hear her. It's whirring electric saws and chop, chop, chop from early morning to late evening. I generally make a note of what time she starts and what time she finishes. I'm sure it's illegal to make the noise she used to make. There have been times when she started before six in the morning and, often on light evenings she didn't stop until ten o'clock.'

'Did you hear her working on the day of the murder?'

'Yes. I had a headache. If you look at my notes I think you'll see she started at eight o'clock in the morning.'

Trevor recalled George Howells saying that he had left with the children at around half past seven, so within half an hour of him leaving, his wife was out on the farmer's land at the back of her house cutting down his trees. He looked at the notes again. 'The sound of sawing and chopping stopped around one o'clock.'

'When a post office delivery van drew up outside her house. It was parked there for three-quarters of an hour.'

'The sawing started again at three.' Trevor was relieved that the window of the time of Kacy Howells' death was finally narrowing.

'And didn't finish until three fifty-five,' Mrs Walsh complained.

'At last.'

'That means something to you?'

Trevor glanced up from Sarah's notes. 'Until this moment all we knew was that Kacy Howells had been killed some time between midday and eight o'clock in the evening. Your evidence has been most helpful in narrowing the gap. Are you sure that you didn't hear Kacy Howells chopping or sawing wood after three fifty-five?'

'Quite sure.'

'And you heard no other noises?'

'None, other than the arrival and departure of Alan Piper's car and various other neighbours. And a taxi that turned at the head of the cul-de-sac. The driver either spent a long time turning or dropped someone off. I couldn't see who it was because the taxi parked out of my view.'

'What time was that?'

'Twenty-two minutes past seven, I believe, it's in my notes.'

Trevor checked, as before, Mrs Walsh was accurate. 'You didn't see anyone approach the

Howells' house?'

'If the taxi had dropped someone off in the Howells' drive I wouldn't have seen them until they left – and no one did. Not before it grew too dark to see out of the window. The post office van delivery driver was the last person to knock on the Howells' door.'

'No one else went near the Howells' house,' he reiterated.

'Alan Piper went next door. But there's a high fence between him and the Howells. He had it erected and I don't blame him. In my opinion Kacy Howells was mentally ill. No normal person would have behaved the way she did.'

Trevor found Mrs Walsh's declaration ironic given her own voyeuristic activities.

'Your nice Constable Merchant is walking up our garden path, Inspector. I saw a team of white-suited officers enter Alan Piper's house eighteen minutes before you and the constable arrived here. Did Mr Piper kill Kacy Howells?'

'Everyone who knew Mrs Howells is a suspect until we make an arrest, Mrs Walsh. We have to keep an open mind. Thank you for the tea.'

Yes, thank you, Mrs Walsh,' Chris echoed. 'I'll go and see what my colleague wants.' Chris went to the front door where Sarah had been waylaid by Mick Walsh.

'Should you want to check any of my diary entries again, Inspector, you know where to find me. I can't get out of this chair and run away like my neighbours.'

'Do you think one of your neighbours might be tempted to run away from the street because of Kacy Howells' murder?' Trevor asked.

'If the person who hacked Kacy Howells to death came in and out of the Howells' garden the front way I would have seen them. Of course, it could have been a stranger who walked through the woods and climbed over the back fence. In which case they would only be seen if Mick was out in our back garden or the farmer was looking down in this direction from his land.'

'What do you mean; Kacy Howells was hacked to death?'

'The paper said she'd been killed with an axe. Wasn't she?'

Not for the first time Trevor regretted his superiors' openness with the press when it came to discussing an ongoing investigation. 'Do you have any particular neighbour in mind as the murderer, Mrs Walsh?'

'If I were you I'd start looking at the delivery men who visited Kacy Howells on a regular basis. Come to think of it, you should also take a good look at that path I mentioned. The one that runs down from the farm, through the woods at the back of our gardens. Strangers wouldn't know about it, but the locals do. If someone approached the Howells' garden from that direction, killed Mrs Howells and returned along the path and up the lane, they might not have been seen.'

'I thought the footpath cut across the farmer's land. Isn't his land fenced off?'

'It is, but most people in this street can step over their fences and access it from the backs of their gardens. From what I recall when I still had the use of my legs the farmer's fence was broken in more than one place. It used to be a popular place for children to play years ago.'

Trevor heard Chris talking to Sarah. 'I must go, Mrs Walsh. Thank you, you have been most helpful.'

'It's good to know that, given the way I am, I can still help someone. Goodbye, Inspector.'

'Anything?' Trevor asked Sarah and Chris when he joined them.

'Forensic want you on site, sir. At the back of Alan Piper's house.'

They walked along the pavement, through Alan Piper's front gate, around the house and up the steps on to the garden. The officer in charge was waiting for Trevor.

'Hi, Joseph. Long time no see.'

'What have you got?' Trevor asked.

'We used equipment that detects ground disturbance. It picked up on an area that was covered by bark. We dug down and found a coat.'

Trevor stood back and watched a technician in boots, overalls, cap and gloves tease a heavily stained coat from the dirt.

'Blood?' he asked.

The technician looked up. 'We'll have to do tests, sir, but it smells like it and looks as though it's been washed in it, sir.'

'The forensic team have photographed the coat?' Trevor checked when Sarah climbed into the back of the car Chris was driving.

'Yes, sir, but I thought you'd want some photographs right away so I took a few as well.' She leaned forward and handed a digital camera to Trevor in the front passenger seat. 'You can call them up now. The ones forensic took are being e-mailed to the office. I'll print them off as soon as we get back.'

'I never cease to be amazed by your efficiency. Thank you.'

'She thinks it will get her promotion before me, sir.' Chris started the car,

'It will,' Trevor said semi-seriously.

'The team is continuing to conduct a thorough search of the house and the garden. I told them to contact the incident room if they find anything else of interest. They've promised to start testing the coat as soon as they get it to the lab, sir, but it will take time.' Sarah fastened her safety belt.

'The one thing I've learned with forensics is they can't be hurried.' Trevor pulled down the sun visor as Chris drove off. A mirror had been inset into the back. He used it to take a last look at the Walshes' house. He detected movement behind the vertical blinds in the living room. As Mick Walsh was putting the lawnmower away in the garage, he assumed Mrs Walsh was monitoring them. Possibly through her binoculars. He glanced from the house to the detached garage.

'There are a lot of boxes in the Walshes' garage. Have you two checked them out?'

'Yes, sir,' Chris slowed at the end of the street. 'Mick showed me the paperwork. The Walshes store chemicals for a cleaning firm. They take delivery and keep them until they are picked up by the operatives. As neither he nor his mother has been able to work since the car accident that killed his father and injured him and his mother, it gives them a small income.'

'I trust they declare it to the taxman and social services.'

'That, I didn't ask, sir.' Chris turned the corner.

Five minutes later they were on the main road heading into town. Another ten minutes and they'd be in the office. Trevor would not only have to face Alan Piper but Peter as well, and he wasn't looking forward to resuming the interview.

He suspected that there was only one way it could end.

CHAPTER ELEVEN

'Do you recognise this coat?' Trevor set the photographs Sarah had printed out in front of Alan Piper. They had been taken after the garment had been spread out on a plastic sheet, arms extended. It probably had begun life as a lightweight, chain store shower-proof jacket. It might have been beige, or possibly cream. The original colour, smudged with dirt and mud could still be seen in rare spots around the edges, but the front panels either side of the central zip fastener and the sleeves were a deep blotched, blackened burgundy. Lumps of matter were stuck to the cloth. Trevor hoped they were dirt not Kacy Howells' brain tissue.

Alan studied the pictures. 'It could be mine.'

'You don't know?' Silence followed Trevor's question. He continued to sit listening to Alan's steady breathing, very aware of Sarah, still and concentrating beside him.

He thought of Peter. He knew the sergeant would be listening outside the interview room, noting every word he and Alan said.

'I had a beige zip-up casual jacket similar to that. I bought it in Marks and Spencer's a couple of years ago. I haven't seen it for a while and although I've looked for it, I haven't looked very hard.'

'Why?' Trevor questioned.

'Because I have plenty of others I can wear.'

'You lose a coat and just forget about it?'

'When I couldn't find it in the house, I assumed I'd left it in the back of my car. Or the boot, or in work, the pub or Judy's. I drive most places. If I need a coat I reach for the nearest one. I must have half a dozen or more.'

Trevor looked at Sarah. He didn't need to say a word. She was already making a note directing the search team to check the number of coats and jackets in Alan's house.

'Would you like to know where we found it?' Trevor asked.

'I have a feeling you're going to tell me.'

'Buried in your garden.'

'Buried …' Alan paled.

'You didn't notice the ground had been disturbed?' Given that the forensic team had told him the area had been covered by bark, Trevor felt he was being unfair.

'I've hardly gone into my garden since Joy died.'

'You were there two nights ago, on the evening of the day Kacy Howells was murdered,' Trevor reminded.

'I went there to walk off my annoyance at being dragged out on a wild goose chase and to look at the stars. Not to dig holes.'

'So you've no idea how a coat that "could be" yours became soaked in what looks like blood – we'll know more when the results of the forensic tests come in – or came to be buried in your garden?'

'None.'

'Or how chewing gum and tissue impregnated with your DNA came to be on the deck in the Howells' garden?'

Alan kept his voice even. 'Other than to say that it looks like someone is planting evidence to make it look as though I killed Kacy Howells, no.'

Trevor opened a file and extracted the pages of Mrs Walsh's diary that Sarah had typed and the notes that had been made of his earlier interviews with Alan. 'I'd like to go back over your movements on the day Kacy Howells was murdered.'

'I've told you all I know.'

'I need to verify the time-line of your initial statement. You don't want to alter your statement in any way?'

'No.'

'You're certain.'

'Absolutely.'

'You had lunch with Peter Collins in the Black Boar and left him at around two o'clock.'

'Yes.'

'You returned to your office and stayed there until four thirty?'

'Somewhere around then, I can't be exact about times. I don't live my life by clocks and watches.'

'After which you drove up to Connor's Lake, taking the scenic route to meet someone who telephoned you at the office, someone who said that he or she – you couldn't be specific about sex – would be there between six and nine o'clock in the evening?'

'Yes.'

'And they didn't show.'

Alan allowed his impatience to surface for the first time. 'I've told you all this.'

'Connor's Lake is a fifty-five mile drive from your house, "door to door" in your own words.'

'Yes.'

'Less from town. Shall we say about forty-five miles if you travel on the mountain road, which you did.'

'Probably.'

'Even allowing for country roads and the vagaries of rush-hour traffic leaving town between four and five or clock I'd say that's approximately an hour and a half's drive.'

'About that.'

'Then why did you leave your office at half past four to reach there by seven o'clock?'

'I'd finished for the day. Possibly I thought that it could be nearer an hour and a half or two if I had a problem with the traffic getting out of town. And, some of those lanes around the lake are very narrow.'

'So you were thinking about the traffic?'

'I also had a few personal problems. I probably wasn't thinking clearly.'

'What kind of personal problems?'

'Problems with a friendship that have absolutely nothing to do with Kacy Howells being murdered.'

Trevor allowed the matter to drop – for the moment – but filed the information in his mind.

148

'What time did you get to the lake?'

'I'm not sure.'

'You must have checked the time when you arrived as the caller had been so specific in asking you to be there between seven and nine o'clock.'

'I probably did check,' Alan conceded, 'but I can't remember doing so. I suppose I simply noticed that I was within the time the caller had asked me to be there.'

'You drove directly to the lake from your office?'

'Yes – no.' He hesitated. 'I dropped by my house.'

'Why didn't you mention this earlier?'

'Because it slipped my mind. I didn't think it was important. I wanted to pick up a sleeping bag. I wasn't sure when, if at all, the contact was going to show or if they did show, if they'd want to move on. I like to be prepared for all eventualities. I wasn't home for long.'

'You pulled up outside your house at fourteen minutes past four in the afternoon,' Trevor informed Alan.

Nonplussed, Alan stared at Trevor. 'I should have known, Mrs Walsh's famous – or should I say – infamous – diary.'

'You know she keeps a diary?'

'Of all the movement in the street? Yes. Everyone who lives there knows about it. She watches us all. When kids lived in the street she used to open her window and yell at them every time they did something she disapproved of.'

'You didn't think that was public-spirited of her?'

'Although Joy and I never had any kids of our own, like most people living in view of Mrs Walsh, I had another name for it.'

'Which was?'

'The polite term would be voyeurism.'

'But you agree that you drove up the street and parked your car at fourteen minutes past four on the day Kacy Howells was murdered.'

'I'll take Mrs Walsh's word for it. If she was clocking me in and out I don't doubt the timing is spot-on.'

'Yet, you said earlier that you left your office at half past four that day.'

'I also said that I don't live my life by clocks and watches.' Alan was making an effort to keep his voice steady but Trevor could detect strain.

'When you reached your house, you parked your car outside, left it and walked across the road to Judy Mason's house '

'Judy was out.'

'But you let yourself in.'

'She gave me a key after Joy died. I use it to check her house and pick up the mail from behind the door when she's away.'

'Does she have a key to your house?'

'No, but only because I rarely go away.'

'But Judy wasn't away that afternoon.'

'She was out, not away.'

'How long were you in Judy Mason's house?'

'I don't know.' Alan's irritation finally surfaced. 'A couple of minutes, maybe more.'

'Try five.'

'All right, I was in Judy's house for five minutes.'

'You knew she'd be out?'

'I know she usually goes to the hairdresser at that time, yes. You've spoken to her about it?'

'No.'

Alan shook his head. 'Mrs Walsh told you it was Judy's regular day at the hairdresser's.'

'If you knew she was out, why did you go in?' Trevor asked.

'We'd had a stupid argument the night before, I wanted to make amends.'

'An argument over what?'

'My relationship with Judy Mason has nothing whatsoever to do with Kacy Howells' murder or my dispute with the Howells …'

'If I were you, before saying any more, I'd think very carefully about the evidence we've accumulated and the errors in the statements you made yesterday. Would you like to telephone your solicitor?' Trevor asked.

'No. I've better things to do with my money than pay solicitor's bills.' Alan clasped his hands together and leaned forward, across the table. 'Judy and I are friends. She's been divorced for four years and wants our relationship to be something more than it is. I am recovering from the death of my wife. I need more time to grieve, and Judy and I argued about it. On my way back from the court yesterday I stopped in town and bought her a small box of luxury chocolates. She likes fruit-flavoured ones. I left them in her living room as a peace offering.'

Sarah was making notes again and Trevor didn't doubt she'd follow Alan's story up with Judy Mason at the first opportunity.

'It took you five minutes to leave a box of chocolates in Judy Mason's living room?'

'I bought her a card as well. I hadn't written in it. It took me a few minutes to decide what I wanted to say to her.'

'So, after you wrote the card and left the chocolates ...'

'As we're being pedantic, on her living room table next to the TV remote so she couldn't miss them when she went in.'

'On her table next to the TV remote,' Trevor repeated. 'You left Judy Mason's house, locked the door and went to your own house. How long were you there?'

'I would have said ten minutes but given that you've just told me I spent seven minutes in Judy's, it was probably nearer twenty.'

'What did you do in your house?'

'What I always do when I walk through the door. Check my answer phone messages and ...'

'Were there any?'

'Pardon?' Alan looked blankly at Trevor.

'Answer phone messages? It was only the day before yesterday.'

'It feels like it all happened months ago,' Alan said.

'Were there any messages?' Trevor repeated.

'Yes – but nothing urgent. I wrote them on the pad next to the phone. There was one from an old friend cancelling a squash session.'

'You play squash?'

'Obviously, as he was cancelling the session. I think there were others but you'll have to check the pad in the living room.'

'What else did you do? Trevor pressed him.

'Went upstairs and took a sleeping bag out of the airing cupboard as I've already said. I also switched on my computer and opened my mail box.'

Sarah continued making notes. A computer was the best witness in any case simply because all activity was timed and recorded.

'You had e-mails?'

'Mostly advertising spam but there were a couple from friends who are working abroad.'

'How long were you on your computer?'

'I'm not sure. After checking my e-mails I glanced at the breaking news headlines, looking for more information on the missing beauty queen, there wasn't anything that I hadn't already read, so I took the sleeping bag, locked the house, got in my car and drove off.'

'And you believe that you were in your house for around twenty minutes?'

'I can't be sure. I just told you I don't plan my day by the clock.'

'According to Mrs Walsh you left your house at five twenty which means you were home for forty-one minutes.'

'Doesn't time fly when you're having fun?'

Trevor felt that given the circumstances it was an inappropriate remark, even for a relative of Peter Collins.

'While you were in your house, did you go outside into your back garden?'

'No.'

'Given your uncertainty about your answer phone and e-mail messages you seem very sure.'

'I am, and not just because Mrs Walsh can't see into my back garden I didn't open the back door of my house.'

'Did you hear Kacy Howells sawing or chopping wood when you arrived in the street?'

'She does it so often, if she was, it didn't register.'

'But if you'd heard the sound, you would have known it was her.'

'No one else spends all their time chopping trees at the back of the gardens at the end of the street.'

'Do you monitor the Howells' activities?'

'I began to after they started stealing my property but I told you this yesterday. I also volunteered to give you a copy of the diary I kept on their activities when you interviewed me earlier.'

'It's on your computer?'

'In my document files titled – Howells, diary of events.'

'Do you have any objection to us examining your computer, Mr Piper?' Trevor glanced at Sarah.

'None whatsoever.'

Trevor nodded to Sarah. 'We'll take a break at this point.'

'Yes, sir.' She left the room.

Trevor sat back in his chair and switched off the recorder. 'Would you like another coffee?' he asked Alan.

'No thanks, I'm coffee'd out.'

'Soft drink and a sandwich?'

'How much longer do you intend to keep me here?'

'That rather depends on you, Mr Piper, but,' Trevor flicked through the papers in his file, 'I have about another hour's worth of questions here.'

'I'll take the sandwich.'

'I'll have it sent in.'

As Trevor had expected Peter was waiting outside the door. He pounced as soon as Trevor closed the door on the interview room.

'You can't read anything into Alan forgetting that he called into his house before driving up to Connor's Lake. He wasn't expecting to be questioned about it ...' He faltered in the face of Trevor's stern look.

'That is exactly why Sarah is sitting alongside me across the table from Alan and not you.'

Sarah walked past them. 'Coffee's on your desk,

sir.'

'Thank you, see that a sandwich and soft drink are sent into the interview room for Mr Piper and ask someone to keep him company until we resume the questioning in twenty minutes. Oh, and, Sarah?'

'Sir?'

'When we go back in, bring a file with a copy of the porn magazine and photographs of the items we found in the Howells' shed.'

'Yes, sir. Forensics rang a few minutes ago with a preliminary report on the jacket found in Alan Piper's garden. The blood is Kacy Howells' and there was an empty envelope in the inside pocket, addressed to Alan Piper.'

Peter followed Trevor into his office. 'Are you going to arrest Alan?'

'Given the evidence we've accumulated what would you do?'

Peter didn't hesitate. 'Arrest him.'

When Trevor and Sarah returned to the interview room they found Chris and Alan Piper discussing the form of the local football team. Trevor wondered if constables followed sport simply to have a relatively safe topic they could discuss with suspects in between questioning.

He dropped the file Sarah had given him on the table. Chris cleared the tray and closed the door behind him. Trevor and Sarah took their seats.

'Ready?' Trevor asked Alan.

'The sooner this is over, the better, as far as I'm

concerned.'

Trevor switched on the tape, noted the time, opened the file Sarah had given him, removed the photographs of the sex aids and handed them to Alan. 'I am showing Mr Alan Piper the photographs A1 A2 A3 and A4,' he said for the benefit of the tape. 'Do you have any comments to make, Mr Piper?'

'That's quite a collection.'

'You've never seen any of them before?'

'That's a leading question.' Alan registered the grim expression on Trevor's face and emulated Trevor's formal attitude. 'I've seen individual items like these but I haven't seen sex aids grouped together like this before.'

'What about this?' Trevor opened the magazine at the advertisement page for Kacy Howells, and turned it around so it faced Alan.

Alan blanched.

'Judging by the expression on your face, I'd say that you have seen that advertisement before, Mr Piper.'

'Yes.'

'When?'

'When the magazine came out a few days ago.'

'Is it a magazine you subscribe to or look up on the internet?'

'No.'

'You just came across the advertisement by chance?'

'No.' Alan raised his head. 'You're going to find

out anyway so I may as well come clean. I drafted the ad and paid for it to be placed in the magazine.'

'With Kacy Howells' knowledge?'

'No. I hoped to embarrass her into taking down that ridiculous platform and shed.'

'How did you pay for it?'

'I applied for a credit card in her name but put it on my address. I hoped the postman would only look at the house number. He did.'

'What about Kacy Howells' details. Her date of birth, bank details ...'

'I applied for a card with an astronomical interest rate in the hope they wouldn't check too carefully. I went for one with a low limit, I think it was around five hundred pounds, used it to place the advert in the magazine and on the internet, pay for subscription copies to be sent to the Howells' office and buy sex toys, also on the internet which I sent to the Howells' home address. I paid off the card after I used it. Then I destroyed it.' He looked at Trevor. 'I know I shouldn't have done it. But I was furious. Furious that Kacy Howells had ruined the last few months of Joy's life. Furious with them for stealing my property and making me paranoid and distrustful of all my neighbours.'

'Furious enough to kill Kacy Howells, Mr Piper?'

'No.'

Trevor picked up the telephone at his elbow. 'Constable Brooke, would you come to interview room three please and assist Constable Merchant in

158

formally charging Mr Alan Piper with the murder of Kacy Howells?'

CHAPTER TWELVE

Sarah and Chris walked into the interview room to find Trevor, Peter and Dan Evans sitting around the central table, polystyrene cups of congealing coffee abandoned in front of them. As usual, Peter was playing with his cigars.

'We telephoned Mr Piper's solicitor, sir, and put the case on the court list,' Sarah reported.

'Alan will be remanded in custody. There's no way he'll get bail on a murder charge.' Peter left his chair and paced to the window.

'He might,' Dan said. 'Given the overcrowding in prisons some magistrates are prepared to give defendants the benefit of the doubt.'

'Only brainless idiots who never travel further from their interior-designed homes in well-patrolled suburbs, to their personalised car parking space outside the courts. If they walked the streets in the inner cities or looked outside their narrow horizons once in a while, they might begin to mete out punishments that fit the crimes,' Peter growled.

'You can't have it both ways. Tough on crime means tough on everyone, even the Alan Pipers of this world when they're up on a murder charge. And, I've always been of the opinion that a murder charge warrants "remanded in custody".' Dan rose to his feet. 'But, the Kacy Howells murder is no longer your case, Sergeant Collins. I can do with all the help I can get. As of this moment you're seconded to the Drug War murders. I'll update you in my office.'

It was a request Peter couldn't refuse. 'Yes, sir.' He glanced at Trevor. 'You'll keep me informed?'

'If Dan agrees. Off the record.' Trevor looked to Dan.

Dan nodded agreement. 'The pub in an hour for a quick one?'

'If nothing turns up.' Trevor watched Dan and Peter close the door behind them, before turning to his team. 'Right people, I don't want anyone sitting back and assuming this case is closed because we've made an arrest. We need all the hard evidence we can dig up if the charge is going to hold up in court. Chris, first thing tomorrow you and I will visit Kacy Howells' father to check out his alibi. If necessary we'll interview every elder in that chapel.'

'Yes, sir.'

'I'll meet you here at nine. Sarah, head down to Kacy and George Howells' office, take as many uniformed constables as can be spared from the station with you. I want everyone who works with George and worked with Kacy Howells interviewed. I'd like you to personally interview the man Kacy Howells lived with for seventeen or eighteen years …' Trevor searched his memory for his name.

'John Evans, sir?'

'That's him. After you've finished there, contact the owner of the magazine again. We need to know if Alan Piper's story about the credit card in Kacy Howells' name pans out. After you've spoken to him check the bank that issued the card.'

'Yes, sir.'

'And, if you and I have any time left after we've interviewed the chapel elders, Chris, we'll visit the farmer and walk the footpath that leads to the back of the Howells' house that Mrs Walsh mentioned. I'll be in my office for the next half hour if anyone wants me. Anything new comes in ...'

'We'll inform you right away, sir.' Sarah was already at her keyboard. When Trevor walked past her computer screen he saw that she was already scanning lists of George Howells' colleagues.

'Pint?' Dan asked Trevor when he joined him in the bar of Platform 10.

'Please.' Trevor stood back and looked around. The bar was crowded with office workers from the town's call centres, shops and offices. Dan saw him studying the room.

'Cheaper to have one drink on the way home, than go home change and make a night of it,' Dan commented.

'Incidentally easing the load on the poor beat coppers who have to patrol the town centre on the graveyard shift. Cheers,' Trevor took the pint Dan handed him. 'Have you made plans for the evening?'

'You have something in mind?'

'You and Peter are welcome to visit your godson. Lyn can always cobble together a scratch meal.'

'The godfathers have imposed on their godson's mother's hospitality too often since Marty's arrival. And Lyn never cobbles anything together. It's always a banquet. With the Kacy Howells case progressing the way it is, snatch some family time while you can. Peter and I are going for a curry after this drink. I haven't finished updating him. Although I doubt there's any point. That brick wall I was talking about appears to be set in six feet of solid concrete.'

'But you have to keep trying.'

'With the body count escalating daily, upstairs are piling on the pressure.'

'More today?'

'Three missing, seven dead. One up on yesterday,' Dan divulged.

'Time upstairs realised this drug war's doing the town a favour by scrubbing out the scum.' Peter joined them and frowned at Trevor. 'It's getting harder and harder to park around here. 'You have some secret bay hidden in town that I don't know about?'

'This time of night, back of the library. Lyn's mother works there part-time. The family use her space when she doesn't need it.'

'Some buggers always get jam on their bread.' Peter picked up the pint Dan had bought for him. 'Here's to the good guys.'

'Our friend has arrived,' Dan warned Peter.

Trevor glanced over his shoulder. 'The station's favourite nark.'

'He wasn't mine the last time I saw him,' Peter complained. 'He wanted a grand for telling me that Lofty was flashing money after a Red Dragon hit.'

'When we know the Nape brothers carried out the last four killings,' Dan explained to Trevor. 'Not that we can prove it.'

'He's making a bee-line for you, Peter,' Trevor warned.

Peter braced himself for an "accidental" collision, but Snaggy coughed as he passed their table on his way to the door that led to the outside yard and toilets.

Dan grabbed an empty table and pulled out a chair. 'What plans have you made for tomorrow, Trevor?'

While Trevor outlined the orders he had given his team, Peter finished his pint. 'Another?' he asked Dan and Trevor.

'Not for me, I promised Lyn I'd be home for dinner.'

'Rub in Daisy's absence, why don't you?'

'I wasn't, and you like Indian.'

'Dan told you?'

'You bachelors enjoy your working dinner.' Trevor left the table.

'Any …'

Trevor interrupted Dan. 'I'll keep in touch.'

'Unlike some people I could mention, you always do.' Dan pushed his empty glass towards Peter.

'Drinks on me tomorrow.'

'I'll hold you to that, Joseph.' Peter pulled out his wallet.

'One more and we'll move on to the restaurant,' Dan warned Peter.

'I'll pick them up on the way back.' Peter gave the barman his order, paid for the drinks in advance and walked outside.

'He's a good copper,' Trevor observed when Peter was out of earshot.

'If he wasn't, he wouldn't be on my team.' Dan moved his chair so he could watch the doors.

Peter walked into the Gents but there was no sign of Snaggy. He saw him as he left, standing in a corner of the smoking area puffing a Lambert and Butler. Peter ambled close to him and filched a cigar from the pack he kept in his shirt pocket.

'Got a light, mate?'

Snaggy took a cheap plastic lighter from his pocket and flicked it. 'Where's my money?' he hissed, bending his head close to Peter's.

Peter deliberately blew out the flame. 'What money?'

'I gave you a tip-off. I want a grand.'

'You gave me the wrong name, sunshine. The Nape brothers …'

'Nape brothers nothing.' Snaggy flicked the lighter again and lowered his voice as a man walked past the yard on the way to the Gents. 'Lofty did that suburban job. And sorted it so someone else would take the rap.'

'What suburban job?' Like Snaggy, Peter lowered his voice to a whisper.

'That woman who was axed. I gave you Lofty. I know he's still on the streets because I saw him today but that's down to you, not me. I gave you good merchandise. I want my money.'

'How did he sort it?' Peter thought of the forensic evidence that implicated Alan.

'Planted evidence so you lot would find it.'

'What sort of evidence?'

'Lofty said something about rubbish from a bin. You want details, you pay for them.'

Peter finally lit his cigar. 'Thanks for the light, mate.' He glanced at two men who were leaving the Gents. They were apparently deep in conversation but it was difficult to tell whether one of them was listening in. He moved away from Snaggy but the snitch was having none of it. He waited until the men went into the bar then followed Peter across the partially tented area.

'Money,' he repeated.

'Why would someone pay Lofty to axe a suburban housewife and finger someone else?'

'I don't know the why, only the who.'

'Spit it out,' Peter demanded.

'The Red Dragon.'

'Do I look as though I've just hatched out of the egg and I'm waiting with an open mouth to swallow anything that's fed me?'

'I'm risking my life here for you lot. I want my money, tomorrow at the latest.'

'And if you don't get it?' Peter challenged him.

'I know people.'

'Put a price on me, sunshine, and it'll not only be your business you'll be waving goodbye to,' Peter threatened.

Snaggy turned defensive. 'You're a sergeant aren't you? I've given you bloody good information over the years, enough to get you promoted ...'

'And you've always given me time to check it out.'

'You've had your time.'

'Not enough,' Peter snapped.

'What am I supposed to do while you check what I've told you?' Snaggy clenched his fists.

'Crawl back into the hole you crawled out of and hide,' Peter advised.

A woman left the bar and walked towards the Ladies. Peter caught the door before it swung shut, put out his cigar in an ashtray, pocketed the stub and called back, 'Thanks for the light, mate.'

'He said what?' Dan eyed Peter over the top of the menu. As Dan had hoped the restaurant was empty apart from the waiters who were laying tables and preparing for the late-night rush.

'"The suburban wife murder" – which I presume is Kacy Howells', was ordered by the Red Dragon and carried out by Lofty who sorted it so someone else would take the rap by planting evidence from a bin.'

Dan raised his eyebrows. 'You bought it?'

'I didn't say I bought it. I'm simply repeating what Snaggy said. He was very antsy, even for him. Nervous, looking over his shoulder every five minutes, asking for money …'

'Money has always come first with Snaggy. The amount we've paid him over the years, he should be a multi-millionaire.'

'He would be if he'd invested it in a bank, as opposed to fixes.'

'He's excelled himself this time.' Dan shook his head from side to side. 'The Red Dragon put a price on Kacy Howells' head?' he queried sceptically. 'Did you ask him why?'

'Yes, he said he didn't know the why, only the who, then people came into the yard. But the last thing he told me to do – practically threatened me – was meet him there tomorrow with a grand.'

'In grubby pound notes in a brown paper bag no doubt.' Dan beckoned the waiter over. 'Special for two do you?'

'If you're paying make it number four.'

'That's the most expensive.'

Peter flashed an insincere smile. 'Is it?'

Trevor didn't waste any time the following morning. At nine thirty he and Chris were sitting in the Jenkinses' living room. Trevor took his notebook from his pocket, opened it and looked up at Kacy's father.

'Mr Jenkins, on the day your daughter was murdered, you left the house to go to a chapel elders' meeting at two o'clock in the afternoon. Is that right?'

'We've already been through this, Inspector,' Sam Jenkins retorted. 'I fail to see how you knowing my whereabouts on the day my daughter was murdered is going to help you catch her killer.'

'Please, Mr Jenkins, humour me. Your whereabouts could be extremely important.'

'How?' the old man barked.

'If you were in the habit of visiting your daughter at her home …'

'Which I wasn't. I last saw her over a month ago. As I've already told you.'

Trevor calmly continued the questioning. 'You left this house at two o'clock. Did you walk or drive to the chapel?'

'I walked. As my wife told you yesterday, I don't drive. And I didn't leave at two o'clock. The committee meeting started at two o'clock and I abhor unpunctuality. I left the house at one thirty.'

'And arrived at the chapel when?'

'Ten minutes later. It's in the next street.'

'Why so early?'

'To put the boiler on ready for tea, and to make sure the chairs were set up around the table. I am Vice Chairman of the elders and I regard preparing the hall for meetings part of the duties that come with the position.'

'The meeting went on for how long?'

'As I've already told you, the meeting finished at four o'clock.'

'Then a few of you stayed on to paint the chapel.'

'It needed it.'

'When did you finish?'

'Not until ten o'clock. Then I visited another of the elders, Matthew Clarke. His wife recently died, he invited me in for a cup of tea. Knowing he was lonely I accepted.'

'Where does Matthew Clarke live?'

'Next door to the chapel.'

'What time did you leave his house?'

'Look at your notes,' the old man snarled irritably.

'Around midnight?'

'About then,' Sam Jenkins confirmed.

'You had several cups of tea?' Trevor looked directly into the old man's eyes.

'Matthew made some cheese sandwiches. We ate them and talked.'

'What did you talk about?'

'I can't remember.'

'You must have talked about something, Mr Jenkins,' Trevor persisted patiently.

'Mainly chapel business.'

'The same things you talked about in the elders' meeting?'

'I can't remember.' His voice grew shrill. 'You should be out looking for whoever murdered my daughter ...'

'When you left Mr Clarke's house, did you walk straight back here or call in anywhere else?' Trevor interrupted.

'Call in anywhere? At that time of night?' Sam Jenkins said indignantly. 'I came straight back here.'

'Mrs Jenkins was asleep?'

'As I told you.'

'Do you have the minutes for the elders' meeting?'

'No. The chairman takes them from the secretary, his wife types them up and we receive a copy at the next meeting.'

'You have a full list of the elders' names, and contact details including addresses and telephone numbers?'

Mr Jenkins squirmed uneasily on his chair. 'Somewhere.'

'Not to hand?'

'I don't need the information.' He tapped his head. 'I keep it filed up here.'

'In that case you can dictate the list to us, Mr Jenkins, so we can validate your statement.' Trevor continued to watch the elderly man. 'Could you begin by giving us Matthew Clarke's address and telephone number. The man who invited you into his house for tea and cheese sandwiches.'

Matthew Clarke was a tiny, wizened man who looked like an animated garden gnome. He spoke quickly, his words tumbling out one after the other, answering Trevor's questions before he finished asking them. Trevor suspected that Sam Jenkins had

171

telephoned ahead to warn Matthew Clarke that he was about to be interviewed.

'That's right, Inspector Joseph, I invited Sam Jenkins in for tea after the meeting. It was late, but he came anyway. I made cheese sandwiches and tea and we sat talking. We'd been painting the chapel. It needed it.'

Trevor noticed that the phrase "it needed it" was the same one Sam Jenkins had used. 'What time did you leave the chapel, Mr Clarke?'

'It must have been quite late, around eleven o'clock. We talked a bit – and played a game of chess. Sam's a good player. I never win against him but he humours me.'

'And he left when?'

'After he'd eaten the sandwiches and drunk his tea. I suppose he must have been here for about half an hour.'

'You'd been together since the meeting started at two o'clock, is that right?'

'It is, Inspector.'

'And the meeting finished, when exactly?'

Matthew Clarke looked distinctly uncomfortable. 'I'm not sure. I wasn't looking at my watch but it was a long meeting.'

'Three … four … five … six o'clock?' Trevor hazarded, hesitating between each number.

'Probably around six o'clock.'

'And after the meeting?'

Matthew Clarke ran his finger around the inside of his collar to loosen it although it was already hanging on his scrawny frame. 'We painted the chapel.'

'How many of you?'

'Pardon?'

'How many of you stayed behind to paint the church?' Trevor asked.

'Six or seven of us. I can't be sure; we each took a different part of the chapel. One – or maybe two of the elders were working upstairs in the gallery.'

Trevor again referred to the notes he had made the first time he had interviewed Sam Jenkins. *A few of us stayed behind to paint the chapel.*

'Could you give me their names?'

'I really couldn't say.' Matthew Clarke jumped up from his chair. 'I am very busy I have a lot of ...' he paused, 'letters to write,' he said suddenly. 'My late wife's business affairs. You know how it is.'

'What I do know, Mr Clarke is that you're uncomfortable with and strangely reticent to answer my questions about what you and the other elders did the night Kacy Howells was murdered. Do you have the keys of the chapel?'

'Yes – I mean no. Normally I would have them but the chairman ...'

Trevor looked him in the eye. 'You live next door to the chapel, Mr Clarke, surely as an elder you hold a key for emergencies.'

'Yes, but this hardly an emergency. I can't hand over the keys to every Tom, Dick and Harry who asks for them. The chairman and the elders would be very angry ...'

'You wouldn't be handing them to just anyone, Mr Clarke. You would be giving them to a police officer who requested them in order to further his enquiries into a murder investigation.'

'Kacy Howells hasn't been in the chapel for months … years … I really don't see how this can help you in any way …'

Trevor held out his hand wordlessly.

'This is highly irregular,' Matthew Clarke blustered. 'The keys are in my safekeeping. I have to get permission from the chairman of the elders…'

'Then get it.' Trevor indicated the telephone.

'He won't be in at this time of day.'

'He works?'

'No. He's retired.'

'In which case you won't know whether he's in or not until you try.' Trevor waited for a full minute during which Matthew Clarke remained silent. 'I could go back to the station, fill out a search warrant, return here and force you to hand over the keys so we could look inside the chapel. And, if you still refused to hand over the keys, batter the door down. While I was getting the warrant I would be fully justified in keeping you in custody.'

'There is no need for that,' Matthew chimed peevishly.

'Shall we go next door and open up the chapel?'

Matthew Clarke left his chair, went to a desk and opened a drawer. He withdrew a large bunch of keys of varying sizes. 'I have to accompany you?'

'I have no objection.' Trevor walked to the front

door and Chris followed. As they left the house, Trevor noticed that Matthew was meticulous about locking the door.

'Burglaries a problem around here?'

'There are vandals here the same as everywhere in Britain today.'

Trevor looked up and down the neat street of terraced houses. There was no graffiti or any other obvious signs of vandalism. 'Seems a quiet area to me.'

'Appearances can be deceptive, Inspector.' Matthew Clarke's hand shook as he tried to insert the Yale key into the lock of the church.

'Allow me.' Trevor took the key from him and unlocked the door. It held fast.

'You have to unlock the main lock as well, Inspector, this is the key.' Matthew pointed to a six-inch key on the ring.

Trevor inserted it in the main lock, turned it and unlocked the door before turning the Yale key again. The door opened. He stepped inside. The outer hall was small, no more than six feet square. He pushed the door and entered the chapel. The pulpit and organ were screened off from the congregation by sliding doors.

'I don't smell any paint,' Trevor commented.

'You can get ones that don't smell these days. They cost a little more …'

'And are totally invisible and useless for the purpose?' Trevor ran his fingers over the grimy walls. Smudges greyed the paintwork. Alongside the chairs in the congregation the paint had been scuffed down to the bare plaster.

Matthew flushed. 'We talked about it. We're going to buy the paint – this week …'

'Mr Clarke, I have to ask to you to accompany me to the station.'

Matthew Clarke looked as though he were about to burst into tears. 'Are you arresting me?'

'Not at the moment, Mr Clarke, but wasting police time and giving false statements are serious offences. If you would like a solicitor to be present while you are questioned, we can send for yours, or find you one. Constable Brooke, please escort Mr Clarke to the car.'

'I have to lock up.'

'I will secure the building, Mr Clarke.'

Trevor waited until Chris had left with Matthew Clarke before telephoning the station and asking the duty constable to arrange an escort to bring Sam Jenkins in for questioning.

CHAPTER THIRTEEN

'We've put Mr Jenkins and Mr Clarke in separate interview rooms, sir.' Chris Brooke went to the coffee station in the incident room and poured himself a cup.

'Did they see one another?' Trevor asked.

Chris smiled. 'As ordered.'

'When you've finished your break, check on the search warrants. As soon as they come through organise searches of the Jenkinses' house and Matthew Clarke's. After they're completed we'll track down and interview their fellow chapel elders.'

'Like a coffee, sir?' Chris asked.

'Please.'

'You take it black, no sugar?'

'I do.'

Chris poured Trevor a cup and carried it over to the computer where Trevor was inputting and cross-referencing Matthew Clarke's and Sam Jenkins's witness statements.

'How did you know Sam Jenkins was lying?' Chris pulled up a chair.

'I didn't. But there was something odd about the way he related his movements on the day his daughter was killed. And, besides his peculiar manner, a two hour meeting followed by a six hour painting session didn't ring true to me. Not for six or seven men. Most people who decide to tackle a job like repainting a chapel would start first thing in the morning. Not sit around discussing chapel matters for two hours, then start painting. A late start would cut into their evening, and most wives of Sam Jenkins's generation want their husbands home in the evening to share a meal.'

'I didn't think of that.'

'And there's the timing. How long does it take to splash on a coat of emulsion?'

'Depending on the size of the room, a couple of hours.'

'You saw the chapel and we're talking six or seven men. Strange neither Matthew Clarke nor Sam Jenkins could give us the exact number,' Trevor mused.

'Glossing would take longer.'

'It would. But most chapels have stained and varnished pulpits, benches and skirting-boards. As this one did, when we finally persuaded Matthew Clarke to open it up.'

'You really had nothing more to go on than the timing and "there was something odd" about Sam Jenkins's story?'

Trevor pressed "print" on the list of discrepancies he'd compiled and pushed his chair back from the computer desk. 'It's called instinct. When I first joined the force I was told to distrust it, but the longer I serve and the older I get, the more I find myself relying on it.'

'What do you expect to find in the searches?' Chris asked.

'What we expect to find in every search, Constable.' Dan walked into the room. 'We don't know until we see it, and when we see it, we'll know it.'

'Yes, sir.'

'Can I have a word in my office, Trevor?'

'I'll be with you in a minute. Do me a favour, Chris, copy this print-out into evidence and distribute them in the files. Then compile a list of the names and addresses of the other chapel elders.'

Trevor followed Dan into his office. Peter was sitting in front of Dan's desk poring over the PM report on Kacy Howells. He looked up when Trevor walked in.

'Heard you've brought in Kacy's father and one of the chapel elders for questioning.'

'You can't keep anything quiet around here,' Trevor grumbled.

'Does that mean Alan's off the hook?'

'It means that chapel elders who should know better are telling porkies about where they were on the afternoon of the murder. Why are you looking at Kacy Howells' PM report? You're off the case.'

'He is and he isn't.' Dan squeezed past Trevor who'd perched on the edge of his desk. 'Snaggy told Peter last night that the Red Dragon ordered the killing of a suburban housewife and paid Lofty to do it.'

'Kacy Howells?' Trevor looked at Dan.

'She's the only murdered suburban housewife on our patch this year.'

'And you believe Snaggy?'

'You're the one who always insists on following every lead, no matter how bizarre.' Peter tossed the report onto Dan's desk. 'For what it's worth I think Snaggy's theory is plausible.'

'More plausible than nailing Alan Piper as her murderer?' Trevor suggested.

'I don't buy Alan as the killer and if you think that's down to sheer bloody prejudice because he's my cousin and unlike most of my relatives, likeable, you'd be absolutely right,' Peter conceded.

'She was axed to death and inexpertly at that. Hardly the method of a professional. They generally use knives or guns,' Trevor picked up the report Peter had discarded.

'Suppose someone wanted to frame Alan for Kacy Howells' murder?'

'What possible motive could anyone have for doing that?' Trevor asked logically.

'I can think of half a dozen reasons. One, that wet wimp apology of a gay husband of hers discovered she was unfaithful and paid someone to get rid of her. And the hired killer fitted up a neighbour to take the rap for the murder to put us off the scent? Snaggy said Lofty fingered someone else using rubbish from a bin. The tissue and chewing gum could well have been in Alan's bin bags.'

'And Alan's coat?' Trevor asked.

'If Alan left it in a pub or his unlocked car it could have been taken any time.'

'It's a story worthy of Hollywood, but it wouldn't explain the Red Dragon's involvement. There's no evidence to connect Kacy Howells to drug dealing. If she was a user it would have been spotted at the PM.'

'There's her father,' Peter conveniently ignored Trevor's mention of drugs.

'Why would he ask a drug dealer to kill his daughter?'

'Because he's a Bible-thumper and holds extreme views. I was there when he started spouting about her "being cloaked in glory" remember. He could have discovered her sexual antics and arranged for the death of her earthly body because it would purge her sins …'

'That's one hell of a jump, Peter,' Trevor interrupted. 'And, it presupposes that he knew about her sexual activities and was friendly with the Red Dragon. An entity we're all trying to pin down.'

'Her sexual activities are there in black and white and cartoon colours.' Peter pulled the porn magazine from his pocket.

'You said you could think of half a dozen motives,' Trevor reminded.

'Even allowing for my usual exaggeration, you'll make me go through them, won't you?' Peter made a face. 'The back of the Howells' house is secluded. It could be used to drop drugs. What if Kacy Howells saw something she shouldn't have?'

'A drug drop? A dealer in suburbia.' Even as Trevor said it, he saw the possibilities. What better cover than a quiet suburban street. Even allowing for the monitoring of the Mrs Walshes of this world, there would be any number of tradesmen and delivery drivers visiting the cul-de-sac on a regular basis – particularly in this age of internet shopping. Who was to say exactly what they were delivering? Catalogue goods or drugs? And some firms employed private drivers who used their own vehicles.'

'It's feasible, isn't it?' Peter said.

'If Kacy saw something she shouldn't have, the chances are it was in the woodland at the back of her house and the farmer has a prime view,' Trevor pointed out.

'He's not there all the time.'

'You're seriously suggesting that a professional walked into Kacy Howells' garden and killed her rather messily with an axe?'

'A professional who had been seen dealing by her.'

'The axe suggests spur of the moment murder,' Trevor declared. 'Snaggy told you it was funded by the Red Dragon, which would mean a certain amount of planning.'

'Planning that included the framing of her next door neighbour,' Peter argued. 'The axe could have been planted in front of Alan's car by the killer. He told me about the axe being in front of his car before Kacy Howells was murdered, remember. And as he had to move it, his fingerprints would be all over it.'

Trevor thought for a moment, much as he'd like

to investigate Snaggy's story he didn't have the manpower. 'My team are working flat out at the moment.'

'On Sam Jenkins's alibi?' Dan asked.

'You are keeping up with developments. Sam Jenkins and Matthew Clarke have concocted a story to hide something. I'm not sure what. Sarah is supervising a team in the office both Howells work in and interviewing the Howells' friends and colleagues.'

'I wasn't aware they had any – friends that is.' Peter left his chair before Trevor could press him about any other theories he might have.

'Can we talk about this tonight? Dinner my place?' Trevor asked.

'As long as it's a take-away and Peter buys,' Dan said, 'he let me pick up the tab for last night.'

'I'll phone Lyn and tell her to warm the plates. But now I have people to interview.'

'Chapel elders,' Peter mocked.

'I'm starting with the two we have in custody. Bearing in mind that they've already lied about painting the chapel, it'll be interesting to see how they try to explain their reasons for lying before we tackle the others. I'd also like to go through Sarah's interviews when she gets back. And, if there's time before the sun sets, I intend to take a look at that path that runs from the farm behind the Howells' house down to their garden.'

'Busy man. Good luck.' Peter reached for his coat.

'You going out?'

'Snitches to see and narks to shake down.'

'You paid Snaggy for his tip-off?' Trevor asked.

'No, and until I'm one hundred per cent certain he's right he won't get a penny from me.'

'How will you know if he's right?' Trevor asked.

'Tell you if I find out one way or the other. Good luck with your elders.' Peter left and Trevor returned to the interview room.

'Have Sam Jenkins and Matthew Clarke been given tea?' he asked Chris.

'Yes, sir,' one of the duty constables answered. 'Do you think either of them had anything to do with Kacy Howells' murder, sir?'

'I don't know,' Trevor poured a coffee, not because he wanted it but because the cup would give him something to do with his hands in the interview room.

'Which one do you want to start with?' Chris asked.

'Matthew Clarke. That will give Sam Jenkins time to sweat a little longer.'

Sarah Merchant sat in the tiny private office she had borrowed from the executive officer of the section Kacy and George Howells had worked in. She opened her briefcase, set a notepad in front of her, took out a pen and read the notes Trevor had made of his interview with Kacy Howells' brother, Mark.

Last time I bumped into John, he told me he had

been trying to kick Kacy out for years. He finally resorted to paying her thousands to get her out of his house, although she never gave him a penny towards the mortgage and every month he had to fight to get her to pay anything towards the bills. He told me it was worth every penny to be rid of her because he couldn't stand her having sex with other blokes in their garden in full view of him and their neighbours. It was her speciality at barbecues. A couple of vodkas and she was any- and everybody's.

An arrestingly good-looking young man knocked the open door and entered the cubicle at Sarah's "come in".

He held out his hand. 'John Evans. You wanted to see me?'

'Yes. Thank you for coming in, Mr Evans. I'm DC Sarah Merchant, one of the team investigating Kacy Howells' murder. Please sit down.' She indicated the chair in front of the desk. She looked into John Evans's eyes and decided the only attraction plain, mousy Kacy Howells could have possibly held for him was kinky sex. Then she remembered she was a professional – and that meant impartial with no preconceived ideas.

'The entire office is shocked by Kacy's murder. It's a dreadful business.' John Evans shook his head.

'It is. Which is why we are interviewing all her friends and colleagues. You lived with her?'

'For eighteen years.'

Sarah closed the file that contained her notes.

'Why did you split up?'

'It's no secret I fell in love with someone else.'

'Someone who worked in the same office as you and Kacy?'

'Yes.'

'Did you remain on good terms with Kacy?'

'I tried but she was having none of it. She became extremely bitter. Tried to sue me for half the value of the house we were living in. Fortunately it was in my name. I'd bought it with money I'd inherited from my grandparents and could prove it.'

'So Kacy moved out?'

'Not before I served a legal eviction notice on her. Even then, she refused to go until I paid her several thousand pounds she had no claim to and I could ill afford.'

'But you still paid her?'

'I had virtually moved into Emma's rented flat – she was my girlfriend now she's my wife – to get away from Kacy. Which had left Kacy in my house. I was afraid she'd try to claim squatter's rights. She had no sense of property.'

'Property?' Sarah queried.

'To say she was light-fingered was putting it mildly. I've always tried to get on with my neighbours but Kacy tore down the boundary fences between us and tried to claim part of their gardens. She also used to pick up any tools they left lying around and put them in our garage. She was just the same in the office. Ask anyone what she was like and they'll tell you the same thing. Chocolate bars, sandwiches, pens, her motto seemed to be, "see it, like it, take it".'

'It bothered you.'

'When I first started going out with her, I made excuses for her. I thought I had to be mistaken. She couldn't really be constantly thieving. Then, after she moved in with me and I saw what she was really like, the excuses became a bit thin.'

'It took eighteen years for that to happen?'

'The last three years we were together were bloody. Look, I don't want to speak ill of the dead but it wasn't just that. I'm ashamed to say that she had a sort of hold on me.' He averted his eyes.

Sarah took the pornographic magazine from the file and handed it to him. 'Have you seen this?'

'Everyone in the office has. A parcel of them arrived the day it was published.'

'Were you surprised to see Kacy in it?'

'Yes and no. When I was with her she was wild but she didn't publicly advertise the fact she slept around. She kept her activities within a tight circle.'

'She was unfaithful when you were together?'

John Evans shifted uneasily on his seat. 'She was into open relationships, swinging – wife-swapping – whatever you want to call it, and I went along with it, but after a few years I tired of it. She didn't.'

'But you had an open relationship?'

'I suppose you could call it that although it was more open on Kacy's side for the last ten years we were together than mine, which is why I fell head over heels in love with Emma. She's the exact opposite of Kacy. Sweet, loving and faithful. Just being with her made me want to settle down and have a family. Something I never wanted to do with Kacy.'

'When was the last time you saw Kacy?'

'Last week in the office.'

'You spoke to her?'

'I haven't spoken to her since she moved into George's house.'

'Were you surprised when she married George?'

'Again yes and no. As I said she was vindictive. We both knew, in fact the entire office knew, George was a closet gay. Not that anyone gives a hang about sexuality these days. But George had been brought up by elderly parents whose ideas were fixed in the last century. And George had a bigger house than me and more money, that he'd inherited from his parents. Kacy is obsessed with money and possessions. She went after him and like a ripe plum he fell into her hand.'

'Is Kacy's eldest child yours?'

'She told me he was after he was born. She wanted me to pay her maintenance for him. A thousand pounds a month.'

'What did you say when she asked you for the money?'

'I offered to have a DNA test and make the results public but only because I knew she'd back off. George was already showing baby photographs around the office and receiving congratulations. It was the ultimate proof he'd been searching for to announce his masculinity to the world.'

Sarah looked down at the notes she'd been making. 'How long did Kacy stay in your house after you asked her to leave?'

'Two years?'

'That's a long time not to get along with someone.'

'As I said our relationship broke down years before that. I suppose the best you could say about us was that we were still living under one roof. And occasionally sharing a bed. Looking back I realise now, I never loved Kacy. But Kacy knew everything there is to know about sex and exactly how to use that knowledge. There wasn't anything she wouldn't do and she was good at inciting others to join in with her. In the end her antics sickened me, especially after I fell in love with Emma. I hated the hold Kacy had on me and I hated myself for going along with the things Kacy did,' he confessed. 'Two years before she finally left my house I moved into a separate bedroom and put a lock on the door so she couldn't get in. I was determined to get away from her. I used to get up ridiculously early in the morning to drive to work to avoid giving her a lift and stay behind late in the evenings until she'd caught the bus home.'

'And during this time she went out with George Howells?'

'No.'

'Did she have any boyfriends that you knew of?' Sarah asked.

'Boyfriends? I wouldn't say that, but she'd sleep with anyone. She also worked for some agency or other. A woman used to call and ask for her. That in itself was strange. In all the time we were together, Kacy never went out with the girls in the office. In fact she had no female friends. I think she saw them as competition.'

'How did you know that Kacy was working for this woman?'

'Because she would leave messages on the answer phone.'

'What kind of messages?' Sarah probed.

'Something along the lines of, "Hi Kacy, Susie here. I have a job and a party right up your street if you're interested." The mention of a job made me think it was an agency.'

'You didn't ask Kacy about it?'

'No. By that time we'd stopped talking.'

'You can't remember the name of the agency?'

'I don't think I ever knew it. I'm sorry,' John apologised. 'I wish I could be more help. To be honest my break-up with Kacy was so acrimonious, there were times when I wished her the other side of the world and not the nice side. Siberia or the Gobi desert comes to mind. But dead?' He bit his lip. 'I never wished her that ill. It had been good between us in the beginning when we were both young and sex-crazy. And then there are her kids. I have two of my own …' he continued to fight his emotions.

Sarah thought back to her first love affair when she felt as though she had just invented sex, and knew exactly what John Evans meant.

'Just one more thing, Mr Evans, where were you last Monday between four o'clock in the afternoon and nine o'clock in the evening.'

'Clearing out my uncle's house. He died last month.'

'I am sorry.'

'He had dementia, it was a blessing.'

'Did anyone see you?'

'I doubt it. Although my car was parked in the drive, you can't see his house from the road. My uncle planted trees when he moved in. He would never cut them.'

'The address?'

'Park View, number nineteen. Surely you don't suspect that I had anything to do with Kacy's murder?'

'We're checking the movements of everyone who knew Kacy on the day of her murder, Mr Evans.' Sarah made a note of the address. 'Thank you. You have been most helpful.'

He reached for a tissue as he rose to his feet. 'I hope you catch the bastard who did it.'

'We'll do our best, Mr Evans.'

'I'll send the next one in, shall I?'

'If you should happen to remember anything more about this Susie who used to call Kacy, please give us a call.' Sarah handed him a card with the station telephone number printed on it.

He hesitated, his hand on the door handle. 'I think her surname was Cleopatra.'

'Cleopatra?'

'I know it sounds strange, but it was either Susie Cleopatra or Susie from Cleopatra's, I'm sure of it.'

CHAPTER FOURTEEN

'What time did the elders' committee meeting finish?' Trevor asked Matthew.

'As I told you I wasn't wearing a watch. It could have been any time between four and six o'clock.'

Trevor tried not to allow his irritation to show. 'Let's try another approach. Where did you go after the elders' committee meeting finished?'

'As I've already told you, I stayed in the chapel.'

'The elders met at two o'clock; you had a meeting which lasted until?' Trevor looked at Matthew enquiringly.

Matthew clutched his head theatrically. 'I remember now, it was four o'clock. I recall the secretary noting the time and putting it on the report before he handed it to the chairman.'

'And then?'

'As I said, a few of us stayed in the chapel.'

'Why? And please don't tell me, "to paint it" when there's no evidence of paint in tins or on the walls.'

'To discuss serious chapel matters.'

'What kind of serious matters?'

'Do I have to answer your questions?'

'Not if you are prepared for me to draw my own conclusions as to why you don't want to answer them.'

Matthew slumped. 'I feel ill …'

Trevor left his seat. 'Escort Mr Clarke to a cell,

Constable Brooke, and ask the duty officer to call the police doctor. When you return we'll drive to the chapel and see how the search of the premises and Mr Clarke's house is progressing.'

'You can't search the chapel or my house,' Matthew protested.

'The searches have already begun, Mr Clarke. I requested warrants when I brought you here. I can and I will do anything to further this investigation. I have already questioned Mr Jenkins and your accounts of the events of that night vary considerably. I will warn you as I have warned Mr Jenkins, wasting police time and giving false statements are serious charges.'

'We didn't do anything illegal.'

'What did you do, Mr Clarke?'

The old man clamped his lips shut.

Trevor's patience finally deserted him. 'Take Mr Clarke to the cell and arrange for him to see a doctor. I will speak to you again, Mr Clarke, after we have visited the officers conducting the searches of the chapel and your and Mr Jenkins's houses.'

The officer standing guard outside the Jenkinses' house looked bored but he stood a little straighter when he saw Trevor approaching.

'Is the search still going on?'

'Yes, sir. I saw the sergeant walking up the stairs an hour ago.'

Trevor found the sergeant directing the four officers assigned to him in a search of the bedrooms and bathroom. 'Have you found anything?'

'Nothing you wouldn't expect to see in your average house lived in by elderly people, sir. But Mrs Jenkins wasn't very keen on allowing us in. Neither was Mr Howells. They both wanted to stay while we conducted the search but Mr Mark Jenkins persuaded them to go next door until we'd finished.'

'Have you much more to do?'

'After this floor, the attic and the garden, sir.'

'Telephone me when you've done.'

'Even if there's nothing to report?'

'Especially if there's nothing to report.' Trevor walked down the stairs to where Chris Brooke was talking to the duty constable. He hated wasting time. Officer man-hours were costly and the search had done nothing to further the case. He looked through the open door and saw Mark Jenkins standing in the wasteland of his parents' "garden", arms crossed tightly over his chest, staring belligerently at him.

'Mr Jenkins,' Trevor stepped through the door to meet him.

'My mother is in a terrible state. You've arrested my father and you won't say what you suspect he's done. None of us can see how he could possibly have had anything to do with my sister's murder. He was with the elders of the chapel all that day …'

'Was he?' Trevor asked.

'Of course he was. He said he was and I've never known my father tell a lie in his life. You've sent police officers into my parents' house to search through their private property without reason …'

'The investigation we are carrying out into your sister's murder is reason enough.'

'You can't possibly believe my father killed her?'

Given Mark Jenkins's previous honesty Trevor was reluctant to resort to the standard police line. But given the stage of the investigation and the lies Sam Jenkins had told them about his whereabouts on the day of the murder, he had little choice. 'I can't say any more at the moment than your father is helping us with our enquiries, Mr Jenkins.'

'When will he be home?'

'I can't tell you that either, Mr Jenkins.'

'Look here …'

'Mr Jenkins, I will update you and your family as soon as I am able. The team should finish in your parents' house in the next couple of hours, then your mother will be able to return home.'

'And what about the damage they will have done to my parents' home in the meantime?' Mark demanded.

'Our search teams are trained to handle people's property with respect. However, should there be any inadvertent damage, compensation will be paid.' Trevor glanced at Chris.

'Time to move on, sir?' Chris asked perceptively, with a sideways glance at Mark who was obviously having difficulty reining in his temper.

'Yes. We have several more visits to make before we can finish for the day.'

'The chapel was clean, sir. There are very few places to hide anything in a building like that,' the sergeant overseeing the search of the chapel and Matthew Clarke's house said in response to Trevor's query. 'We checked behind the wall panelling and found bare brick walls. But we did find a metal crucifix hidden in the pulpit.' He held up a foot-long cross that bore an agonised figure of Christ.

Trevor took it from him. It was surprisingly heavy.

'Personally, I thought it a bit odd to hide something like that in a chapel.'

'Depends on the denomination of the chapel.' Trevor rubbed the surface of the metal to try and determine what it was made of. 'Most Protestants regard crucifixes as Catholic artefacts. The only Christian symbol you'll see inside most chapels is a plain cross. Generally made of wood.'

'We found soft porn DVDs and magazines locked in this suitcase. It was on top of a wardrobe upstairs, sir.' The officer opened the case that had been lifted onto a table in Matthew Clarke's living room. The covers look racy but there's nothing illegal in them that I can see. Although I thought you might want to turn them over to the Vice Squad for closer examination.'

Trevor picked out three DVDs at random. *The Three Libidos, Fly Virgin Fly, Ten In a Bed*. He studied the boxes, and found what he was looking for. A seller's sticker.

'These could explain why Mr Clarke and Mr Jenkins won't tell us their exact whereabouts after the meeting, sir,' Chris suggested. 'If it became generally known that chapel elders watched porn films after their committee meetings, it might ruin their reputations.'

'Would, not might. And looking at where these were bought they could be into more than just watching porn films.' Trevor returned the DVDs to the suitcase. 'I'll take them down the station. Have you found anything else?'

'These in the recycling bin.'

Chris picked up one of half a dozen empty bottles of vodka.

'How often are the bins emptied in this street?' Trevor lifted the box from the table.

'Every fortnight, sir,' the sergeant replied. 'Next collection is due in four days.'

'So either Mr Clarke has been collecting these for a while or he drinks. Thank you, Sergeant, most helpful.'

Chris followed Trevor out to the car and unlocked it so Trevor could stow the case in the boot. 'What about the other eleven elders on the committee, sir?'

Trevor glanced at his watch and shook his head. 'We can't hold Sam Jenkins and Matthew Clarke much longer without either charging them with wasting police time or releasing them with a caution. We'll return to the station and see how

198

much luck the team has had in contacting the other elders by phone. Sarah should be back and I want to look over her interview notes.'

'And the farm, sir?'

'Like Scheherazade's head in the Arabian Knights, it will have to wait another day.'

Sarah was thumbing through her notes when Trevor arrived back in the incident room. A bright young constable had put a sheet of the elders' telephone numbers on his desk and the responses she'd received when she'd asked if they could be interviewed the following day. Six had consented; five had stated they were too busy.

Trevor picked up the internal telephone and ordered the duty officer to move Mr Jenkins and Mr Clarke back into adjoining interview rooms. Chris was already playing one of DVDs they'd picked up in Matthew Clarke's house on a computer.

'It's low-quality soft porn, sir,' he said when he saw Trevor watching the screen over his shoulder.

'So I see. Which reminds me. Vic,' he called to a sergeant who was working at a desk on the other side of the room. 'Susie still in business?'

'Cleopatra's going from strength to strength, sir.'

'Did you say Cleopatra's, sir?' Sarah flicked through her notes until she found John Evans's interview.

'I did.'

'Kacy Howells' ex, John Evans, mentioned Susie Cleopatra. Could there be a connection?'

'That depends on what he said.'

'He said that when he lived with Kacy, messages were left on their answer phone by someone called Susie Cleopatra who was offering Kacy work.'

'Did he say what kind of work?'

'He assumed agency work and given Kacy's interests, something to do with sex for sale. Do you want me to sit in when you re-interview Mr Clarke and Mr Jenkins, sir?'

'In ten minutes.' Trevor went into his office and closed the door behind him.

It didn't take Trevor long to track down Susie's telephone number. If the telephone rang the other end of the line it could only have rung once. A deep throaty, sexy voice echoed down the line. 'Cleopatra's palace. What is your pleasure?'

'Susie, please.'

'Who shall I say is speaking?'

'Trevor Joseph – inspector as in police.'

The voice became shriller and brisker. 'I'll see if she's in.' Seconds later she reconnected and said, 'Putting you through.'

'Trevor, darling, you warning me about a raid?'

'Last I heard your place was legal and above board.'

'And I'm making sure it stays that way.'

'Of course you are.' Trevor had known Susie for years. He'd arrested her for streetwalking when he was a rookie, only for his sergeant who'd considered her the proverbial "whore with a heart of gold" albeit a kid still in care, to let her off with a caution. When one of her "punters" died and left her enough money for a comfortable retirement – if it had been invested wisely – Susie had used it to buy and open a massage parlour-cum-brothel where young girls could ply their trade away from the street and, more importantly, the pimps who creamed off most of their "wages".

'If it's not a raid, you must want a favour?'

'How do you know?'

'Because, despite all the social events I've invited you to over the years, the only time you ever ring me is when you're conducting police business and want information.'

'Do you know a Sam Jenkins or Matthew Clarke?'

'Darling, where's your discretion. We use nicknames in Cleopatra's, remember?'

'In their case, Zimmerman and Geriatricman might be appropriate.'

'How unkind. You'll be old one day.'

'I'm getting older by the minute. These two are chapel elders,' Trevor rattled off their addresses.

'Means nothing to me.'

'How about films, you still do rental?'

'Sale not rental.'

'And special shows for group outings?'

'I warned you discretion is our keyword.'

'These two old men would be extremely embarrassed if it became common knowledge they patronised your establishment.'

'As would one hundred per cent of our happily married customers, and a fair proportion of our bachelors.'

'I think they're too embarrassed to admit where they were last Monday. As a result they've become suspects in a murder case. Suspects that are wasting police time. I'm tempted to throw the book at them. Whereas if I knew for certain they were at your place … you can fill in the dots.'

'You'd let them go?'

'After a dressing down for irritating and annoying me. And given the proviso that they haven't committed any other crimes.'

'Give me a time?'

'As I said – last Monday, four-ish to ten-ish.'

'You didn't get this from me?'

'Absolutely.'

'Swear on Peter Collins' life, on second thoughts don't. I don't love him any more.'

'What's Peter done to you now?' Trevor asked in amusement.

'Arrested one of my best clients and sent him down for two years.'

'What did he do?'

'Receive stolen goods and screw the DSS.'

'In which case he deserved to be sent down.'

'He probably did but the four hundred pounds a week he spent in here isn't easy to make up. Four-ish … old guys … Nothing at four.'

'Try later.'

'Six o'clock – seven o'clock –?'

'Could be?'

Peals of laughter echoed down the line. 'You must be talking about our fishing club.'

'Fishing club – as in rods, lines and fish?'

'I've never seen them hunched over a pier or a river bank. But seven old guys turn up in taxis once a month. They buy films, drink coffee and spirit chasers, see a live show and sometimes book girls, although according to the girls not one of them can get it up, let alone keep it up.'

'And they book into your place as a fishing club?'

'You don't expect me to question punters or turn down business?'

'Describe them?'

'Old, grey and wrinkled and bald, what more is there to say?'

'Names?'

'How would you expect me to know that?'

'Your girls would.'

'Hang on.'

Trevor waited patiently while a hurried whispered conversation was conducted the other end. 'We have a Sam, a Bill and a Cyril. Any use to you?'

'Might be. Thanks, Susie, you're a gem.'

'Our live shows are tasteful, I'll arrange one down the station for you cost price so you can see for yourself. It pays to advertise where the police are concerned. None of you have visited us socially for months.'

'Upstairs would throw a fit and me out of the force if I booked one. See you around, Susie.'

'Not with a whistle in your hand I hope.'

'Before you go, this is something of a wild shot but have you heard of a girl called Kacy Howells?'

'The only Kacy I knew was a Kacy Jenkins. She did the odd bit of filming for us, years ago. Strange girl would never allow the boys to film her face, only her body but it worked She even had a cult thing going for her. She wasn't exactly what you'd call stunning; her body was flabby in places but keep the punters guessing and they always imagine better than it is.'

'How long since she worked for you?'

'Seven or eight years.'

Trevor did a quick calculation and worked out that if they were talking about the same Kacy Jenkins, she had stopped working for Susie round about the time she married George Howells.

'Do you have a list of the films she made for you?'

'Somewhere … Trevor I have a business to run …'

'I'd be really grateful if you could courier the DVDs over.'

'You're talking money …'

'Invoice me for the DVDs and taxi.'

'And you'll pay?'

'By return out of my own pocket. I'll get it back on expenses from upstairs and take the hit on interest for the sake of justice.'

'For a copper, Trevor Joseph, you're not so bad. I'll see what I can dig up. And now, I really must go.'

Matthew Clarke's eyes were dark, reproachful. He seemed to have shrunk in the few hours that had elapsed since Trevor had last seen him.

Trevor set down the file he was holding and sat across the table from him. 'Mr Clarke, you'll be pleased to know that our team will have finished searching the chapel and your house today.'

'Did you find what you were looking for?'

Trevor nodded to Chris who was carrying the suitcase the search team had found on top of the wardrobe in Matthew's house. 'Do you recognise this case?'

'I've never seen it before in my life,' Matthew lied stoutly.

'You've no idea who put it on top of the wardrobe in one of your bedrooms?' When Matthew didn't answer, Trevor continued. 'I've never heard of someone breaking into a house to put a suitcase on top of a wardrobe but I suppose there is a first time for everything. We'll need to take your fingerprints, Mr Clarke ...'

Matthew clenched his shrunken fists. 'All right, it's mine.'

'And the DVDs?' Trevor lifted the case on to the table and snapped the locks open.

'I bought them in a shop.'

'You didn't buy them in a shop.' Trevor held up

the copy of *The Three Libidos*. 'You bought them in a massage parlour called Cleopatra's.'

'So? They're not illegal.'

'No, they're not.'

'But you want to tell the world they were on the top of my wardrobe ...'

'Mr Clarke, all I want to know is where you and Mr Jenkins were last Monday between the hours of four o'clock and midnight. Once you have told me, I will try and corroborate your story. If it is the truth, you may take your suitcase and go. After I have given you another warning about wasting police time.'

'Seven of us go to Cleopatra's after committee meetings. We go to my house first, get a take-away of fish and chips ... there's a place at the end of my street that delivers, eat while watching a film ...'

'A Cleopatra special.' Trevor held up one of the films.

Matthew nodded, averting his eyes from the naked girl on the cover. Then we book two taxis to take us down to town.'

'To Cleopatra's?'

'We get the driver to drop us off at the taxi rank around the corner and go into Cleopatra's through the back entrance.'

'Next to the art gallery,' Trevor guessed.

'There's no law ...'

'Against a few friends having fun in Cleopatra's,' Trevor finished for him. 'No, there's not. How long do you stay in Cleopatra's?'

'We usually leave my house about half past six. By then the traffic is going the other way, out of town so the taxis have a clear run. We get there about a quarter past seven.'

'And then?'

'You know?' Matthew mumbled.

'No, I don't know, Mr Clarke, that is why I am asking,' Trevor spoke briskly.

'We have a drink and see a show.'

'A film or a show with girls.'

'With live girls.'

Trevor had to suppress a smile as he recalled one of Peter's tirades. *"Look at that. All live girls. What's the point in putting that up over the door. Do they really believe that anyone would think the girls were dead?"*

'And afterwards?'

'We have another drink, talk to the girls …'

'Do any of you see them privately?'

'Sometimes,' Matthew admitted guardedly.

'All of you?'

'Not always.'

'What time do you leave?'

'Never later than ten o'clock. Susie – the lady who owns the club – lets us have the small theatre until then. Any later and the price doubles.'

Trevor reflected that it was good deal for Susie. Monday nights were traditionally the quietest. The parlour would be busy from five thirty to seven with people leaving the offices in town. There'd be a lull until eleven. The "Fishing Club"'s business would be a welcome boost. 'And then what?'

'We take taxis back to my place.'

'All of you?'

'We all chip in and I buy tea, cheese and biscuits. Everyone leaves around midnight. It's our once a month jaunt,' he said defensively. Repeating, 'It's not illegal,' as if he couldn't quite believe it himself.

'So last Monday you and Sam Jenkins weren't alone, you were with five other members of the elders' committee.'

'I was with five of them. Sam wasn't. He had fish and chips with us, and he went into town with the rest of us, but he left us when we got there. Said he had to see someone on urgent business and he'd catch up with us later. He joined us in Cleopatra's about half past nine, in time for a last drink. Then he got in one of the taxis and went back to my house with us.'

'Did he tell you where he went?'

Matthew shook his shrunken head. 'No. But he was short-tempered when he joined us. I remember thinking that his business couldn't have gone well.'

CHAPTER FIFTEEN

'So where were you, in the afternoon and early evening last Monday, Mr Jenkins?' Trevor was tired. It was heading for evening on what had become the longest of long days.

'I told you …'

'You told me a pack of lies, Mr Jenkins,' Trevor interrupted. 'Mr Clarke has given us a sworn statement. He and five elders went on their usual monthly jaunt to Cleopatra's parlour expecting you to accompany them. But last Monday you left them in town after telling Mr Clarke that you had to see to some urgent business. You rejoined the party at approximately nine thirty in Cleopatra's. You arrived in time to have a drink with them before returning to Mr Clarke's house in the taxis Mr Clarke and the other elders had ordered to ferry the party back to Mr Clarke's house.'

'I want to see my solicitor.'

'Give Constable Brooke his name.' Trevor went outside.

Peter was in the corridor. 'A prospect?'

'Prospects are the problem with this case. We have a woman axed to death on her deck and a neighbour who had a running feud with her, who has no one to verify his movements at the time she was murdered. That same neighbour admits to obtaining a fraudulent credit card in her name and using it to purchase a lewd advertisement offering the said neighbour's sexual services in exchange for "presents" as well as copies of the magazine which he arranged to have sent to her workplace. His DNA has been found at the scene of the crime and a jacket he admits "could be his", soaked in the victim's blood was buried in his garden.'

'Alan engineered the credit card and the ad because he was angry.'

'Most people scream and shout when they're angry, not commit fraud in order to place bogus character-assassinating adverts in obscene publications.'

'Alan admits he was wrong. And he lied. But her father …'

'I'll say it before you do. He's religious. That in itself is not a crime.'

'If he saw the ad with Kacy's picture, it could have tipped him over the edge.'

'In which case, Alan would be morally in the wrong for placing it and would have to shoulder some of the blame for Kacy's murder.'

'Morality has nothing to do with the law.'

'Granted, and her father may or may not have seen the advertisement in the pornographic magazine. He is also without an alibi for the time of the murder. But to confuse the issue even more we have a farmer who was furious with the victim for chopping down trees on his land – and again, I bet without someone able to substantiate his alibi at the time of Kacy Howells' death, and …'

'An ex-boyfriend who says that he spent the day

clearing out his uncle's house. There are no witnesses and I just checked the address.' Sarah handed Trevor a slip of paper.

'Park View. Just around the corner from the farm that overlooks the Howells' house.'

'There's more, sir. Forensic took DNA samples from the Howells' colleagues. They found traces of John Evans's DNA in the Howells' shed and on the deck.'

'Fresh?'

'Yes, sir. His fingerprints were on a whip and a chair and one of them was bloody.'

'Any advance on three suspects?' Peter asked blithely.

'What do you want to do, sir?' Sarah asked Trevor.

'Bring John Evans in for questioning.'

Sarah glanced at her watch. 'Now, sir?'

'Now,' Trevor answered.

Peter made a face. 'I guess our meal's off in your place.'

'Haven't you work to do?' Trevor snapped.

'Not at the moment, Dan's gone to prison to interview the White Baron again to see if he can pick up a clue – any clue – as to the identity of the Red Dragon.'

'Sir,' one of the constables came running out of the interview room. 'Forensic team's on the telephone.'

'Put it through to my office.' Trevor walked down the corridor, Peter followed, but Trevor closed the door firmly in Peter's face.

'Hi, Trevor.'

'Alison, what do you have for me?'

'I'm calling from the Howells' house. We've found traces of blood on the outside tap and the drain in the garden.'

'Kacy Howells' blood?'

'Haven't tested it yet. It's possible the murderer washed her blood away there. We've also found shoes, socks, trousers, shirt and underwear in the drain, all soaked in blood. I'm taking them back to the lab, now.'

'Make and sizes?'

'All George – it's an ASDA brand. Shirt's fifteen and half collar, trousers 29 inside leg and 34 waist. Shoes are size ten. Shirt's pale blue, trousers beige and shoes brown lace-ups. Synthetic upper and sole.'

'Thanks Alison.' Trevor scribbled a note on his pad.

'You sent samples of a Sam Jenkins's DNA and fingerprints to the lab?'

'Yes. He's Kacy Howells' father.'

'We found his fingerprints in the kitchen and all over the master bedroom.'

Trevor sank down on his chair. 'Anything else?'

'Isn't that enough for you to be going on with? You got my message about the fingerprints and DNA we found on the deck planking we took back to the lab?'

'John Evans's DNA and prints, one bloody?'

212

'That's the one. You can't complain about the quantity – or quality of evidence.'

'No I can't. Thanks, Alison.'

'I like dark Belgian chocolates and Chardonnay.'

'I'll see what I can do at the end of the case.' Trevor hung up.

There was a tap at the door, Peter opened it. 'Dan's back, he suggested you pack up for the day and we have that take-away … what's the matter? Forensic definitely identified the murderer?'

'No such luck.'

'They can't decide between the father and John Evans?'

'They're both suspects, as is your cousin,' Trevor said firmly. 'But it's possible that whoever did it stripped off in the Howells' garden and washed at their outside sink. The search team's found traces of blood, and clothes dumped in the manhole.'

Peter picked up the notepad on Trevor's desk. 'Sizes are wrong for Alan.'

'He looks bigger,' Trevor agreed.

'Looks nothing, he's the same size as me, I know because I went on holiday with him and Joy and the missus before our divorce. Stupid airline lost Alan's bag, so I loaned him clothes – but not shoes. He's a size twelve, but we both take 17 in shirts, 33 inside leg and 38 waist in trousers.'

'His coat was soaked in Kacy's blood and buried in his garden.'

'I don't need you to remind me. But you heard

him. He hadn't seen that coat in weeks. He could have left it anywhere. That coupled with the axe …'

'And the tissue and the gum,' Trevor interrupted.

'The tissue could have been in the coat pocket, or both could have been in a rubbish bag – which Snaggy suggested. It's what I've said since the beginning, someone's trying to fit him up.'

'He fitted himself up when he applied for that credit card and took out that advertisement.'

'I don't want to discuss it any more.'

'A sure sign you're losing the argument.' Trevor almost smiled.

'Forget it for tonight. We'll pick up fish and chips …'

'I told Sarah to have John Evans brought in, remember.' Trevor took his notes from Peter. 'See you in the morning.'

'You're going to wear yourself out, Joseph. And then what use will you be to your wife and son?'

'More than you can be to Daisy at the moment?'

'There you go, rubbing her absence in again.'

'You could try putting in some overtime against Daisy's return,' Trevor suggested.

'I would, if I knew where to start looking for the Red Dragon. Well, if I'm not going to get my take-away, I suppose I may as well call into my favourite Indian restaurant and see what's cooking.'

'When's Daisy back?'

'The weekend. Think of me in my lonely bed tonight when you're cuddling up to Lyn.'

Peter hung about the station, reading files until seven o'clock. When Dan didn't return, he left the station and drove towards the High Street. He changed his mind halfway through town and manoeuvred his car in a sudden U-turn that earned him a blast of horn from an oncoming elderly driver who was travelling at half the speed limit.

Recalling Trevor's tip about parking, he drove into the library car park, left and locked his car and walked around to Platform 10. He bought a pint and went out into the yard. It was deserted. He looked at his watch. The surroundings weren't particularly pleasant but he had nothing planned for the evening. He pulled up a rickety plastic chair, sat down, lit a cigar and waited.

Trevor tried to shake off a sense of depression when he walked into the interview room, ahead of Sarah Merchant. The bland beige and brown décor, strong lighting, and the small window that overlooked the walls of the station car park, weren't inspirational at the best of times but at the tail end of a long day after dealing with lying witness after lying witness, it was the last place he wanted to be.

'Good evening, Constable Merchant.' The clean-cut, good-looking man rose nervously from his chair.

'Good evening, Mr Evans.' Sarah slapped a file down on the table. She opened it. The notes she'd made that morning of her interview with John were on top.

'I'm Inspector Trevor Joseph; please sit down, Mr Evans.'

'I know why you want to speak to me ...'

'Please wait until I've switched on the recorder, Mr Evans.' Trevor forced himself to be polite although he found it hard to forget that one of the reasons that his and Sarah Merchant's day was extending to twelve hours plus was this man's lies.

John Evans clasped his hands together and leaned over the table. 'You've found out, haven't you?'

'Mr Evans, I'd like you to think very carefully about where you were last Monday between the hours of midday and eleven o'clock in the evening. When you've remembered your movements you can tell us exactly where you were, and when.'

Sarah sat forward alongside Trevor, pen poised over her notebook. Trevor sat back in his chair and waited.

'It's like I told Constable Merchant. I was at my uncle's house clearing it.'

'The entire time?'

'No. I must have got there about ten o'clock in the morning.'

'Did you visit Kacy Howells that day?'

'Isn't that why I'm here?'

'We are the ones asking the questions, Mr Evans, not you. Did you visit Kacy Howells at her home last Monday, or not?'

'I hated going there.' John hung his head and looked down at the table. 'The last thing I wanted was for Emma – that's my wife – to find out that I was still seeing Kacy. But it's like I said to Constable Merchant this morning. Once Kacy gets her claws into any man it's impossible to break away.'

'How often have you called in on Kacy Howells at her home?'

'A couple of times a month.'

Trevor concealed his surprise. 'For how long?'

'Since three weeks after she married George.'

'And your wife doesn't know?'

'We have flexi-time at work. I've been taking Monday afternoons off to look after my uncle and do odd jobs around his house. Kacy found out about it somehow and suggested I call in on her afterwards.'

'Can I ask a question, sir?'

'Go ahead, Constable Merchant,' Trevor consented.

'You said your break-up with Kacy was acrimonious. That you didn't want anything more to do with her, after you moved in with your wife and that was why you paid her off. So why did you agree to call and see her?'

'Blackmail,' John said simply.

'For seven years?' Trevor was incredulous.

'When we were together Kacy had filmed us doing all sorts of things. I didn't know she was doing it at the time. She threatened to send the tapes to my uncle and parents and work as well as publish them on the web.'

'When you say "all sorts of things" you mean illegal things?' Trevor probed.

'Things I'd rather my family, colleagues and friends didn't see me doing,' he answered.

'Involving other people?'

'Sometimes. Kacy was into sado-masochism.'

'People got hurt?'

He nodded.

'Did they complain?' Trevor asked.

'One ended up in hospital.'

'All the same you've been seeing her for the last seven years …'

'My wife would leave me if ever she found out.'

'Did George Howells know?'

'I don't know. But he'd have to be blind and stupid if he didn't know that Kacy was being unfaithful to him.'

'With you?'

'And others. Sex was like an itch with Kacy.' Bitterness crept into his voice. 'She wanted it scratched all the time.'

'So you called in on Kacy almost every other Monday afternoon to have sex?'

'It's like I said to Constable Merchant this morning, I didn't want to, but it was the things Kacy would do. Things no normal woman would think of doing. She was worse than a drug. Every time I tried to end it between us and stop visiting her she threatened me with the films she'd made. I couldn't risk her telling Emma. The last thing I wanted was to lose my wife and children …' He finally raised his eyes and looked at Trevor, 'although I suppose Emma will find out all about me and Kacy now you've arrested me.'

'You were asked to come along and help us with our enquiries.' Trevor rubbed the back of his neck. It was stiff with tension.

'I am helping …'

'Then start by answering my question,' Trevor snapped, exhaustion making him irritable, 'think very carefully about where you were last Monday between the hours of midday and eleven o'clock in the evening and tell us exactly where you were and when.'

The sun was sinking below the rooftops surrounding the yard of the pub when Snaggy finally appeared. He crept along in the shadow of the wall, glanced over his shoulder and pushed a cigarette in his mouth before approaching Peter who was nursing a cigar and the remains of his second pint of beer.

'Got the money?'

'No.' Peter flicked his lighter and lit Snaggy's cigarette. 'We need to talk about Lofty and the man he fitted up for the suburban housewife murder.'

'I need my money …'

'My car's behind the library. Follow me in ten minutes. The back door will be open, lie on the floor. I'll drive us somewhere we can talk.'

'I can't be seen with you.'

'You won't be.' Peter returned his lighter to his pocket, finished his beer and strolled out of the pub.

'Like I told Constable Merchant, I went to my uncle's house. I worked there all morning clearing it. Kacy always wanted me to visit her at two o'clock. But that day she rang me in my uncle's house and asked me to make it at half past four because George and the kids were away and she'd be busy until then.'

'You walked up the cul-de-sac to her house?'

'I always went the back way down the farm track so no one would see me.'

'You never walked up the street?' Trevor checked.

'No, Kacy said she had a neighbour who used to watch everyone who walked up and down the street. Even noted how long delivery drivers took when they dropped off goods. Although given the way Kacy was I've no doubt she offered all of them special favours too.'

'Did you drive up to the farm?'

'Yes. I park my car on the track and walk down through the woods.'

'Make and model of your car?'

'It's a Vauxhall Astra, a convertible. Emma wanted one and we share it.'

'So you drove from your uncle's house to the farm track, which took you how long?'

'A couple of minutes. I parked the car and walked down the track through the woods.

'You reached there at half past four?'

'It was about twenty to five when I got there. I

checked my watch. I knew Kacy would be angry. She liked me to be there at whatever time she wanted me. It was one of her foibles. She hated hanging around waiting after she'd made all the preparations.'

'What preparations?'

'There was a false panel in the summer-house. She'd fixed handcuffs and ankle straps to the wall behind it, and she had a selection of whips and other things. She was always naked when I arrived. She'd make me strip off, handcuff and buckle me to the wall and begin by whipping me.'

'She was a dominatrix?'

'She was a sadist who liked whipping people.'

'She left marks?'

'Sometimes.'

'How did you explain them to your wife?'

'I told Emma I'd got them gardening in my uncle's house.'

'She believed you?'

'It was like a jungle; every time I went there I tried to cut something down and usually ended up hurting myself.'

'So you walked down through the woods to Kacy's garden at around twenty to five. What then?'

'I climbed over the fence as I usually did and went to the decking.' He closed his eyes. 'It was horrible. She was lying there naked with an axe in her head. Flies were swarming all over her …'

'What did you do when you saw her?'

'I retched. If I'd eaten anything that day I would

have been sick but my stomach was empty.'

'You didn't think to call an ambulance?'

'It was obvious Kacy was dead and past any help that a paramedic could give her.'

'What about the police?'

'I didn't want to have to explain why I was there so I turned and ran back the way I came.'

'And left her lying there.'

'And left her lying there,' John echoed dully. He looked at Trevor. 'Am I under arrest?'

'You will be formally charged with withholding evidence, making false statements, wasting police time and attempting to pervert the cause of justice.'

'But you believe me, don't you?' John pleaded.

Trevor left his chair. 'Frankly, Mr Evans, I no longer know what to believe in this case.'

'After you've charged me, I will be free to go?'

'Procedures have to be followed. Fresh statements taken.' Trevor turned to Sarah. 'I will send in officers to relieve you. As soon as they arrive you are to go off duty.'

'Thank you, sir.'

Trevor went into the incident room where a dozen officers were hard at work correlating evidence and witness statements.'

Dan was sitting drinking coffee and chatting to Chris Brooke. He looked up as Trevor entered the room. 'I hear you've found yourself yet another suspect.'

Trevor nodded. 'One who insists Kacy Howells was dead at twenty to five.'

'Before or after he killed her?'

'I wish I knew, Dan,' Trevor answered.

Peter drove into a deserted car park on the seafront. He pulled up facing the sea, and wound down his window before taking out his cigars.

'Anyone watching will assume I'm a lonely copper appreciating the view after a day's hard graft down the station,' he muttered over his shoulder.

'Not if they see your lips moving, they won't,' Snaggy mumbled from the floor of the back.

'It's almost dark and I could be talking to myself. Besides, the only signs of life are the lights twinkling across the bay.'

'Have you got my money on you?'

'No.'

'Then there's nothing for us to talk about.'

'There's plenty for us to talk about if you want money. Who's the Red Dragon?'

'Do you think I'd be asking you for a measly grand if I knew that? It would have to be worth at least half a million.'

'You think so?'

'I gave you Lofty as the killer of that suburban tart. I want my money.'

'Where's the proof that Lofty's the killer?'

'Lofty was bragging about it in the Casino when he lost the money. He said she was stark naked and such an obvious tart he didn't even want to rape her.'

'How do you know it was the Red Dragon who

'paid him to do it?'

'Because he told me.'

'Just like that.'

'He was drunk.'

'Enough to give you the identity of the Red Dragon?'

'I don't talk to coppers without money.' The door opened.

Peter turned in time to see Snaggy running down the cliff path that led to the sea. Tired and hungry, he grabbed the handle on the back door, slammed it shut and drove off. Halfway into town he made a detour and swung into the station. Lofty was known to every beat constable in the town; it shouldn't take too long to pick him up.

CHAPTER SIXTEEN

Trevor drove his car into the parking space at the back of his house. It was one o'clock in the morning, eight hours later than he'd hoped to be home. He thought of what he'd missed. Helping Lyn bath Marty and put him to bed. A quiet supper and a film with Lyn. A discussion about the playroom they were planning to build for Marty by extending the utility room into a new conservatory.

He looked at the garage doors and decided against putting the car away. There was little point when he'd be returning to the station at the crack of dawn. He only hoped he could clear his head long enough to get a few hours sleep. But, given the way ideas were buzzing, he doubted he'd succeed. He switched off the ignition and opened the door.

How could he have complained – was it really only a couple of days ago – about the slow start to the case and the wait for forensic evidence? Now, when he felt as though he were drowning in false and conflicting witness statements and a plethora of scientific test results, he would have welcomed a more leisurely pace and a few clear hours to spend with his family.

He climbed out of the car, locked it, opened the garden gate and walked towards the back of the house. A full moon shone down, silvering the white petunias Lyn had planted in tubs, troughs, planters and every available inch of ground between the perennials dotted around the courtyard garden.

He paused for a moment, drinking in the beauty of the quiet moonlit scene and admiring the lines of the simple white art deco garden furniture Lyn had chosen. He found himself comparing the elegant simplicity of this small space with the oversized ramshackle deck, shed and messy garden of the Howells. Some women had the knack of turning a house and its surroundings into a home, some didn't. He was grateful Lyn belonged to the former group.

He unlocked the back door, walked through the back porch into the kitchen and switched on the light. The black and white units, tiled worktops, walls and floor gleamed pristine, clean and orderly. Even with a new baby to care for Lyn kept the house immaculate. He opened the fridge and reached for a bottle of orange juice.

'I thought I heard you.' Lyn joined him, tall, slim and beautiful in her floor-length black and silver kaftan; her mass of black hair tied back, away from her face.

'What are you still doing up, sweetheart?' He set down the orange juice, opened his arms and hugged her, lifting her off her feet.

'I've just given Marty a feed. If we're lucky the little darling will sleep through until six, like he did last night.'

Trevor smiled. 'He's saving us a lot of wear and tear in batteries for the alarm clock.'

She returned his kiss. 'Rough day?'

'The worst.' He lifted the bottle of orange juice. 'Want some?'

'No thanks, it'll give Marty colic. But I will have a glass of water. You hungry?'

'I'll forage for cheese and biscuits.'

'There are fresh rolls in the bread bin, but I could cook you something.'

'I had something sent into the office from the canteen.'

'A fry-up?' she guessed.

'Sandwiches.'

'What kind?'

'The healthy sort. You go on in; I'll bring a tray into the living room.'

'I was sitting on the balcony.'

'Better still.' Trevor loaded a tray and carried it up the stairs, through the master bedroom and out on to the balcony that extended across the full width of the house. It overlooked the bay and, as there was no road between the front of the house and the sea, the view of sands, distant cliffs, and the even more remote lighthouse was uninterrupted.

Lyn was curled on a lounger, her hands wrapped around her knees, her face turned towards the horizon where sea met sky. The night was still and warm and moonlight silvered the sea just as it had done the garden. Although not for long. Clouds were already edging over and blotting out the stars. Trevor breathed in, savouring the sea air before setting the tray on the table.

'I love it out here.'

'So much, you're smug about it,' Lyn teased.

'Two things sold me on this house. This balcony and the view. And you look perfect sitting on one and framed by the other.' He sat beside her.

'The balcony wouldn't have been much good without the view. You have an early start tomorrow?'

'Unfortunately.'

'So we'd better not stay out here too long.'

'Want a cheese biscuit?' He placed a slice of cheese on a cracker and held it out to her.

'No thank you, darling,' she shook her head. 'I'm too tired to eat.'

'Marty wearing you out?'

'I had no idea such a small thing was capable of sapping so much energy.'

Trevor finished his orange juice, pushed the plate of cheese and biscuits aside and held out his arms, 'Come here?'

'That lounger isn't big enough for you, me and all the baby weight I'm carrying.'

'Rubbish and you're not carrying any baby weight.'

'Yes, I am. I need to start doing some exercises.'

'Not now this minute you don't. Please come here, I need reassurance.'

Lyn left her chair and sat on his lap. 'Why don't you ask for a transfer out of serious crimes? You know you hate investigating murders.'

'I do and this particular one is foul.'

'Because the victim was a young mother?'

228

'What do you know about it?' he asked.

'Only what's in the papers. They're painting a lurid picture of the victim's past and double life.'

'Journalists always seem to be days ahead of poor coppers in the information stakes. But you can never be certain if they print the truth or titillating gossip cooked up to serve their readers. They'll pay anyone a couple of grand for a story they think will sell newspapers. And when a dubious source serves them up a giant-sized helping of cock and bull they generally swallow it, principally because they have to fill their column inches with something.'

'Then it's not true that the victim had hundreds of lovers and worked as a prostitute?'

'I'm not sure about the working as a prostitute. From what we've discovered it looks like she'd have sex with any- and everyone for nothing.'

'The case is getting to you because she had young children?' Lyn guessed.

'Partly,' he conceded. 'She was a lousy wife and mother. We're scarcely a couple of days into the investigation and I'm beginning to wonder if there's a man in this town she didn't sleep with. No one who knew her apart from her mother and husband – and he's gay – has a good word to say about her. Her brother couldn't wait to tell us about her exploits when she was still a schoolgirl and one of her long-term lovers spoke about her as if she was a drug he was addicted to, and hated using. The only comment her father made, was that she is now in heaven and, in his words, "cloaked in glory".'

'That's an odd thing to say about your murdered daughter.'

'What I can't understand is why some husbands put up with the antics of sexually incontinent women. I know in this case the husband is gay but, even so, you think he'd be annoyed by the gossip. And there must have been some. They worked in the same office. You're the psychiatric nurse; tell me, why do so many married women sleep around?' Trevor tightened his arms around her waist to stop her slipping downwards on his lap.

'The simple textbook answer would be lack of self-confidence.'

'You're talking about a woman who made low-grade porn films for a massage parlour.'

'Exactly. She felt she had to prove something.'

'What?'

'That she was desirable. That she was more proficient at satisfying men than other women. Or it could be that, unsure of herself, unloved, she felt she had to "buy" her worth by giving people what she thought they wanted.'

'Unconditional no-strings sex?'

'From what I read in the paper and you've just said, it would appear so.'

'Her lover said she would do things no other woman – including his wife – would do.'

'In which case it could be a simple case of sex-addiction.'

'There is such a thing? It's recognised by professionals? Not just dreamed up by the tabloids

230

when they want to print stories about the antics of celebrities?'

Lyn laughed. 'Of course. How do you think the word nymphomaniac came into common use?'

'This one liked to take risks – have sex in public places.'

'You need to talk to the police psychologist. If he's built a profile on your victim, he'd know things about her that aren't in the paper and you won't tell me.'

'I suppose it's academic now the woman's dead.'

'Do you know who killed her?'

'After today I feel like writing all the suspects' names on slips of paper tossing them into a pot and asking one of the raw recruits on my team to draw one out.'

'That bad?'

'I've told you too much. Remember the rules we laid down. No work discussions at home.'

'That aside, have your discoveries about the victim's private life worried you about us?'

'No,' he answered truthfully. 'Because whatever she was, you are the exact opposite. Beautiful, inside and out.' He kissed the back of her neck.

'It's odd that she married a gay. Lack of sexual fulfilment could provide a reason for her wayward ways. Do you think he married her for security, children and family life?'

'And to prove to the world that he isn't gay.'

'No one gives a toss about people's sexuality in this day and age.'

'Normal reasonable people don't. Some religious fanatics of many faiths do. It's a fair bet that at least one of the victim's children isn't his.'

'That wouldn't matter if all he wanted was a normal family life.'

'It makes for a weird marriage.'

'A lavender marriage. Apparently there were a lot of them in Hollywood in the 1930s, 40s and 50s when everyone in the media had to be seen to be squeaky clean.'

He buried his face in her hair. 'You smell gorgeous.'

She rose to her feet and held out her hand. 'Forget about the case and other people's marriages and come to bed. That's an order.'

'Bully!'

'That's me.'

He smiled at her in the darkness. 'What would I do without you, Mrs Joseph?'

'Be a lot richer.'

'Love you.'

'Love you back.' She pulled him through the French doors into the bedroom and closed the blinds.

Peter lifted his feet onto Trevor's desk, sat back and flicked through the files on Trevor's computer until he came to *Alan Piper Witness Statements*.

'What do you think you're doing?' Dan was standing in the doorway watching him.

'Working.'

232

'Does Trevor know you're in his office?'

'Yes. He went home over an hour ago.'

'It's where you should be. It's two a.m.'

'I know.'

'Perhaps you need reminding that you've been transferred to the Drug War Murders case.'

'I am working on the Drug War Murders, but I keep thinking of something Alan said. I can't quite put my finger on …'

'If you have it in mind to ask Alan if he discovered the identity of the Red Dragon when he was researching his piece on the White Baron, forget it.'

'I doubt he knows it.'

'After spending an hour with him in prison this afternoon, I doubt he does too.'

Peter stared at the screen. 'But Alan did say something significant which didn't register at the time and it's bugging me.'

Dan sat in the visitor's chair. 'I've very little time for most journalists. Ninety per cent would sell their mother, children and grandchildren for a story and not necessarily a true one, but I had Alan Piper pegged as different.'

'Until you spent time with him this afternoon?' Peter guessed.

'He refused point-blank to give me the name of the snitch who tipped him the information on the White Baron.'

'Can you blame him?' If he had done, no snitch would every trust him again – or give him a lead to

233

a story.'

'I suppose so,' Dan allowed grudgingly.

'You haven't been visiting prison until now?'

'No, they kicked me out at five o'clock. But before they did and after I saw Alan, I visited the White Baron. For all the good it did me I may as well have talked to the wall. But he does have some very nice stuff in his cell. I had a chat with the governor about it.'

'And he promised to take the Baron's toys away?'

'He promised to look into it.'

'Which means the poor druggies, alcoholics, and schizophrenics on the streets have a tougher time than convicted murderers and rapists who can sit inside in their nice cushy cells ...'

'It's a quarter past two in the morning, Peter. I'm not in the mood for one of your rants. Especially as I've just driven around town four times looking for snitches and found none. If nothing happens to break this case in the next twenty-four hours, I'll have to go upstairs, admit I've drawn a blank and offer to hand the case over to another officer.'

'I talked to Snaggy, tonight.'

'What did he say?'

'Apart from "I want my money", in repeat mode, not much.'

Dan shifted on the chair. 'Lucky Trevor being home.'

'He should be in bed by now,' Peter said enviously.

'I can tell Daisy's still away.'

'After Snaggy ran out on me, I came back here and put out a request to the beat constables to look out for Lofty and Snaggy, and bring them in. I thought they'd have checked out all the casinos by now.'

'You've established that Snaggy is broke and Lofty could be, so it's unlikely they'll be gambling.'

'That sort always manages to lay their hands on money. And will continue to do so while there are little old ladies to mug and people to kill.' Peter leaned back in his chair.

'You can't really think there's anything in Snaggy's story that Lofty killed Kacy Howells.'

'He's capable of it.'

'Only if someone paid him well to do it,' Dan qualified. 'And can you really see Lofty using an axe?'

'If he was told to frame Alan.'

'As Trevor would say, "that's one hell of a jump".'

'I went back through the forensic reports.'

'Anything?'

'Kacy's father's, Sam Jenkins's, DNA is in the house. Trevor intends to question him about the bloodstained clothes that were found in the drain tomorrow. If they were his and he dumped them because they were soiled, stripped off and washed under the tap in the garden before going upstairs and borrowing George Howells' clothes, it might explain why they were under the manhole.'

'Not to mention finger him as his daughter's murderer.'

'Trevor's hoping for some answers tomorrow.'

Dan left his chair. 'Want a coffee?'

'Please, if it's only for the joy of seeing a superior officer bringing it.'

'One more quip like that and you'll be bringing it.' Despite his grumble, Dan left. He returned a few minutes later with two full china mugs and a plate of Danish pastries.

'Oh joy. Where on earth did you get these?' Peter grabbed an iced cinnamon roll.

'My office, I have a hidden store.'

'I might ask for this posting to be permanent. The only thing in the food line Trevor keeps hidden in his office is the odd health biscuit.' Peter stared at Alan's statement on screen again.

'Take a break. You're addling your brains,' Dan advised. He picked up his own coffee.

'And you're going home I suppose?'

'Going to take a last look at all the evidence we have to see if I can mine some nuggets of information.'

'Happy mining.' Peter continued to study the computer screen.

'Please ... please ... I didn't say nothing to no one ... I didn't do anything ... I know it's more than my life's worth ... please ... please ... you can't do this ... you can't kill us ... you can't ... we did everything you asked us to ...' Snaggy was terrified beyond words. He didn't know what he was gibbering behind the gag that that had been pushed into his mouth. Could they hear him or were the words only in his head?

He didn't even know what he was saying. Only that he didn't want to die. He looked across at Lofty. Not even the gloom of a cloudy night could conceal the fact that the big man had been so badly beaten his face and hands had been reduced to bloody pulp.

'Lofty, wake up,' Snaggy pleaded, thrashing around, fighting to loosen the plastic ties that held his ankles together and his wrists firmly behind his back. It was hopeless. He was trussed like a chicken for the oven. 'Lofty, they're going to kill us. Don't you care ...'

Snaggy stared at Lofty. Was he already dead? Was that it? They'd killed Lofty, and now they were going to kill him?

Snaggy tried to scream, he managed a grunt and earned himself a boot in his face for his trouble.

'We're going to die, Lofty. We're going to die, you stupid bastard, don't you care? Help ... help ...'

The subsequent grunts earned him another blow to his head.

Snaggy fell whimpering, next to Lofty. The big man was warm, breathing. He was still alive. They hadn't killed Lofty after all. A warm tide of relief flooded through Snaggy's veins. They were teaching him and Lofty a lesson; that was all.

A lesson not to talk to policemen. He'd promise not to do it again and they'd let him go. That's all he had to do – promise …

Strong hands picked him up and thrust him next to Lofty. They were hauled to their knees, their bodies pressed together and held steady while a chain was wrapped tightly around their chests, binding them together, face to face. When Snaggy felt he'd never be able to draw breath again, a padlock was snapped on to the links of the chain.

Strong arms lifted them, bundled together as they were, and pushed them over the side into the water.

Seconds later Snaggy managed another sound as cold water seeped through his clothes to his skin, freezing the blood in his veins. He tried to fight, but, immersed in water, his hands and feet bound together and his chest tied tightly to Lofty's, he was helpless.

He sank downwards. Water closed over his head. Lungs bursting he struggled but he was hauled upwards before he had time to save himself.

A second padlock clicked.

Snaggy creased his eyes against the glare of a narrow blinding beam.

The chain cut painfully into Snaggy's chest, he felt as though ice-water was swirling inside as well as outside his numbed body. Lofty was a dead weight that pulled him downwards again. The torch beam still shone directly into Snaggy's eyes.

'You can't … you can't …' Snaggy was aware of a face staring at him beyond the narrow beam of light.

All around the beam of light was shadow, water

and – bitter darkness.

Was it his imagination or was the tide already creeping upwards? It was at the bottom of his chin. This was it! The end of his life! The end!

His mouth filled with water. Desperate, he tilted his head back. Lofty wasn't moving. He couldn't hear him breathing any more. His weight continued to pull them both downwards. A grey ceiling closed over their heads. Heavy, oppressive. His lungs were bursting. Pain – hot agonising pain filled his body. He was pain.

When it ceased a soft, gentle warmth stole upwards blotting out the cold. His last thoughts were of escape. They would be rescued. It couldn't be the end. Not for him. Not for Lofty. It simply couldn't be.

CHAPTER SEVENTEEN

'Good morning, sleeping beauty, you can carry on your nap in your own office.'

Peter woke to see Trevor clearing his mug and plate onto the windowsill. 'I must have fallen asleep.'

'It's difficult to know who was snoring louder, you or Dan. I need this space. Sarah is bringing in the files and photographs of the clothes that were found in the Howells' sewer and I need to go through them before I interview Sam Jenkins.'

'Lying Sam Jenkins.' Peter groaned as he lifted his legs down from Trevor's desk. 'I'm stiff.'

'Serve you right for sleeping in my office when you have your own.' Trevor opened the window.

'Bloody freeze me, why don't you?' Peter griped as a blast of fresh morning air whipped in.

'Have to get rid of the whiff of eau de Peter.'

'Dan awake?'

'Not sure, why don't you go and see?'

'I can take a hint.' Peter recalled the events of the previous night. 'Has Lofty or Snaggy been brought in?'

'No, desk sergeant said neither has been seen.'

'Buggers have gone to ground.'

'Don't they always when you are looking for them. But, given what Snaggy's saying about Lofty, wouldn't you go to ground if you were him?'

'Snaggy's word of mouth isn't proof.'

'No, but up until now it has usually pointed us in the right direction.'

'Good luck with Sam Jenkins.'

Sarah knocked and entered and Trevor took the photographs she handed him. 'Ready for the interview room again?' he asked her.

'Yes, sir.'

'I'll make a prediction.' Peter stretched his arms above his head, levered himself out of Trevor's chair and moved his feet over the floor in a search for his discarded shoes. 'Sam Jenkins will open with, "I went to see my daughter because I was worried about her …"'

'Why would Sam Jenkins be worried about his daughter?' Trevor asked.

'Because he'd seen the ad offering her services,' Peter explained. '"And when I got there, Mr Policeman",' Peter continued in a fair imitation of Sam's rustic accent, '"there she was lying on the deck with an axe in her head. I did what any father would do. I tried to help her. By the time I saw she was past help, I was covered in her blood. Then I panicked. I thought what if the police suspect I killed her …"'

'And why would we do that?' Trevor demanded.

'"I was shocked, Mr Policeman, I wasn't thinking straight. And I had to get Kacy's blood off me. So I went to the outside tap, took off my blood-soaked clothes, lifted the manhole, dumped them in, washed, then went into the house to borrow a change of clothes from my son-in-law …"'

'Get out of here,' Trevor ordered.

'A week's wages say I'm right.'

'Out!'

'I'm going, I'm going.' Peter backed out of the door.

'And consider your colleagues. Go home, shower, shave and change for the sake of everyone who has to work with you today.' Trevor pushed his window wider.

Peter grinned, stubble dark on his cheeks. 'You're not my boss any more and I bet Dan's in a worse state than me.'

'What don't you understand about the word "out"?'

Ten minutes later, Trevor was sitting alongside Sarah, opposite Sam Jenkins and his solicitor in interview room 3. He listened as Sam Jenkins stammered out his revised alibi.

'I'd come across the porn magazine with the advertisement and our Kacy's photograph. I thought it had to be a mistake. A girl who looked like her. So, I went to talk to her about it and I found her lying in her garden with an axe in her head. I tried to help her, got covered in her blood and without thinking what I was doing stripped off my clothes threw them down the drain, washed her blood off me under the garden tap and went in the house to borrow my son-in-law's clothes ...'

If Peter had been with him, Trevor would have thumped him.

* * *

Peter was in Dan's office when Trevor emerged from the interview room and joined them. Trevor saw that they had both shaved and changed and, judging from the dampness of Peter's hair – and what was left of Dan's – showered.

'Am I a fortune teller, or am I a fortune teller?' Peter grinned at Trevor.

'You bastard, you were listening in.'

'I didn't have to. Given the size of the clothes it was obvious what Sam Jenkins was going to plead. And, when we interviewed him in his home he and his wife were both wearing George clothes.'

'You recognised the brand?' Trevor was amazed.

'Where do you think I get my working clothes from?' Peter asked.

'I have no idea.'

'Some of their designs aren't bad.'

'What have you done with Peter Collins?' Dan smiled in amusement. 'I want a police officer not a fashion guru.'

'Daisy's educating me in shopping. Another six months and I'll be ready to sit my NVQ examination.'

'Don't joke,' Trevor said, 'the way things are going it'll be on the school curriculum along with media studies next week. My blood runs cold at the thought of what Marty might be studying.'

'Nothing useful if the educational pundits have their way,' Peter suggested.

'Any sign of Lofty?' Trevor changed the subject

back to business.

'No, but he's never been easy to find whenever he's been implicated in a case,' Dan said.

'Snaggy's usually easy to find.' Trevor sat on the windowsill.

'I probably scared him off last night when I asked him to identify the Red Dragon.' Peter picked up a pen from Dan's desk and unscrewed it.

'But the Red Dragon is our problem, Trevor, not yours.' Dan retrieved his pen and picked up the mountain of paperwork in his in-tray. 'Sergeant Collins and I are going to spend what could be our last day on this case brainstorming. I can't justify any more officer hours on a case that's stalled. You?'

'Off to see the farmer.'

'And Kacy Howells' father?'

'We've charged him with the same offence as her one-time live-in lover.'

'We police officers hate witnesses who waste our time. But I doubt the magistrate will give them custody like Alan.' Peter failed to keep the bitterness from his voice.

'There is a difference between lying, perverting the course of justice and admitting fraud. Alan held up his hand when we asked him about the credit card and advertisement in the porn mag, remember?' Trevor reminded.

'There is such a thing as mitigating circumstances.'

'I'm not in the mood for splitting hairs.'

'Think the farmer will be able to tell you something you don't know?' Dan handed over the files he'd taken from his in-tray to Peter.

'Possibly. John Evans said she was dead when he arrived in her garden at four forty in the afternoon and Mrs Walsh last heard her working out the back at three fifty-five. That puts Kacy Howells' death in a forty-five minute time frame.'

'Either one or both could be lying,' Peter warned.

'I just wish ...' Trevor hesitated at the door.

'What?' Dan asked.

'That we had less forensic evidence and fewer suspects.'

'If you gave us one of your suspects and a little of your evidence, we might get somewhere with our case.' Peter opened one of the files Dan had given him.

'Pity it doesn't work that way. If it did this station would have a great clean-up rate.' Trevor walked out of the door, but instead of going into the incident room to pick up Chris Brooke, he went into his office.

He re-read Mrs Walsh's diary and he didn't leave his chair until he was almost word perfect.

Chris bumped the police car along the track that led to the farm behind the Howells' house. 'You'd think the farmer would put chippings down to fill some of the bigger potholes, wouldn't you?' he complained when his head jerked against the ceiling of the car for the third time in succession.

'Farmers are too busy to think about the comfort of anyone who has time to waste visiting them. And you don't feel bumps in a tractor the way you do in a car.'

'We must have taken a wrong turn. The farmhouse can't be this far along.'

'We haven't passed any turns.'

'Perhaps it's set back behind a gate.' Chris slowed as they passed a field of grazing sheep.

'Farms need tracks or roads of sorts if only for deliveries. There's a slate roof ahead.'

'I hope there's a turning point in the farmyard. I don't fancy reversing up this lane.' Chris drew up beside the entrance to the farmyard and they both climbed out. Trees surrounded the old stone buildings that enclosed the yard and Trevor heard the cry of a falcon. The sound generated a sudden, unexpected wave of longing for the farm that had been his childhood home.

He walked the few yards to the end of the lane and looked down. The farm had been built on the crest of a hill that bordered a steep-sided valley. To his right a lake stretched in the distance, below him a stream meandered through thick undergrowth and on his left he could see the back of the Howells' garden and the skeletal remains of the oversized deck and shed. All that remained after the forensic team had taken it apart and removed pieces for testing in the laboratory.

'You looking for something?' A short, square-built ruddy-faced man demanded suspiciously from the entrance to the yard.

'Yes, the farmer.' Trevor turned and walked back.

'You've found him.'

'Inspector Trevor Joseph, I'm investigating the murder of Kacy Howells. This is my colleague, Constable Chris Brooke.'

'Bob Guttridge.' He shook the hand Trevor offered. Two sheepdogs moved in behind the farmer and growled at Trevor and Chris as they approached. Bob snapped an order and they retreated to the barn. Half of it was piled high with bales of straw. Half a dozen had been left in a corner near the door, and a nest of new-born kittens were attempting to crawl on the topmost one under the watchful eye of their mother. Chickens scratched the dirt floor and a piglet ran loose.

It wasn't a picture of streamlined, modern hygienic farming. More like the chaotic old-style farming his brother practised on the family farm in Cornwall, following in the footsteps of generations of their forefathers. Trevor loved it. But only in small doses. He'd recognised early on that farming wasn't for him.

'Nice place you have here,' he complimented Guttridge.

'I like it, but I was born here. Farming is in my blood.'

'Mine too, but I walked away from it. Too much like hard work.'

'Your family farm round here?'

Trevor knew Bob Guttridge was fishing for information. The farming families were well acquainted in any given area. Most intermarried at least once in every two or three generations. 'No, Cornwall.'

'Dairy?'

'Mixed arable and livestock, including tourists.'

The farmer laughed then became serious. 'Kacy Howells' murder is a bad business, not that she didn't have it coming to her.'

'You gave one of my colleagues a statement, saying that you saw Mrs Howells on the day of the murder.'

'Like I told the young girl who came here, I saw Mrs Howells about four o'clock. She was chopping branches from trees on my land and tacking bird boxes on to the trunks. Frankly she's a bloody nuisance. Never stayed in her husband's garden from the day she moved in. But that's women for you. Nothing but trouble.'

'You're a bachelor?'

'All my life and I intend to die that way.' The farmer spoke with the vehemence of a man who'd been crossed in love.

'You told my constable that you last heard her about four o'clock?'

'About then, although I don't wear a watch so I couldn't tell you the exact time. I intended to go down and have a word with her after I cleaned out the pigs. But just as I finished in the sty, the feed lorry came. There was a car blocking the lane. He had a devil of a job to get past it.

'Did you notice the make?'

'A Vauxhall Astra. Convertible.'

'Do you know who it belonged to?'

'Haven't a clue. I've seen it here before. But whoever drives it down the lane never walks past the farmyard. Always avoids me, sneaky bugger that he is, probably afraid I'll tell him off for parking on private land. God knows he deserves it. I assume it belongs to someone who comes here to do a bit of shooting in the woods. Illegal of course, but you can't watch everyone all the time and if they stick to crows I don't mind – provided they park somewhere that doesn't annoy me. Bloody birds kill at least a couple of lambs every spring, and that's without the damage they do to my soft fruit crops.'

'You hear shots when the Astra's parked in the lane?'

'Not particularly but then I hear them so often, they hardly register. The man who owns the golf course on the other side of the valley is always shooting something or other. Shot himself in the foot one day. That pleased the dog walkers. He's always threatening their dogs whenever they come near his land, even the ones who keep their dogs under control.'

'You don't mind people walking on your land with dogs?' Trevor asked in surprise.

'I can't object seeing as I have three rights of way over the land. And provided the walkers treat my land and property with respect, stick to the path and keep their animals under control, what is there to object to?'

Trevor was amazed. Most farmers he knew did everything in their power to stop people rambling on their land, which only served to illustrate how easy-going Bob Guttridge was and how much Kacy Howells had annoyed him as well as Alan Piper and Mrs Walsh. 'Don't suppose you noted the number of the Vauxhall?'

'Didn't think to. I've been hoping to catch him and give him a piece of my mind but only about his parking. Like I said, I don't mind people walking down the lane but I do mind them blocking it. The feed delivery lorry had to drive into the hedge to avoid it, and it ended up damaging the bushes. Whoever the car belongs to, I hope the bugger doesn't come back. Not on feed day anyhow. But by the time I'd given the driver a hand to unload and fed him tea and biscuits the car had gone.'

'You're sure Mrs Howells was using a saw when you spotted the car parked in the lane?'

The farmer scratched his head. 'If it wasn't then, it was shortly before. Come to think of it, it was before I started cleaning out the pigs. I was fixing the hen-house when I heard her. Foxes are a problem and the bloody things had got in and killed four chickens the night before.'

'And after your feed delivery the car had driven away without you seeing the driver?'

'That's right. If the driver had walked over the

fields to the lane he wouldn't have had to come near the farmyard.'

'Did you hear Mrs Howells after the car left?'

'Not that I can recall.'

'Did you see her?'

The farmer shook his head. 'No, and nor did the driver.'

'He went to look?' Trevor asked in surprise.

'The drivers always do. She often cavorts naked in front of her shed. Some of the drivers even changed their schedules in the hope of catching sight of her. Not that she was that much to look at. Bit flabby and past it for me.'

'What kind of neighbours were the Howells?'

'He was quiet enough. He's lived there for years since he was a boy but things certainly got livelier when she moved in. After she built that deck she started performing on it with any man who would join her. She knew I had a grandstand view from up here because you could see her head turning this way when she was with someone.'

'Did she offer to have sex with you?'

'I didn't give her a chance. The couple of times I tackled her about cutting down my trees I asked Mick Walsh to go round to the Howells' house with me. I figured she wouldn't proposition me if I had a witness. She was shameless. Mick's presence didn't stop her from getting suggestive. In fact she tried it on with both of us. But I never stayed with her long enough for her to get past the talking stage.'

'So you did have a word with her about the work

she did on your land.'

'Work! You call that work … bloody woman …'

Trevor was saved from a tirade by his mobile phone. 'Excuse me.' He walked away before answering it. 'Trevor Joseph.'

It was Peter. 'We've found Lofty and Snaggy.'

'Are they talking?'

'No, when I say found, I mean found. At low tide. They'd been chained together and fastened to a mooring ring on the pier below high-tide level.'

'Were they dead when the tide came in or did they drown?'

'We're waiting on the PM report. It could take until tomorrow.'

'I'll be back in an hour or so.'

'Any luck with your farmer?'

'Not your case. I'm going to call in on Mrs Walsh on the way back. See you in the station.' Trevor rejoined the farmer.

'You're going to see the village clarion?' Tirade forgotten, the farmer watched Trevor switch off and pocket his phone.

'Is that what you call Mrs Walsh?' Trevor asked in amusement.

'It's her nickname in the village.'

'Since when?'

'Since as long as I can remember.'

'You known Mrs Walsh long?'

'Since the day she and her husband and Mick moved into the village about twenty-five years ago. The builder hadn't put up a fence between their garden and my land. I went down to do it, and unlike the Howells, the Walshes have always respected the boundary. Since the accident Mick's helped me out now and again with small things like taking deliveries when I've had to go to market and feeding the animals when I'm pushed for time.'

'And acting as a bodyguard when you visited the predatory Mrs Howells?' Trevor added.

'Mick may look as though he's not quite all there but I assure you he is. He's just a bit slow in his movements, that's all. But it is a pity about Mrs Walsh. She's a shadow of the woman she used to be. She used to do an enormous amount of charity work but after her accident when her husband was killed, precious few people around here remembered her good deeds. Hardly anyone offered to help her, and Mick was in hospital himself at the time. I did what little I could when they finally came home but if you grew up on a farm you know how much work is involved in running one.'

'Yes, I do.'

'She struggled for a while financially. When the compensation came through it wasn't much because the truck driver who crashed into their car wasn't insured. But since her husband's insurance paid out she seems to have managed on her savings and the little she makes from storing cleaning materials in her garage.'

'You help them?' Trevor guessed.

'Not much and not any more. She's too proud to take it, although I don't know what I would have done without her help when my mother was dying. Cancer … horrible way to go and it took months. That was before the accident that took Mr Walsh.'

Trevor took a last look at the barn. The kittens were rolling on top of one another and two tiny chicklets had appeared behind them.

'Nice sight.'

'New life always makes me feel good,' Bob Guttridge grinned.

'Me too. I'd love my son to see it.'

'Bring him and your wife up one day. I usually get on with other people's wives. Just not exhibitionists like Kacy Howells.'

'I'll wait until he's old enough to appreciate it. Perhaps it could be a first birthday treat in ten months or so.'

'Any time.' Bob whistled to the dogs. 'Time to bring the cows in for milking.'

'Nice man,' Chris commented as they walked to the car. 'Must be a lonely life for him, though, up here by himself.'

'Must be,' Trevor agreed absently. He was reflecting on Kacy Howells and her legacy. He hadn't spoken to a neighbour who regretted her loss and now that the press had got hold of the more lurid details of her sex life, even her husband would probably be relieved that she was dead.

CHAPTER EIGHTEEN

'Stop here.'

Chris obediently parked the car at the end of the cul-de-sac. Trevor wound down the window and looked up the street. The air was still and so quiet he could hear bird-song in the woods behind the houses.

'Nothing stirring,' Chris commented.

'Except Mrs Walsh's blinds,' Trevor observed when he saw them flick marginally to the right, he presumed so she could get a better view of their parked car. Trevor's thoughts turned to Dan and Peter back at the station. He felt he ought to be with them, which was ridiculous given that there wouldn't be anything they could do until the PM reports on Snaggy and Lofty came in; and probably not much then.

Snaggy and Lofty had probably been murdered on the orders of the Red Dragon because Snaggy had been seen with Peter, either in Platform 10 or leaving Peter's car. The Red Dragon was known to pay professionals to do his dirty work and professionals rarely left tangible clues or DNA. And, even if they had in this case, the sea water would have washed them away by the time the corpses had been found.

The double murder would become just another unsolved drugs war case unless someone was prepared to leak the identity of the Red Dragon.

Which given that Snaggy had been a known nark wasn't very likely.

'How long do you want to sit here, sir?' Chris asked when he saw Trevor glance at his watch.

'Seven minutes.'

If Chris found Trevor's precise directive odd he didn't comment.

Trevor continued to watch the street intently. 'Do you have an opinion on Bob Guttridge?'

'Seemed a nice enough bloke, sir.'

'A "nice enough" bloke isn't a precise police officer evaluation,' Trevor criticised.

'He seems to be involved in his farm and animals, sir. To the exclusion of all normal life – in my opinion,' Chris added diffidently.

'What's "normal"?'

'I'm not sure, sir.'

'I'm sorry, it's hardly fair to throw a question like that at you after you've given a fair assessment of Bob Guttridge, and another couple of hundred farmers like him,' Trevor conceded. 'Farming's not a job.'

'More of a vocation, sir.'

'I'd say an all-consuming lifestyle. If you're prepared to sacrifice your social life and a large part of family life and work all the hours of the day and night and then some, for little remuneration, then it's for you.' Trevor changed the subject. 'Are you up to date with the witness statements and forensic evidence on this case.'

'I think so, sir,' Chris replied guardedly. 'Or at

least I was last night.'

'Do you have any ideas on who murdered Kacy Howells?'

'Too many, sir.'

Trevor rubbed the back of his neck. 'Then you can join every other officer on this case. Want to try naming some suspects.'

'It could be the father …'

'Motive?' Trevor broke in.

'Some religious people are intolerant of other people's failings. Especially family members. Sam Jenkins admitted to seeing that advertisement in the porn mag and visiting Kacy to discuss it. If she was on the deck when he arrived and the axe was lying around and they argued, he might have lost his temper and killed her in a rage.'

'How do you explain the fact she was naked?' Trevor checked his mobile phone.

'We know from the farmer that she often walked around her garden naked. If she wasn't wearing clothes when her father arrived that could have tipped him over the edge.'

'Could have. But the timing is wrong if John Evans arrived at four fifty-five and found her dead. Sam Jenkins spent the whole of that afternoon with the chapel elders.'

'He and they could be lying about that, sir to give him an alibi if they felt that he was justified in killing his daughter, which they would do if they held the same intolerant beliefs.'

'You could be right.' Trevor opened the message

box on his phone.

Chris couldn't decide whether Trevor was humouring him or thinking the theory through. 'Or it could be the husband. I know he has a cast-iron alibi, sir,' Chris pre-empted the obvious. 'But there are plenty of people willing to kill someone for a price. George Howells also admitted to seeing the advertisement. And, given the evidence we've accumulated concerning Mrs Howells' sex life, he couldn't have believed she was faithful to him. Most men take exception to their wives sleeping around.'

'Women have been murdered by their husbands for a lot less than Kacy Howells did and we're not in a position to disregard Sergeant Collins's tip-off about Lofty – yet,' Trevor said cautiously.

'Although an axe in the head isn't the style of a professional.'

Trevor recalled Peter's theory that someone had been trying to frame Alan Piper. Was it that outlandish? He glanced at his watch again. 'Another three minutes. What are your thoughts on Alan Piper?'

'I'm not sure, sir. Again in my opinion …'

'You're a police officer, Chris, you don't have to apologise for having an opinion.' Trevor knew that Chris wanted to ask what he was doing sitting in a parked car at the end of the cul-de-sac instead of interviewing Mrs Walsh. But he decided to keep him guessing – unless he asked outright. Timidity wasn't a quality a police officer should possess.

A post office delivery van overtook them at

speed and raced up the street. Halfway along, the driver slammed on the brakes in an emergency stop. Leaving the engine idling, he jumped out of the cab, ran round to the back, opened the doors and lifted out a small package. He charged up to a house and hammered on the door. After a few seconds which wouldn't have given the occupants time to walk to the front door if they'd been at the back of the house, he returned to his van, jumped back into the cab and drove to the end of the cul-de-sac.

Mick Walsh opened his front door before the driver reached it, took the parcel from him and signed the electronic box. They chatted for a few moments. Mick watched the driver return to his van before closing the door.

Trevor checked his watch again. 'Drive to the end of the cul-de-sac and park in front of the Howells' house.'

Chris did as Trevor ordered. Trevor opened the door and stepped on the drive. A police van was stationed in front of the Howells' garage. The forensic team's paraphernalia was stacked, awaiting loading, behind it. Plastic sheeting and tenting had been returned to their containers and two operatives were working in the garden, filling in the areas that had been excavated. They saw Trevor and waved. He returned their acknowledgement, walked into the alley between the garage and the house, opened the back door and entered the kitchen. Chris followed.

The work surfaces, sink and cupboard were covered with greyish-white fingerprint powder. The floor bore stains Chris recognised as chemicals used for testing for the presence of blood. Trevor strode into the open-plan dining room and lounge area. Sarah Merchant, dressed in a white boiler suit and boots, a paper cap covering her hair, was sitting in a chair set back in the centre of the room. Her laptop was open on a table by her side. Trevor noted Sarah's view of the street was only marginally narrower than Mrs Walsh's grandstand vista.

'You've been making notes?' Trevor asked.

Sarah handed him her computer. 'And e-mailing them to your mobile phone, sir.'

'I noticed. Thank you.' He scanned the computer screen. 'Give me a run-down on everything that happened here this morning.'

'Four delivery vans. In reverse order, one post office ...'

'Which we've just seen.'

'One Home Delivery, one FedEx. No one was in any of the houses to take deliveries, so all the parcels were dropped off at the Walshes'.'

'The only occupied house in the street during the day?'

'Looks like it, sir. And there was one plain white van with no logo or markings that parked in the Walshes' drive. Mick Walsh helped the driver and his companion load boxes into the back of it. I took the number. The descriptions of all the delivery van drivers are in my notes too.'

'Thank you. When you get back to the station run a check on the contract cleaning firms and find out which ones use the Walshes' garage as a storage facility.'

'I will, sir.' Sarah looked back at her notes. 'The milkman, paperboy and the postman were all in the street before nine, I noted the exact times, and also the times when the families in the street left their homes. All in cars except for two women, one lives halfway down the street, the other at the end. I checked their interviews, and the bus timetable. Both of them work in town and they left in good time to catch the eight ten.'

'Excellent work, Constable.'

'I've been in touch with the station, sir,' she hinted.

'You heard about Lofty and Snaggy's murder?'

'Yes, sir. Do you think Snaggy was right about Lofty being the killer?'

'As Chris suggested, given the advertisement in the porn magazine at least two members of Kacy Howells' family had reason to kill her. Snaggy could have been right about Lofty but wrong about who hired him.' He pulled his mobile phone from his pocket and scrolled down the messages again. 'Thank you for these. I'll arrange for you to be relieved in a couple of hours when the forensic team pull out. With luck our Mrs Walsh might not notice you going. She didn't spot you coming in?' he checked.

'I don't think so, sir. I came in with the forensic team and it's difficult to see who's who, in these suits.'

'See you back in the station after lunch.' Trevor motioned to the door. 'Time to interview Mrs and Mr Walsh, Chris. Who knows they might even give us some new information.'

'I doubt it, sir, given that she's been looking out of the same window as Sarah.'

Trevor pocketed his phone.

Chris was clearly baffled by his behaviour but the constable still held back from asking a direct question.

'Inspector Joseph. Nice of you to call and see us again. Mick put the kettle on, make tea and set up a tray.' Nothing had changed in Mrs Walsh's living room since the last time Trevor had been there. He had the oddest feeling that time had stood still in the Walshes' house since he had last interviewed her.

'Not on our account, Mrs Walsh,' Trevor demurred.

'Are you here socially or on police business, Inspector?' Mrs Walsh asked.

'Police business,' Trevor answered.

'I thought as much. Mick saw you talking to Bob Guttridge this morning.'

'We went to the farm,' Trevor confirmed.

'Mick saw you through the kitchen window when he was washing the breakfast dishes.'

Trevor recalled standing on the ridge of the hill looking down at the houses.

'Bob Guttridge is one of the best neighbours and men you could hope to meet.'

'He seems a nice chap.' Trevor unconsciously reiterated Chris's words.

'Was he helpful?' she fished.

'Very,' Trevor said tantalizingly. 'I came to ask for your help again.'

'Anything I can do for the police, any time, but I told you that last time you were here.'

'I know you use your own shorthand. Could you tell me how many delivery vans have driven up this street this morning?'

'I'll have to read from my notes. I haven't had time to transcribe them.'

'That will be fine, Mrs Walsh, Constable Brooke will write out what you say for me.' Trevor looked to Chris who immediately took his notebook and pencil from his top pocket.

'Milkman's float at 7.45 a.m.'

'Not a delivery van,' Trevor said quietly.

'That's right, you asked specifically about delivery vans. Any reason in particular?'

'Just trying to establish a pattern for the street.'

'There were three. A FedEx van which delivered computer parts to Mr Lewis in number six. He teaches computing in the Further Education College. We took the parts in for him because they had to be signed for. Mick will take them down to his house when he returns home at four thirty. You can set your clocks by Ron Lewis. A very punctual man. A Home Delivery van brought Mrs Merick's latest order. She buys all her clothes from catalogues. And not the cheap ones either. We have her parcel as well but Mick won't be able to take that to her until eight o'clock this evening. She goes to the gym after work. A widow doesn't have a man to cook for so she can afford to gad about. A post office van was the last to drive up the street. But you would have seen it.' She looked enquiringly at Trevor.

'We did,'

'It brought Mr Jones's latest Amazon order. That man spends a fortune on books and DVDs.'

'That was all.'

'So far today, Inspector.'

Trevor glanced at Chris who was still writing. 'You have all that?'

'Yes, sir.'

'You'll stay for a cup of tea, Inspector, Constable?'

'No, thank you, Mrs Walsh, as I said earlier, we have to get back to the station.'

'When will Mr Piper be in court?'

'I couldn't tell you, Mrs Walsh.'

'You have charged him?'

Trevor opened the door. 'I'm afraid I can't tell you that either, Mrs Walsh.'

She tapped her nose. 'I understand – confidentiality. I also understand Alan Piper killing Kacy Howells. As I've said before, she had it coming to her.'

Trevor waited until Chris had returned his notebook and pencil to his pocket.

'Mick,' Mrs Walsh, called to her son. 'Show the officers out.'

Mick appeared in the kitchen doorway. 'You're not staying for tea, Inspector Joseph, Constable Brooke?'

'I'm afraid we can't, not today, Mick,' Chris apologised. 'We have to work.'

Mick looked crestfallen. 'But I've made the tea the way you like it, Constable. And laid out our best Belgian chocolate biscuits on Mum's silver salver.'

'Thank you, Mick. That was very kind of you, but I'm sorry we really do have to go, perhaps next time. Goodbye, Mrs Walsh, Mick.' Trevor shook the hand Mick offered him as he left the house.

'The station, sir?' Chris asked when they climbed into the car they'd left on the Howells' drive.

'Yes.'

'Anything wrong, sir?' Chris asked curiously.

'Did you notice anything odd about Mrs Walsh's diary of events?'

'No, sir. It tallied with Sarah's, didn't it?'

'Almost.' Trevor brushed fingerprint powder from his trousers. The stuff got everywhere. Then he thought back to Mrs Walsh and wondered at her private life, and Mick's. There weren't many sons – even brain damaged ones – who wouldn't resent Mrs Walsh's constant orders.

Peter looked up from the computer when Trevor walked into Dan's office. 'Snaggy and Lofty drowned.'

'Hardly surprising given where they were

found.'

'It's very surprising that they drowned in chlorinated fresh water not sea water. And, according to Patrick they'd both been beaten about – Lofty more than Snaggy. Bruising points to them being chained together while still alive, drowned in a pool, taken out then ferried to the pier where they were chained to the mooring ring. I found a fisherman this morning who remembers seeing a motor boat sailing close to the pier around four o'clock this morning.'

'When this morning?'

'Six o'clock. I went out as soon as Dan called me to interview the angler who spotted the bodies. One of his mates had been out all night fishing from the pier. I think upstairs should ask all criminals in the area to commit their crimes in the vicinity of the pier. That way we'll ensure a good supply of witnesses. Anglers are an observant lot.'

Trevor took out his mobile phone and forwarded the e-mails Sarah had sent him to his computer before sitting on the edge of Dan's desk.

'Made progress?' Peter asked him.

'Possibly, possibly not.'

'I can hear your brain ticking. If you don't tell me what's bothering you it's likely to explode.'

'Nothing is bothering me. Where's Dan?'

'Where do you think,' Peter replied irritatingly. 'Upstairs,' he added in response to Trevor's sour look.

'Pulling the plug on the Red Dragon case?'

'He has little choice given the lack of evidence.' Peter eyed Trevor suspiciously. 'You have something, haven't you? Something that links the Howells murder to the Red Dragon.'

Trevor shook his head. 'I only wish I did. But I've drawn a complete blank on that one. Snaggy must have mixed up the Kacy Howells murder with one out of our jurisdiction.'

'Snaggy was greedy, not unreliable.'

'Give me one good reason why a drug baron would risk blowing his secret identity by hiring a killer to waste a suburban housewife.'

'Given Kacy Howells' private life and taste for the kinky it has to be sex.'

'A drug baron, clearing a fraction of what the Red Dragon is making, would have the money to buy any woman he wanted. And, in my experience, drug barons go in for young, glamorous, nubile girls. Kacy Howells falls short in all three categories.'

'The password on your files still Tamar, or did you change it this morning?'

'Why do you want to know?' Trevor demanded.

'I want to go through Alan's statement. Something he said is bugging me …'

'Oh no, you don't.'

'Oh yes, I do,' Peter echoed pantomime fashion. 'If you won't give it to me all I have to do is go into the incident room, listen to the transcripts of Alan's interview and demand a copy. Alan was a material witness in the White Baron trial. The one who gave

267

us the evidence we needed to put the Baron away.'

Trevor conceded. 'Rome.'

'Roam as in wander? Why pick that? You hate rambling.'

'As it happens I enjoy going for long walks with my wife. But it's Rome as in city, you idiot.' Trevor finished forwarding his e-mails and wondered why he'd bothered. Given Sarah's efficiency she would have undoubtedly copied them on to his office computer.

'You a sudden fan of sex and gladiator epics?'

'Lyn wants to go there for a long weekend. She's been before and has friends in the city. I've never been and she wants to show me round before Marty's old enough to grizzle at sightseeing.'

'And before you have another six or seven kids clinging to your trouser legs and Lyn's skirt,' Peter joked. 'Where you off to now?'

'As Dan's not around, to my office and then I suppose I'd better see if John Evans or Sam Jenkins is in a more talkative mood.'

'You think they're holding something back?'

'One of them might be.'

'They might not. It has been known for witnesses to tell the truth.'

'I wonder why we put up with you, Peter. Whenever the situation is depressing you can always be counted on to make it worse.'

Peter opened Trevor's document folder on the computer and read Alan's original statement before moving on to the second one he'd made. He read through both carefully. When he finished he closed the file and reached for the phone.

'I need to speak to Alan Piper. I know he's on remand in prison,' he snapped testily. 'Just arrange it will you?' He glanced at his watch. 'An hour; that will give me time to drive over there.'

'Drugs?' John Evans shook his head. 'I told you, Inspector. Kacy was into sex not drugs.'

'Are you sure she never took anything?'

'Drink – she'd down three quarters of a bottle of vodka in a night but never drugs.'

'She didn't know any dealers?'

'That I couldn't tell you. She could have slept with half a dozen for all I know. I tried not to discuss her bed mates with her. Honestly, Inspector, I've told you everything I know. I realise it looks bad for me …'

'You were one of the first, if not the first, person to find her corpse and, you didn't alert anyone or seek medical help for Kacy.'

'I told you, I could see it was useless. She was dead.' John fought to maintain his composure. 'But I didn't kill her. I swear it, on my children's life.'

Trevor considered the melodramatic statement. He was inclined to believe John Evans simply because there was only one bloody fingerprint, and Evans's confession that he'd been there, to link him to the murder scene. Whereas there was more than enough bloodstained clothes, shoes and fingerprints to link both Alan Piper and Sam Jenkins to the victim, murder weapon and scene.

He turned to Chris who was sitting next to him. 'The original charges remain, but there's no need to oppose bail when Mr Evans is brought before the magistrates.'

John Evans's face crumpled in relief. 'You mean that, Inspector?'

'Giving false statements and attempting to pervert the course of justice are serious charges, Mr Evans. But I doubt you'll try to run away before your case comes to court.'

'Not with a wife and two children to support, I won't. Thank you, Inspector.'

'Save your gratitude until after the trial. If you are given a custodial sentence you might not feel quite so grateful.'

Trevor left the interview room and returned to Dan's office. There was no sign of Peter but Dan was behind his desk, his chair turned to the window. He was staring wide-eyed into the car park.

'The Red Dragon case dropped?' Trevor asked.

'We're now investigating the murder of Snaggy and Lofty so the answer to your question is, not really. Everyone knows why they were killed; it wouldn't even be too difficult to find out who chained them to that mooring ring. But the one thing we want is still eluding us.'

'The identity of the Red Dragon.'

'How about you?'

'I suppose I should interview Sam Jenkins again

but frankly, like you, I've had enough of dead ends.'

'You believe his explanation about the clothes?'

'He could be speaking the truth or he could be lying, but I'd be more interested in your take on this.' Trevor handed Dan the sheets of paper he'd printed off. Sarah Merchant's notes on activity in the cul-de-sac that morning. And Mrs Walsh's notes. Dan read them.

'Do you see what I see?'

'It's not enough for a search warrant.' Dan set the papers aside.

Trevor looked Dan in the eye. 'Are you sure?'

'We need more than this and one of your hunches, Trevor. I know what you're thinking but this leap is almost worthy of Peter Collins.'

CHAPTER NINETEEN

Peter Collins replayed the formal police interviews with Alan in his mind while he drove out of town. He was almost certain that whatever was bugging and eluding him hadn't been said in the station. Not in the interviews he had sat in on, or the ones Trevor had conducted while he'd watched and listened outside the room. Yet the more he tried to concentrate on exactly what it was Alan had said that had triggered his suspicions, the more confused he became.

Was it something Alan had said to him in an informal conversation? Possibly when they had both been standing on Alan's patio the night Alan had discovered Kacy Howells' body? That didn't seem right. He had memories of a convivial atmosphere, both of them laughing – the pub lunch they'd shared. Had it been on the afternoon of the day Kacy Howells had been found murdered? It seemed further back in time. He'd been talking about Kacy Howells' persecution of Alan.

'You don't expect a woman – and I use the word loosely – to stalk her neighbours by snaking around the border of her garden using her elbows and knees like a commando so she can eavesdrop on a private conversation. I can still see the look on her face when she looked up and saw us staring down at her. I expected her to at least say "sorry" before running off into the house. But she didn't say a

word, not a single bloody word.'

'That's not the first time it's happened. One of my ...'

Alan hadn't finished his sentence because he'd noticed him staring.

'Sources?' He'd guessed what Alan was about to say but he'd also anticipated Alan's response.

'Don't ask.'

Alan had never divulged who had tipped him off about the White Baron. Every officer who'd worked on the case had assumed it had been one of the Red Dragon's henchmen. Like Lofty? Had it been Lofty? Dan had been working on the Drugs War case for over a year and the evidence he'd accumulated pointed to Lofty killing at least one of the Red Dragon's rivals on his boss's orders. Evidence based on "hearsay" that would never stand up in court.

As both the White Baron and Red Dragon operated in the same field, the Red Dragon would undoubtedly have had the knowledge and information to shop the White Baron. Had the Red Dragon passed it on to Lofty and asked him to give it to Alan Piper so it could be published? The police didn't have a monopoly on narks' information and he didn't doubt that journalists would pay more for a scoop than the local force would for a tip-off. He also wouldn't put it past narks to try journalists first, especially with sensitive information that came without hard evidence attached to it. On Alan's own admission he'd had to dig deep for the final pieces of evidence that had put the White Baron away. It made sense. One drug lord fitting up another to do gaol time. Leaving the market open for a monopoly. And Dan was convinced that since the White Baron had gone down the Red Dragon was the only major drug dealer in town.

Still preoccupied, Peter parked his car in the prison car park and walked across to the reception area. The towers of the sterile cell blocks rose above and behind the single-storey entrance building. The facility was new, purpose-built and several miles and light years away from the Victorian institution it had been built to replace. But the old and grossly inadequate Victorian prison remained in use. The demand for prison places had risen so steeply that the authorities needed both. Since the new prison had opened, both old and new facilities had been filled to capacity but, whenever possible, the new prison was used for those on remand, if for no other reason than that the cells were cleaner and the leisure activities on offer more numerous. A testament to the British belief of "innocent until found guilty".

Peter signed in, submitted to the routine search, left his mobile phone, pens, wallet and personal items in a locker in the reception area, pocketed the key and steeled himself for the endless routine of unlocking and locking of doors by warders, and irritating waits in submarine-style "holding areas" between the locked doors that separated and secured the different areas of the prison.

Ten tedious minutes later, he sat facing Alan in a

blandly decorated cubicle that stank of antiseptic. A warder stood, his back to the door watching both of them, as Peter took a seat across a table from Alan.

'How are you?'

'That's a stupid bloody question, even coming from you,' Alan growled.

Unfazed by Alan's outburst, Peter continued blithely, 'You look tired.'

'You think I came in here for a rest?'

'I assumed sleeping might be a way of passing the time.'

'Even if I could sleep – which I'm having difficulty doing with a murder charge hanging over my head – it's too bloody noisy and airless in here to rest. Lights-out is a signal for my fellow inmates to start banging out Morse code on their doors.'

'Lack of sleep explains your foul mood.'

'Did you come here for a reason? Or are you just visiting the monkeys in the zoo.'

Peter took the notebook and pencil he'd declared to the warder who'd searched him from his shirt pocket. 'Something you said has been bugging me.'

'I said a great many things. All truthful. I only wish your fellow piggies, starting with Trevor Joseph believed me. If they had, I wouldn't be locked up in here and you'd have no reason to visit this salubrious place.'

'A couple of days inside and you're already calling law enforcement officers "piggies"?'

'Make a civilized man live among savages and he becomes one.'

'Is that a quote or an Alan Piper original?'

'Say what you've come to say and clear off.'

'Can't wait to return to your nice cosy little cell?'

'I needed that reminder.'

Peter gave a bright artificial smile. 'Much as I enjoy chatting to you, I'm here under sufferance and they'll kick me out soon enough. Where did you get the information you published on the White Baron?'

'I don't believe this. First Dan, now you asking me to name one of my sources. I thought you both knew better.'

'Off the record,' Peter emphasised.

'I know you and your "off the record".'

'I'm your cousin. We've been closer than brothers since I was knee-high. In fact a lot closer than we are to our own brothers ...'

'You're also a copper. And with you that will always come first. Whatever I tell you, will only stay off the record as long as you don't need it in a courtroom.'

Peter leaned forward and lowered his voice. 'You're a thick-headed bastard. Can't you see I'm trying to help you?'

'Help yourself to a promotion like your mate Trevor more like.'

'I thought you knew me.'

'Look at where trusting your bloody friend Trevor Joseph's put me ...'

'Look at where you put yourself, you idiot,' Peter retorted. 'It wasn't Trevor who applied for a credit card in Kacy Howells' name or bought an advert featuring her in a porn mag. What was Trevor supposed to do? Ignore fraud because he happens to know you're my cousin and a nice guy?'

'Don't change the subject. And don't ever ask me to name my sources.'

'If that's your last word, you can rot in here until you go to trial.' Peter rose to his feet. 'You might not be treated so kindly afterwards. Lifers can end up in all sorts of funny places. This is one of the jewels in the chain of Her Majesty's pleasure palaces. There are still a few dungeons staffed by Neanderthals in existence, where they put people who refuse to co-operate.'

Alan raised his eyes and looked at Peter. 'You know what my career would be worth if I told you my sources.'

'I said "off the record",' Peter reiterated.

'I don't trust you.'

'Don't expect me to visit you when you're transferred to a cellar full of loonies and I'm not talking about the inmates.'

Alan glanced at the warder who was still standing in front of the door. The man was staring impassively at the blank wall above their heads but Peter and Alan knew he was listening to every word they were saying.

'No names,' Alan mouthed.

Peter hesitated

'No names,' Alan mouthed again, 'but I'll give you background,' he whispered.

Peter returned to his seat. 'Did the Red Dragon shop the White Baron to you, or was it one of his henchmen?'

'Do you think I wouldn't have tipped you off if I knew the identity of the Red Dragon?' Alan whispered.

'Mr "My sources are sacrosanct" wouldn't have.'

'You said it yourself. Half the drugs disappeared from the street when you put away the White Baron. But I wouldn't mind betting that in spite of the drug war and rising body count over market share, the other half has multiplied and you lot are fighting the same number of dealers and addicts that you were before the Baron went down.'

'We might make some inroads if we could take out the Red Dragon as well,' Peter acknowledged.

'If I knew who he was I'd tell you.'

'Then one of the Dragon's henchmen shopped the Baron?'

'You never give up, do you?' Alan clenched his fists.

'Evidence you gathered and wrote about in the paper – before you came to us,' Peter reminded him coldly, 'put away one major dealer and a few minor ones. But whoever the Red Dragon is, he's powerful, invisible and he has people running scared. Snaggy …'

'You know Snaggy?'

'I knew Snaggy.'

'Knew … he's dead?'

'He and Lofty were found early this morning,

fastened to a mooring ring in the Marina. Rumour has it by the Red Dragon's henchman who beat them up before they drowned them in a freshwater pool and dropped them into the sea.'

'Horrible way to go,' Alan murmured. 'Snaggy was a mercenary sod, but occasionally his information was spot-on.'

'He told me that Lofty killed Kacy Howells on the orders of the Red Dragon.'

'Did he now?' Unlike Dan and Trevor, Alan didn't pour scorn on the idea.

'You believe him?'

'It's possible.' Alan remained guarded.

'Because Kacy Howells saw you talking to one of the Red Dragon's narks in your garden.'

'Never stop being a copper for one minute, do you?'

'I'm right.'

'Yes.'

'And, with some narks that would have been enough to sign her death warrant.'

'If the nark thought she'd overheard our conversation and understood it – yes.'

'Did she?'

'If she did, I never heard a hint that she'd made anything of it. So on that basis, I doubt it. I think she was simply crawling around on her hands and knees to bug me. Which as you well know she succeeded in doing.'

'Come on, Alan, give me a name,' Peter demanded.

Alan closed his eyes momentarily.

'This is your freedom you're playing with.'

'The name won't do you any good.'

'I'll be discreet. I'll find somewhere to talk to him where we won't be seen.'

'It won't do you any good,' Alan repeated.

'Who …'

Alan opened his eyes. 'Lofty.'

'He approached you?'

'Yes.'

'At the Red Dragon's instigation?'

'That's what he told me. I had no reason not to believe him.'

'Why would the Red Dragon tip you off about the White Baron?'

'You said it yourself. The drugs war was starting. The town isn't big enough to support two major dealers.'

'Who got in touch with who?'

'Lofty with me.'

'How?'

'I came home one night at midnight and found him sitting on the patio outside my back door.'

'He drove up the street?'

'No, he walked down the path that leads from the farm. I know because he went back that way. We saw Kacy Howells crawling along the ground when I walked him up to the woodland patio.'

'How many times did you see him?'

'Just the once.'

'What did you pay him?'

'Nothing.'

'He gave you information free and for gratis?' Peter was incredulous.

'He did.'

'Did you ask him why?'

'He said his girlfriend had been killed by heroin supplied by the White Baron. You remember that batch that had been mixed with asbestos and cement powder and contaminated with cyanide?'

Peter thought for a moment. 'Two years ago, forty people died. Did you check out the name he gave you?'

'He wouldn't give me one.'

'So there was no way to prove that he wasn't lying.'

'Not now.' Alan watched Peter leave his seat. 'What are you going to do?'

'Some more thinking.'

'You believe me?'

'Now I do. But it remains to see whether or not it will help to get you out of this place.'

'Do you have any biros you can spare?'

Peter saw the warder watching them. 'So you can make it into a bong? No way, mate.'

'And you believed Alan when he told you that Kacy Howells eavesdropped when he and Lofty were talking about the White Baron?' Dan Evans was pedantic in speech and thought. His mannerisms frequently irritated Peter to the point of eruption but Trevor had realised long ago that Dan's insistence on getting every fact straight – no matter how small – had saved, not wasted time on every case they had worked on together.

'Yes,' Peter stated emphatically. 'I saw her crawling along the boundary fence myself when I was talking to Alan. Think about it, Dan. It makes sense. Especially of Snaggy's assertion that it was Lofty who killed Kacy Howells. Alan said he found Lofty sitting on his patio one night, waiting for him to come home. He'd walked down the path that led from the farm down through the woods to the back of Alan's and the Howells' garden. The same path Trevor thinks Kacy Howells' killer might have used.'

'Slow down,' Trevor broke in abruptly. 'I had enough suspects before you brought Lofty into the Howells case.'

'None have a better motive than Lofty.'

'I don't know about better. Her father, husband and ex-lover all had reasons to kill Kacy Howells – as did Alan.'

'Alan, come on …'

'You don't see Alan losing his temper with Kacy Howells after she'd stalked him and generally made his and his wife's life hell while his wife was dying?' Dan questioned.

'Losing his temper, yes,' Peter conceded. 'But there's a world of difference between losing your temper with a neighbour and axing them to death.'

'Even if the axe is lying to hand?' Trevor raised his eyebrows.

'Stop playing Devil's Advocates and open your minds.' Peter left his chair, paced to the window, turned and faced Trevor and Dan. 'Imagine you're the Red Dragon. You're making money supplying drug dealers, not as much as you'd like because the price on the street is falling – just as it was before Alan wrote his article. A rival supplier is undercutting your merchandise. What you'd really like is a monopoly on supply, then you can fix the price at a level of your own choosing. So you look to one of your men and instruct him to shop the White Baron to a journalist. You give that journalist enough information to put the White Baron in the dock plus a number of leads that helps to pile up the evidence against him. But when your man goes to see the journalist – unannounced and late at night – he discovers a neighbour eavesdropping. Has she heard and seen enough to finger him …'

'Him being the henchman?' Dan checked.

'Alan insists he doesn't know the identity of the Red Dragon.'

'And you believe him?' Trevor asked.

'Yes, I believe him.' Peter answered irritably.

'Does that mean that you think Lofty killed Kacy on his own volition, and not on the orders of the Red Dragon?' Dan asked.

'I don't know,' Peter shrugged. 'But if he did kill Kacy Howells, which I think he did, he didn't keep his mouth shut about it because Snaggy got wind of it.'

'There's not one shred of physical evidence to

connect Lofty to the murder scene,' Trevor pointed out.

'There might be. Alan said that he found Lofty sitting on his patio at midnight. He knew the path and found his way to the back of Alan's house in the dark. That establishes that Lofty knew his way to the Howells' garden. He could have killed her and changed and disposed of his bloodstained clothes on the way back to his car.'

'Which he'd parked in the lane that leads to the farm,' Trevor murmured.

'Think about it,' Peter pressed eagerly. 'Lofty was in Alan's garden. He went there without anyone – even that village gossip who sits in her front window all day – seeing him. He could have taken the tissue and a piece of Alan's discarded chewing gum from Alan's bin bags and planted them on the Howells' deck alongside Kacy Howells' body. And he could have planted that axe in front of Alan's car …'

'When it was in the street in full view of the gossip?' Dan observed.

'He could have put the axe there early in the morning before the gossip was up, or late at night under cover of darkness.'

'There's still no forensic evidence,' Trevor reminded.

'Every idiot who watches crime shows on TV these days knows how to fudge forensic evidence,' Peter said dismissively. 'Besides there were smudges on the decking that could have been down

284

to gloves and paper over-shoes.'

'Why would Lofty frame Alan?' Trevor questioned.

'Because Lofty or the Red Dragon was afraid that Alan was talking to us about Lofty's tip-off. I've been around there a fair bit since Joy died. Perhaps one of them thought that I was collaborating with Alan and he didn't stop at passing on the information Lofty gave him, but had started digging for more and got closer than he realised.'

'You think Lofty was watching Alan – and you?' Dan asked.

'I don't know. He could have been.'

'There's a lot of supposition in your arguments,' Dan said shortly.

'Supposition that's worth investigating,' Peter challenged.

There was a knock at the door. Dan shouted, 'Come in,' and Sarah Merchant opened it.

'I'm sorry to interrupt, sir, but I have some information Inspector Joseph asked for.' She gave Trevor a computer print-out.

Trevor read it and looked up at her. 'You're sure about this, Constable?'

'As sure as I can be, sir. Whoever is paying the Walshes to store cleaning materials in their garage, isn't operating a contract cleaning business within a two hundred mile radius of this town.'

'Thank you, Sarah.'

'Sir.' Sarah hesitated for a moment before

leaving.

'That girl is curious and curiosity makes for a good copper,' Dan held out his hand and Trevor passed him the print-out.

'The path at the back of the Howells' house is all yours, Peter.' Dan rose to his feet. 'Take a good look at it in the morning.'

'I will.' Peter smiled.

Dan looked at Trevor. 'That search warrant you wanted?'

'Yes.'

'Use it with care and make sure you get the goods when you do.'

CHAPTER TWENTY

'You're setting up a stake-out in the cul-de-sac, aren't you?' Peter followed Trevor down the corridor to the incident room.

'You're working on the drugs war murders,' Trevor reminded him.

'It's the same case.'

'No it's not.'

Dan opened the door to his office. 'We need to discuss Snaggy and Lofty's PM reports, Peter.'

'We have,' Peter retorted.

'Not the injuries they received before they died.'

'So – they were beaten up.'

'So – they were beaten up somewhere – there could be witnesses. But first we need to find out where it happened. And, if there's no physical clues, we can start by making lists of their known associates.'

Peter watched Trevor disappear into the incident room.

'If the cases converge, we'll be the first to know,' Dan consoled him.

'By working on different aspects of it?'

Dan chose to ignore the scepticism in Peter's voice. 'The sooner we begin on those lists, the sooner we finish. And if your lady love hasn't returned I'll buy you a pint in Platform 10. In return you can stand me a curry.'

Peter faced Dan. 'Daisy won't be home until

tomorrow,'

'That should put a smile on your face.'

'I'll have a bigger one when Alan walks free.'

'Which is why you're working with me and Trevor is working with Sarah and Chris.'

'No personal involvement,' Peter recited.

'Let's make a start.'

Peter glanced back at the closed door of incident room before entering Dan's office.

Trevor stood in front of his assembled team, who were at their desks. 'Four personnel will go into the Howells' house tonight. They will take it in shifts to watch the street and monitor activity around the Walshes' garage and on the Walshes' property. Constables Brooke and Baker will take the first shift, Constable Merchant and Constable Harris the next. One person monitoring the front of the house and the street, the other the back. Shift changes every six hours. You'll be armed. I'll arrange back-up on standby. Keep outside contact and conversation among yourselves to a minimum. You don't know who might be listening in. We're not expecting a pick-up of materials from the Walshes' garage at any specific time. It could happen tonight, tomorrow or the day after so prepare for a surveillance of 48 hours plus. When it happens we won't move in until at least two boxes have been moved out of the garage into the pick-up vehicle. Surveillance to be carried out in darkened rooms, no lights to be switched on. No noise of any kind to be made that could be picked up by Mrs Walsh. That means no flushing of toilets and no turning on taps. Any questions?'

'How do we get in and out with Mrs Walsh watching the street?' Sarah Merchant asked.

'Shortly after sunset I will visit Mrs Walsh to ask if she, as the Howells' other immediate neighbour, had any problems with Mrs Howells concerning the boundary line between their gardens. I'll park my car in the Howells' drive, which I've done before, backing in close to their garage and halfway across the gate that leads into their garden. I will open the hatchback, lift out my briefcase and leave the door ajar. The four operatives will be crouching low in the back of the car below the window line. As the Howells' house is set back slightly from the Walshes' and Mrs Walsh can't monitor that side of the Howells' house she won't see the operatives move out of the car and into the alley between the house and the garage. But, to be on the safe side, no operative will leave the car until I have signalled from the Walshes' house by text to Sarah's phone.'

'What about people in the street, sir?' Sarah asked.

'I will park the car at an angle in front of the garage; if you're quick you shouldn't be seen in the darkness. After parking the car I will check the gate between the garage and the house and the back door, and leave both unlocked. You'll have to carry everything you need, including food, water, night goggles and sleeping bags. You have twenty minutes to make your preparations and any personal calls. Any other questions?'

The four officers who'd been chosen looked at one another. Sarah was the first to shake her head.

'The van will be here in forty-five minutes. I suggest you start packing.'

'Will you be overseeing the operation, sir?' Chris Brooke asked.

'From inside the house. I'll drive off after I leave Mrs Walsh, but arrange for someone to pick up the car and drop me off on the farm track. I'll walk down the path to the back of the house and enter through the back door. I should be with you within an hour of leaving Mrs Walsh. Any other questions?' He looked around. 'See you in the car park, in ...' he glanced at his watch. 'Forty-one minutes.'

Trevor left the incident room, and went into his office. Closing the door he dialled his home number. Lyn answered on the second ring. He pictured her curled up in a corner of the sofa, the phone, a cup of coffee and a bowl of her favourite cheese biscuits at her elbow as she watched an old film.

'I wish I was there with you and Marty.'

'No you don't,' Lyn teased, 'you know he'll be up again in two hours.'

'He's not settling?'

'He needs his father's firm hand. You're not coming back tonight?'

'You have second sight.'

'We'll miss you, but breakfast will be special.'

'It might not.'

'How long?'

'Not sure. This one could take a couple of days.'

She failed to keep the concern from her voice. 'You will be careful?'

'I will. I have a lot to live for these days.'

'Marty sends his love, as I do.'

'Take care of yourselves. Love you.' Trevor fought a lump in his throat as he hung up. Less than half an hour left before he would drive out of the car park. He tried not to think about the body count in the Drug War murder cases that Dan was investigating. If he was right, he – and all his team – would be in the firing line. There wasn't much time left to check out his gun and get his bullet-proof vest.

Peter unlocked the door of the flat he shared with Daisy shortly after midnight. He dropped his keys on the silver tray on the hall table, opened the door to the living room and looked around. The flat was tidy – he was good at keeping mess at bay – but every surface was grey with dust, the carpet could do with a good hoovering – and a change of bedclothes might be appreciated by Daisy, even if he slept in them that night.

Trevor had often mocked him for what he had christened "his over-developed domesticity" but Peter found it therapeutic to set a place to rights. An hour later, every work surface was gleaming, the floor hoovered and the air filled with the scent of beeswax polish. The kitchen took longer because the fridge was packed with out of date food that he hadn't got around to eating – or throwing out.

He cleaned the bedroom, changed the bed linen, and scrubbed the bathroom. The last thing he did was use the shower before cleaning it. Dressed in a robe he took a can of beer into the living room, set it on a coaster and picked up the paper to see if there was a late-night film worth watching. He knew he should sleep, there weren't many hours left until the dawn rendezvous he had arranged with Dan, but he also knew he was too restless to sleep. There was nothing worse than spending the night tossing and turning.

He scanned the TV listings without reading a word. Instead his thoughts turned to Snaggy and Lofty's corpses tucked away in drawers in the mortuary. Lofty was vicious, Snaggy devious, both were somewhere around his age and both had squandered their lives. Where did that leave him?

Daisy was right. It was time to make a commitment. Buy a house with a garden, a cat – and one up on Trevor – a dog – and start the family Daisy wanted. And him? What was so terrifying about the thought of having children? Especially with Daisy. Could something as small and instantly loveable as Marty really drive him and Daisy apart and destroy their very special relationship?

Trevor walked up to the Walshes' front door and rang the bell. Mick Walsh opened it immediately.

Trevor wasn't surprised as he had seen Mrs Walsh's shadow behind the blinds as he had driven up the cul-de-sac.

'I'm sorry, I know it's late. I should have telephoned, Mick, but I've just spoken to an officer who interviewed Alan Piper today, and I wanted to check something with you and your mother.'

'You're not disturbing us. I haven't taken Mum up to bed yet.' Mick Walsh opened the living room door. Two lamps had been lit but as they were both placed on table behind Mrs Walsh, the light from them didn't interfere with her view of the dusky street.

'You're working late, Inspector. Would you like a brandy?' Mrs Walsh lifted her glass and Trevor saw an expensive bottle of Hennessy Cognac on a side-table beside a silver bowl of grapes and an antique salver of marzipan petit fours.

He recalled what Bob Guttridge had said about the Walshes' finances. Mother and son were certainly living well now. Making up for penny-pinching times?

'No, thank you,' he refused politely, moving in front of her and blocking her view of the street. 'I'm on duty.'

'I thought policing was a nine till five job for officers of your rank, Inspector.'

'Unfortunately not, Mrs Walsh. As I was saying, I only called in to check something with you. Did you ever have any trouble with Kacy Howells over the boundary between your two properties?'

'Of course, Inspector. Did you think she reserved her anti-social antics for the Pipers? Haven't you noticed the fast-growing conifers Mick planted along the hedge line between us?'

'Then she tried to take some of your land too?'

'I contacted our solicitor as soon as she started.'

'They sent the Howells a letter?'

'I believe he sent someone around to their house. Afterwards I hired a surveyor to plot the boundary and Mick planted the conifers.'

Trevor's phone vibrated, signalling the alarm he'd set earlier. 'Excuse me, Mrs Walsh, Mick.' He removed it from his pocket and checked that the street was deserted before pressing "send" on the text he'd prepared for Sarah. He returned his phone to his pocket. 'When was this, Mrs Walsh?'

'Within two months of Madam moving in next door. Unlike Alan and Joy, I could see she was trouble from the first day George brought her back to his house.'

'And you had no trouble with the Howells after Mick planted the hedge?'

'I called the social services on a few occasions when her children were left out to wander in the rain all day without suitable clothing.'

'Did they follow up on your information?'

'I believe so. I saw social workers visit the Howells.'

'Was Mrs Howells aware that it was you who telephoned the authorities?'

'If she was, she never spoke to me about it. In

fact she never spoke to me about anything after our solicitor sent someone round there to explain the exact location of our boundary line.'

Trevor's phone buzzed again. He opened the message box and he read *OK*. 'Thank you, Mrs Walsh, you have been most helpful.'

'I fail to see how, Inspector.'

'You have helped establish Mrs Howells' behaviour pattern.'

'In my opinion Alan Piper deserves a medal for killing Kacy Howells. If he needs a character witness to speak on his behalf or against Kacy Howells, tell him I'm ready, willing and waiting.'

'I doubt I'll be speaking to Mr Piper's defence team, Mrs Walsh. I'm sorry for interrupting your evening.'

'No need to apologise. Mick, show the inspector out.'

'Yes, Mum.' Mick opened the door to the living room.

'Enjoy what's left of your evening, Mrs Walsh.' Trevor picked up his briefcase.

'There isn't any of it left, not for me, Inspector. It's past my bedtime. It's not easy living like an invalid.'

'I'm sure it's not. Good night, Mrs Walsh. Good night, Mick.' Trevor walked through the front door and went straight to his car. Trusting that his team had latched the hatchback closed, he locked and unlocked his car – just in case someone was watching him, climbed into the driving seat, and drove off.'

'Any further and your lights will be seen. Drop me off here.'

'Yes, sir.' the constable stopped the car in the lane.

Trevor picked up his briefcase. In it he'd packed the emergency kit he kept in his office. A spare toilet bag that included a toothbrush and razor and a change of clothes. He stepped out of the car and into the shadows that shrouded a recessed gate.

Trevor waited until the constable reversed the car and drove away. It was a moonless night. Shadows lay thick and deceptive around him. He felt as though the trees and the hedge were closing in on him. He leaned against the gate, acclimatising himself to the darkness and the sounds of the night. Sounds that reminded him of his childhood in Cornwall. The screech of a night owl as it swooped low seeking food. The scuttling of small creatures in the undergrowth. The crack of twigs and branches as cats – or foxes – stalked their prey.

He set off down the lane, walking close to the hedge. There were no lights visible in the farmhouse or the outbuildings. He would have been surprised if there had been. Animals woke at dawn and no farmer could afford to waste daylight. Bob Guttridge had probably been tucked up in his lonely bachelor bed for hours.

He made his way to the crest of the ridge with no problem and started down the hillside, feeling his way and clinging to branches and tree trunks on the steeper parts of the slope. Lights shone from the back of the Walshes' house. If the layout was the same as that of the Howells', the illuminated windows were the kitchen, upstairs bathroom and a back bedroom. He continued making his way downwards, treading slowly and carefully.

Any hopes he'd had of sneaking up to the back of the Howells' house dissipated when his foot squelched into a rotten log and he slid the final forty feet to the valley floor, dropping his briefcase in the scramble.

He lay on his back, panting, until he regained his breath. His back hurt. Had he bruised or wrenched it? When he tried to move agonising pains shot down his legs. He braced himself for more pain and rolled over. Crawling on hands and knees he patted the ground looking for his briefcase. It had slid further than he thought, almost up to the Walshes' fence.

He picked it up and tore his hand on barbed wire that had been threaded through the top of the five foot mesh fence that marked the boundary of the Walshes' garden. Stifling a cry he wiped his hand in the sleeve of his jacket. His suit was washable but after the fall it was probably ruined. He had to forget his pain and follow the fence line until he came to the Howells' garden. There the wire fence had been pulled down low, presumably so Kacy Howells could step over it and pursue her hobby of axing other people's trees.

He moved gingerly forward, briefcase in hand, carefully avoiding the top of the Walshes' fence. He reached the line of conifers that marked the boundary between the two gardens and then reeled as a blow landed on the back of his neck. He fell heavily, landing on his knees. A hand clamped over his mouth. He was lifted from his feet. He felt for his phone and hit the speed dial button. He opened his eyes wide, but all he could see was the silhouette of a dark hooded figure and an opening in the barbed wire-topped fence he had believed solid.

Pressure was exerted on the side of his neck. He knew what it meant and fought against the rising tide of numbing darkness that was engulfing him. It was hopeless. He fell headlong into a swirling mist that blotted everything – even thoughts of Lyn and Marty – from his mind.

'The boss drove off an hour and half ago. He should be here by now.' Chris handed out polystyrene cups of coffee before screwing the top back on the vacuum flask.

'He'll be here,' Sarah snapped, failing to hide her own concern.

'It's dark out the back. He could have fallen. Perhaps one of us should look for him.' Constable Harris was keen, eager and fresh out of training.

'He wouldn't thank us if we did. He gave us a job. We should do it,' Sarah said abruptly.

'We are doing it,' Chris pointed out logically.

'What do we do if he doesn't come?' Constable

Baker asked the question Sarah and Chris were trying to avoid.

'Nothing until morning,' Sarah answered decisively. Although she and Chris were the same rank, she had been appointed detective two months before him and assumed seniority whenever they worked together. She knew the day would arrive when he'd challenge her. But so far it hadn't. 'The inspector wants undercover surveillance, there's no sense in blowing our cover.'

'And if he needs help?' Chris asked.

'He has his mobile. He'll call the station.'

'Just like you said he'd be, Mum, he was snooping around the back.' Mick Walsh stood at the kitchen sink washing his hands.

'You've put him in the pool?'

'Like you said I was to do, after tying his wrists and ankles with plastic ties and stuffing a rag in his mouth.'

'You taped his mouth?' Mrs Walsh checked.

'With parcel tape from the garage.'

'And fastened the pool cover back on, firmly – and locked it?'

'I did everything you asked me, Mum. Here's what I took from his pockets.' Mick dropped Trevor's phone, wallet, keys, change, a pack of tissues, warrant card, pen and notebook onto the kitchen table.

Mrs Walsh picked up the phone. She unclipped the back and removed the battery before picking up the notebook and thumbing through it. 'Good, boy. The boys can take him in the morning when they pick up the delivery. You'd better warn them it will be the last for a while. I had hoped that once Alan Piper was charged the police would stop snooping round here. But that inspector didn't seem to have anything better to do.'

'You got the better of him though, Mum,' Mick smiled.

'I did. But the sooner we get him out of our pool and garden the happier I'll be. Tell the boys they'll have to be more careful with this one than the last two. I don't want him left where he can be found. The police never forget the death of one of their own. In fact it would be better if his body disappears for good.'

'What do you think they should do with him, Mum?'

'Weigh him down and dump him at sea. Tell the boys to give him to the couriers who bring in the next shipment. They can drop him off on their return journey across the channel. If anyone tracks the inspector's disappearance to us, we'll be in real trouble. It would mean life in prison – for both of us. And where you might survive to be paroled, I wouldn't. Not with my health problems.'

'Don't worry, Mum. Me and the boys will make sure he's never found,' Mick reassured her. It was the first time his mother had trusted him with an important job. She usually called in her "boys". Did it mean that she was preparing to allow him to manage more of the business? Perhaps even let him take over from her in a year or two and then he'd become the legendary "Red Dragon".

CHAPTER TWENTY-ONE

Peter reached out and grabbed the telephone before it could ring a second time. He glanced at the clock on the wall. One o'clock. Daisy should be at the airport. Had something happened to her – a car accident …

'Peter.'

'Lyn? What's up?'

'Something's happened to Trevor.'

'What?'

'I don't know. But it's not good. I'm sure of it.' Her voice trembled.

'What makes you think something's happened to him?'

'I can feel it. I *know* it …' she struggled to compose herself. 'I got a call from his phone.'

'When?'

'About eleven twenty.'

'Did he say anything?'

'No. I heard heavy breathing, dragging sounds, bangs, voices, too faint for me to hear what was being said, then the phone went dead. I tried calling him back but all I got was "this telephone is not receiving calls".'

Peter said the first thing that came into his head. 'You know what an idiot Trevor is. He's probably lost his phone or dropped it …'

'He's in trouble, Peter,' Lyn contradicted him fiercely. 'Do you know where he is?'

'Yes,' Peter admitted reluctantly.

'Tell me where.'

'You know I can't.'

'Peter …'

'Trevor and Dan will have my head and various other parts of my anatomy for doing what I'm about to, but at the risk of blowing Trevor's cover I'll check on him.'

'Promise?'

'I promise,' he agreed reluctantly.

'And you'll phone …'

'I'll get him to phone you, so you can explain to him exactly why I countermanded his and Dan's orders. Look after Marty and stop worrying, Lyn. He'll be fine.' He hung up the phone and tried Trevor's number. As Lyn said, it wasn't receiving calls.

He sent a text to Sarah Merchant's phone. '*Must speak T J.*'

Thirty seconds later he received a reply.

TJ absent.

He looked the clock again, picked up the phone and called Dan.

Peter left his apartment block to see Dan parked outside.

'That was quick,' he climbed into the car.

'I was still up. You?'

'I'd showered so I had to dress.'

'The driver said he dropped Trevor off in the lane at eleven.'

'Even allowing for darkness he should have reached the house half an hour later.' Peter glanced at the clock on the dashboard.

'He's been missing two and half hours.' Dan didn't need to look at the clock. 'He could have seen something through the back windows of the Walshes' house and decided to monitor them from the woods. Or he could have fallen, hurt himself ...'

'In which case he would have phoned.'

'And if his phone was broken in the fall. That might explain the noises Lyn heard. The laboured breathing and dragging sounds.' Dan stopped at a set of traffic lights and glanced across at Peter who was tapping the window with his fingertips. 'That won't help change the lights to green.'

'You're as on edge as I am.'

'I am,' Dan admitted. The lights finally changed and he drove off.

'You going to the lane at the back of the house?' Peter asked.

'No.'

'You're driving up to the house?'

'The Howells' to roust Trevor's team and then we'll search the Walshes' house. An officer is missing,' Dan said flatly.

Sarah Merchant stared in amazement when Dan Evans and Peter Collins drew up outside the Howells' house. Seconds later they walked into the living room.

'Still no sign of Trevor?' Peter asked.

'No, sir.'

'His phone went out in this area,' Dan informed her. 'You sure you haven't seen or heard him?'

'Absolutely, sir.'

Peter looked at Dan. 'Want me to go and wake up next door?'

'As we haven't a search warrant, we'll have to.'

Peter left his finger on the Walshes' doorbell for a good twenty seconds. Mick Walsh stumbled down the stairs, his eyes bleary and his limbs heavy.

'So sorry to wake you, Mr Walsh, but it is an emergency.' Dan showed his warrant card to Mick.

Mrs Walsh's voice, querulous, thick with sleep, wafted down the stairs. 'Who is it, Mick?'

'The police, Mum.'

'They can't come in, not at this time of night.'

Dan stepped into the small hall, and looked up the stairs. 'I am very sorry to disturb you, Mrs Walsh, but we are concerned about one of our officers who was last seen in this area. Inspector Trevor Joseph …'

'He was here, tonight,' Mick broke in, eager to be of service.

'What time did he leave?' Dan knew the answer to his question because he had spoken to the police driver who had dropped Trevor off in the lane, but now that he was in the house he had no intention of leaving until it had been thoroughly searched. All he needed was an excuse that would hold up with "upstairs". Peter had stepped in behind him and was already edging towards the kitchen.

'He left just before I took Mum up to bed and I always do that around eleven o'clock.'

Peter started to cough. 'Do you mind if I have a glass of water?' Without waiting for Mick to reply he pushed his way into the kitchen.

'Mick, come and get me,' Mrs Walsh shouted down the stairs.

Mick looked helplessly after Peter.

Her voice took on an iron tone. 'Mick?'

'Coming, Mum.' He ran up the stairs.

Peter appeared in the kitchen doorway. He was holding a bunch of keys.

Dan saw them and blanched. 'Trevor's?' He didn't know why he'd asked.

'Do you know any other idiot who'd walk round with a silver teddy bear this size on his key-ring?'

Dan called the back-up team and ordered them to bring dogs. Peter fetched the surveillance team from the Howells' house. Sarah and Chris started searching the upstairs, Constables Harris and Baker the downstairs while he and Dan ushered Mrs Walsh and her son into the living room.

'The inspector had a small brandy and some petit fours with us and accidentally left his keys ...'

'How did he drive away, Mrs Walsh?' Dan asked, watching Peter who was prowling back and forth in front of the back window, staring into the floodlit garden.

'He must have had spares. We didn't notice the keys until after he'd left. I told Mick to remind me to call the telephone number Inspector Joseph had given us in the morning …'

Peter interrupted. 'What have you done with him?'

'I told you. All we did was give him a small brandy …'

'Trevor doesn't drink on duty.' Peter watched Mick stare out of the back window.

'Sit down, Mick.' His mother ordered sharply.

'It's still raining. Raining heavy …'

Peter followed Mick's line of sight. It had been raining steadily for two or three hours. The first rain they'd had after a long dry spell. Water was standing on the vinyl pool cover, but one corner was drier than the rest …

Peter sprung the lock on the patio doors, slid them open and charged outside. He fought with the fastening on the cover. It was heavier than he thought it would be.

It took what felt like a lifetime to wrench back the corner and uncover the edge of the pool. When he succeeded Trevor's face, unnaturally white in a pool of black water looked up at him, the eyes open, staring … then he blinked.

'Another inch downwards and you'd be dead, mate,' Peter muttered as he hauled him out. It wasn't easy. Trevor had wrapped his fingers into the buckles that fastened the cover. Two of them hung limp – and broken.

'I suppose it's a small price to pay for your life.' Peter laid him gently on the sodden lawn.

Dan and Peter sat in the back of the crematorium, not that there were many mourners. Sam and Mary Jenkins and George Howells watched the curtains close around Kacy Howells' coffin to the accompaniment of Mozart's Requiem. When the music died, Peter rose to his feet and walked out.

'Think they'll convict the Walshes of killing Kacy Howells as well as Snaggy, Lofty, the other drug war victims, and the attempted murder of Trevor?' he asked Dan.

'I don't know. Mick Walsh is singing like a bird but the defence may try to make something of his mental disability and ask that his evidence be regarded as inadmissible. But even without the murder charges, I predict that Mrs Walsh is going down for a long, long time. That was quite a haul of heroin and cocaine they found in her garage. Two of the dealers we caught trying to make a pick-up are anxious to cut a deal. They've shopped Mick for murdering Lofty and Snaggy. I'm not sure I believe them, but it's all out of my hands now and up to the courts. We've delivered the evidence and the rotten eggs. It's the judge and jury's job to decide who did what.' Dan watched a man leave by the side door of the chapel and place two wreaths on a concrete plinth. Both were small. One of lilies, the other of roses. After he dropped them he pushed a slip of paper into a holder and set it in front of them.

Peter read the label. '*Kacy Louise Howells.* Not much to show for a life is it? But then what do any of us leave behind?'

'Hopefully more people to miss and mourn us than she did,' Dan commented. 'Want to call in the hospital and see Trevor?'

'He was hoping to go home today. How about a drink?' Peter asked.

'Sounds good to me.'

'But not Platform 10, or anywhere else that narks hang out,' Peter warned. 'I want a nice quiet drink.'

'Call yourself a copper?'

'Later on I might. Not just now.' Peter went to his car and opened the door.

Peter finished reading the article, folded the newspaper and placed it on the rack beneath the coffee table. He looked at Daisy who set a large fruit basket on the table.

'Poor Trevor,' she murmured. 'I hope he's well enough to enjoy this. Pneumonia's not good.'

'Lucky bugger's got a month off work. All he has to do is play with Marty and be fussed over by Lyn.'

'Pneumonia's not a joke.' She took a bottle of perfume and a teddy bear she'd bought in duty free for Lyn and Marty out of a plastic bag and set them next to the basket.

'How many officers do you know who are stupid enough to allow someone to dump them in a swimming pool?'

'Stop doing that.'

'What?' he asked.

'Acting like what happened to Trevor is a huge joke and you don't care about him.'

'Daisy …' he hesitated.

'Yes,' she prompted when his voice tailed.

'I've been thinking.'

'Coming from you, that sounds ominous.'

'About that house you wanted to buy …'

'Yes,' she prompted again.

'I was talking to Alan …'

'About the beauty queen who turned up fit and well in Hollywood, and who was never in a North African harem?'

'He never wrote that article about her being sold into white slavery. And after what happened when he tried to follow her story, I didn't think it wise to bring up the subject with him,' Peter said impatiently. 'He's putting his house on the market. Both he and his lady love Judy are selling up and moving out of the cul-de-sac. They're going to buy a penthouse together on the Marina.'

'Sounds sensible given Alan's lifestyle.'

'He said being locked up in prison made him think about what he wanted to do with the rest of his life.'

'I've no doubt a stint in a cell will do that, although I hope I never experience it.'

'It made me think about his house …'

'No.'

'You don't know what I'm about to say.'

'Yes I do,' she contradicted him.

'It's a nice house and it has a big garden. And

310

now that George Howells has put his on the market as well …'

'And no doubt the Walshes' will either be rented or put on the market.'

'As well as Alan's lady love's. So many houses in one street. It's bound to drive the price down,' he pointed out.

'My answer's still the same. No, Peter, I am not moving into that cul-de sac.'

'I never had you down as superstitious. Just because there was a murder …'

'It's nothing to do with the Howells murder. The houses in that cul-de-sac haven't a view that's a patch on Trevor and Lyn's.'

'They're bigger.'

'I'd like a sea view.'

'Trevor and Lyn only have a courtyard.'

'And the beach on their doorstep with a front gate that opens directly on to it. Tell me, Peter, which one of us has time for gardening?'

'You?' he joked.

'Besides, I've bought a house. I signed the papers when I came back yesterday. I noticed it was for sale the last time we visited Trevor and Lyn. It's two doors up from them. I thought it would suit us quite nicely. And it has three bedrooms, two more than we need – at present – but one of which we'll be needing in about seven months or so. So,' she smiled at the expression on his face, 'was there anything else you wanted to talk to me about before we go sick visiting?'

Also By Katherine John

WITHOUT TRACE

In the chilly half-light of dawn a bizarre Pierrot figure waits in the shadows of a deserted stretch of motorway. The costumed hitchhiker's victim is a passing motorist. The murder, cold-blooded, brutal. Without motive.

Doctors at the local hospital Tim and Daisy Sherringham are blissfully happy. The perfect couple. When an emergency call rouses Tim early one morning, he vanishes on the way from their flat to the hospital.

And Daisy is plunged into a nightmare of terror and doubt . . .

ISBN 1905170262
Price £6.99

MIDNIGHT MURDERS

Compton Castle is a Victorian psychiatric hospital long overdue for demolition. Its warrens of rooms and acres of grounds, originally designed as a sanctuary for the mentally ill, now provide the ideal stalking ground for a serial killer.

Physically and mentally battered after his last case, Sergeant Trevor Joseph is a temporary inmate – but the hospital loses all therapeutic benefit when a corpse is dug out of a flowerbed. Then more bodies are found; young, female and both linked to the hospital.

Everyone within the mouldering walls is in danger while a highly unpredictable malevolence remains at large. And, as patients and staff are interrogated by the police, the apparently motiveless killer watches and waits for the opportunity to strike again . . .

ISBN 1905170270
Price £6.99

MURDER OF A DEAD MAN

Jubilee Street – the haunt of addicts and vagrants is a part of town to avoid at all costs, especially when it becomes the stalking ground of a brutal and ruthless murderer.

A drunken down and out is the first casualty, mutilated and burned alive but his grisly death raises even more problems for the investigating officers, Sergeants Trevor Joseph and Peter Collins. They discover that their victim died two years earlier. So who is the dead man? And what was the motive for the bizarre crime?

While they seek a killer in the dark urban underworld, the tally of corpses grows and the only certainty is that they can trust no man's face as his own.

ISBN 1905170289
Price £6.99